Lethal Lineage

Books by Charlotte Hinger

Come Spring

The Lottie Albright Series
Deadly Descent
Lethal Lineage

Lethal Lineage

A Lottie Albright Mystery

Charlotte Hinger

Poisoned Pen Press

Copyright © 2011 by Charlotte Hinger

First Edition 2011

10 9 8 7 6 5 4 3 2 1

Library of Congress Catalog Card Number: 2010932115

ISBN: 9781590588376   Hardcover
        9781590598390   Trade Paperback

Poisoned Pen Press
6962 E. First Ave., Ste. 103
Scottsdale, AZ 85251
www.poisonedpenpress.com
info@poisonedpenpress.com

Printed in the United States of America

This book is dedicated to the three dazzling daughters:
Cheryl Flink, Michele Crockett, and Mary Beth Bieker

Terrors are turned upon me; they pursue my soul as the wind, and my welfare passeth away as a cloud.
—Job 30:15 (KJ21)

Chapter One

Happiness happens. Collective joy surges, pulses, and is sweeter when it's unexpected. Exhilarated, I looked around at the proud faces of the congregation gathered for the first service in our new church, St. Helena. Only dimly remembered snatches of scripture or poetry seemed powerful enough to say what I felt; my heart leapt, my soul soared.

We did it! The Episcopalians in four counties in Western Kansas had miraculously united to build a church. Overwhelmed by gratitude, I dabbed at a tear. We had a church, and were beginning with a special ceremony. My niece, Tammy Clements, would be confirmed here today. A sunbeam spotlighted a patch of our new celadon blue carpet. The scents of new varnish mingled with new wood and over-perfumed women wafted through the air.

A number of relatives were here. After the service the whole congregation was invited to Fiene's Folly—my husband's family's farm—for a grand picnic and a day of music.

Chords sounded from a boom box. Lacking an organ or a piano, it was the best we could do. We rose to the thunderous notes of "A Mighty Fortress is our God."

The processional began. We lifted our voices unto the Lord. A little acolyte, swollen with self-importance, strutted down the aisle dangerously swinging the brass thurible like it was an aborigine bola meant to bring down little animals. I blinked to ward off the hypnotic attraction of flashing metal.

Beside me my twin sister's face tightened. For a psychologist, Josie could be surprisingly judgmental, and uncontrolled children always brought on a surge of her disapproval.

A bell tinkled and the attendant calmed down and stilled the censer. More beaming acolytes followed. Sunlight prismed off the raised burnished cross.

The priest, Mary Farnsworth, was next in line. I had not seen her in vestments before. Her multicolored stole bore primitive motifs and appeared to be hand woven. As always, she wore a lovely elongated silver cross that displayed a ruby heart off-center on the body of the stylized Christ. I expected her to be all smiles, but her mouth was tense, her hands trembled. Our paths intersect often in our work as she organizes the social work in Northwest Kansas and I am the undersheriff of Carlton County. I am also in charge of our historical society and edit our county's history books.

After Mary came the bishop.

I gasped, stunned. My reaction was irrational, but my mind couldn't stop my heart from speeding up like I'd seen a ghost. The bishop, formally addressed as The Right Reverend Ignatius P. Talesbury, was an Anglican living image of a nineteenth century Catholic bishop I had seen in an old photo. Through my research I had come to look upon that very nineteenth century bishop as Western Kansas' answer to Darth Vader.

Talesbury looked like an El Greco painting; other-worldly, ascetic, and ghastly pale. He carried the traditional shepherd's crook and wore the obligatory mitre.

Sensing my tension, Josie stared at me. Not wanting to meet her eyes I turned toward the altar, determined to keep our niece's confirmation a joyful occasion. We all have a double. Not just we twins. It wasn't fair to assume Talesbury was a cruel man just because he looked like the photo image of a clergyman from the past.

Tammy sat with her parents in the front row in a sweet pink dress. She'd wanted to be confirmed on her eighteenth birthday and that request had required unconventional arrangements. In the Episcopal Church, only bishops can confirm. Katy Poudre, the lady charged with contacting the Diocese of Western Kansas, had reported that there was a scheduling problem and this confirmation could not take place until much later in the year.

Then Mabel Sidwell, Copeland County's most excellent professional clubwoman, came to the rescue. She had triumphantly announced that a friend recommended a suffragan bishop who was willing to come on the Sunday Tammy requested. Mabel assured us it would all be perfectly fine and she'd proceeded with the arrangements.

I am a lapsed Episcopalian and don't know about such things, although Josie and I had attended an Episcopal boarding school and I should have paid more attention. Mabel had explained that these "flying bishops" could just go, well, wherever.

St. Helena was precisely centered on the corners of the four counties initiating the construction. The location had been calculated with a protractor. I'd stayed out of all the debates until Mabel informed me the tentative vestry had approved of an avocado shag carpet for the sanctuary.

Appalled, I'd intervened and offered to donate a blue low plush pile. I'd won the women over by agreeing to perform all necessary Altar Guild tasks. Although I was ignorant of all the responsibilities involved, how hard could it be?

The service progressed. The Bishop had chosen the less familiar Rite One and we responded clumsily, and glanced at our prayer books for phrases usually chanted automatically. More relaxed after the "Glory be to God on High," I took deep breaths.

Then Bishop Talesbury began his sermon.

Shame. Hot Coals. Harsh scolding. Our fault, our most grievous fault, that the diocese was in dire straits financially. Our fault that our land was barren. Our fault that our economy was sinking like the Ogallala aquifer.

Our own grievous fault.

Beside me, Josie looked around at the congregants' shocked expressions. Shrewd, evaluating, no longer a participant in this rite, she became a professional assessing collective damage. I followed her gaze.

While Talesbury ranted, Tammy clutched the skirt of her lovely dotted swiss pink dress, compulsively wadding it while she leaned against her mother's shoulder. Most of the men stared straight ahead, their faces flushed with anger. More than a few of the women dabbed at their eyes with shredded tissues.

Talesbury finally finished. We mouthed the words of the Nicene Creed then stumbled through the ritual required to confirm Tammy and the "laying on of hands" by a bishop. After an eternity, we began the solemn Rite of Holy Communion.

The railing filled once. I tamped down my reluctance to receive the Body of Christ from this man and kept my eyes lowered when I stretched my hands to receive the Host. Then I sipped from the common chalice offered by the Reverend Mary Farnsworth. I looked up at her compassionate brown eyes. They brimmed with tears.

Mary was gentle, kindly, an ideal tentmaker priest, undoubtedly ordained through the provisions of the now defunct canon nine. These priests administered the sacraments to local congregations. But in Mary's case, "local" meant all of Northwest Kansas. These little worker bees served without any financial support from local parishes.

When I'd expressed my surprise over Mary Farnsworth's calling, Mabel Sidwell had explained Reverend Mary went exclusively to little house churches. And there were precious few of those.

I rose, turned, and started down the exterior aisle.

A cry. A thud.

I turned back and froze. Mary Farnsworth had dropped the chalice. Unthinkable. Once consecrated, then spilled, the Blood of Christ cannot be retrieved. Dropping the bread, the Body, is bad enough, but it can be salvaged and then buried.

But the blood? The Blood of the Lamb? Never. It's a dilemma that has haunted both the Roman Catholic and my own Anglican Catholic church for centuries.

"My God," Josie said.

Mary Farnsworth fled. She ran from the rail into the anteroom where the clergy changed.

Bishop Talesbury's hands trembled and if it was possible for his face to become even whiter, it just did. He stepped back to the altar and consecrated additional wine. He resumed placing the Body of Christ in the hands of the remaining parishioners, then started over with the chalice as there were no lay clergy present who had the authority to perform this duty.

Mary Farnsworth would no doubt be stripped of subsequent duties because she served at the pleasure of the Bishop. I doubted Talesbury had a forgiving bone in his body. Once a priest, always a priest. Vesting cannot be undone, but there are ways to push errant clergy off on an ice floe.

We would never find another person with her abilities to serve here again. Mother Teresas didn't grow on trees. I glanced at Tammy. Tears streamed down her face. Her special day ruined by the acidic sermon—and now this.

The grim ceremony concluded. The moment after we squawked through the final notes of the difficult closing hymn, Josie bypassed the crowd starting toward the Bishop's receiving line outside the church. She headed to the little anteroom and knocked gently on the closed door.

I watched but hung back, knowing my sister would do Mary the most good.

There was no reply. I glanced at Tammy to see if I was needed there, but she was surrounded by a comfort of aunts. So I joined Josie. She knocked again. We waited. She turned, shrugged. People were leaving. Cars trailing dust fled from this little church in the middle of nowhere. Why wouldn't everyone want to get the hell out as fast as they could? I did too.

"Josie, I have to stay and take care of the linens. Why don't you go on to the farm and help Keith with the barbeque. Mary's my friend. Perhaps I can help her the most."

"All right." Reluctantly, she turned away from the door. "But please let her know she's welcome to join us. Maybe she'll talk to me later."

"Mary? Are you all right?" There was no reply. I rattled the door knob. "It's locked," I whispered to Josie. I kept all the keys to St. Helena on a separate ring. I reached into my purse and found the one to the anteroom, inserted it, and opened the door.

"My God. Oh my God."

Josie's hands flew to her face and she took a step backwards. Mary Farnsworth's body lay sprawled on the floor.

Chapter Two

"Get out, Josie. Get the hell out. Right now. Just leave. And don't touch anything." She swayed. The color drained from her face, even though she's a clinical psychologist and tough as nails.

As a historian my life should have been an ivory tower existence, but my role at this church had suddenly changed from that of a loving aunt to first responder. Actually, one of the only responders in this county, and now second in charge since I'd been promoted from Deputy Sheriff to Undersheriff of Carlton County. It was supposed to be an honor, but I knew better.

"I'm OK," Josie mumbled. She stared at Mary, and then me.

"Just go on," I ordered. "Right now. Are you OK to drive?" She nodded.

"Leave. Don't say anything to anyone yet."

This was not a crime scene, but as a professional I was required to follow certain procedures. Sheriff Sam Abbott had made that quite clear. I knelt by Reverend Mary and felt for a pulse to check what I already knew.

Dead.

I called Sam. Silence on the line after my terse message.

"At the church?" he asked. "Just like that?"

"Yes, just like that."

"Jesus Christ."

"You'll call Doc Golbert?" Doc couldn't bring her back to life but we needed an official cause of death. Golbert is our County

Coroner. Our county is too small to have a Deputy Coroner. My guess was Mary died of a heart attack, but only because it was the sole reason I knew for an apparently perfectly healthy woman to keel over.

"Nope," he said. "He's out of town and will be gone for a week. Since this is an unattended death we'll have to send her directly to the District Coroner."

I sighed. That would mean a hundred mile trip to Hays. We have six counties in our district.

"OK, Sam, I'll leave it to you to sort this all out." Normally, the ambulance would take the deceased straight to our under-taker. Gateway City has only one mortician. Like a number of men in small rural towns who have families to support he has two jobs, and is a part time electrician.

I watched Josie give a quick nod to the bishop where he stood outside the church. Having greeted the very last person, Bishop Talesbury came inside. Now only he and I remained.

"I would like a word with you sir."

"Yes?"

I gazed into his cold eyes. "I have some bad news, sir. Reverend Mary…" My tongue froze. I simply could not get the words out. Suddenly angry at myself for being intimidated by this cold self-righteous son-of-a-bitch, I matched cold with cold. "Reverend Mary is dead."

He flinched but didn't speak for thirty seconds. "Three," he whispered. "How?" He trembled, then clamped down on his body's betrayal as though he had received ordinary news.

Suddenly conscious that I was in a pale blue linen suit, wearing a corsage of carnations and concerned that he might think I had stayed behind merely as the sole person comprising the Altar Guild, I introduced myself. "I'm Lottie Albright, the Undersheriff of Carlton County. I've made all the necessary phone calls. In fact emergency personnel will be arriving shortly."

"Thank God for that, Miss Albright." Technically, I was Mrs. Keith Fiene, but I did not correct him. I still use my maiden name professionally as I have published so much under Albright.

We were interrupted by sound of a vehicle arriving; gravel crunching, no siren. Sam's instructions, no doubt.

"Sir, we do not have an Altar Guild yet. I had planned to stay after the service and take the linens home with me. Our family was going to remove the flowers too. They are from Tammy's parents and we are having a picnic later." I sounded anxious, incompetent, and hated myself for it. Hated my haste to counter his cold silence.

The EMT's came through the door and we watched in even more conspicuous silence as they laid Mary's body on a stretcher and carried her out to the waiting vehicle.

I collected the few personal items Mary had placed on the table in the anteroom to take to Sam. Her purse lay beside her car keys, a cell phone, and a small plastic bag. I looked inside the bag. It contained miscellaneous health items labeled with the names of the intended recipients.

No doubt she'd planned to visit these people after the service. I dabbed at a few stray tears and vowed to distribute them myself.

I had admired this kindly earnest woman. We'd had a number of conversations due to her job as a social worker. It was my unhappy responsibility to occasionally collect children and place them in foster care. The children of Northwest Kansas had a vigorous advocate in Mary Farnsworth.

The ambulance crew left. Bishop Talesbury turned toward the altar, made the Sign of the Cross, then walked over to the communion elements. He looked back at me reproachfully and I suspected I had ignorantly omitted some duty normally performed by subordinates. Our acolytes had fled with their parents right after the closing hymn.

After dousing the candles, he began consuming the bread and the remaining wine as was required by our church. I waited to gather up the linens to take back to the farm to wash and store. Even under normal circumstances it would have been a while before we used this little church again. We were aiming for once a quarter.

Bishop Talesbury bowed in the direction of the cross. Brass gleamed. The faint aroma of incense still lingered. A residual tang of wine vinegared my tongue. The abnormal silence with which the man moved accentuated body noises. I could hear myself swallow. My breath quickened. If one could hear one's own blood pulsing, I did now. This little church suddenly so desecrated. Tears threatened, but I would not give in.

The pews had been so lovingly refinished. We even had a start on funds for a stained glass window. Once installed, the lovely celadon blue carpet, a hue Josie always referred to as Virgin Mary blue, met with everyone's approval. We had a real church.

Bishop Talesbury bowed toward the altar again. Then he walked over to a small black satchel and drew out a very sharp knife. I couldn't move.

A stiletto.

Chapter Three

I closed my eyes. Prayed. Foolishly, I had left my gun at home. Helpless, I stood frozen as he turned toward me with the knife held stiffly, at an odd angle in front of him, tip upward.

My God, my God. My blood started circulating again. Some small remnant of professional training kicked in.

He nodded toward me, and turned back toward the altar. Then he genuflected, crossed himself, knelt, and raised the knife as though asking God's blessing.

My God. Did he plan to use it on himself? I started toward him, then stopped, afraid I might provoke him. He walked over to the splotch of spilled wine, inserted the tip at the outermost edge, and began to cut around the spill.

Rage seared through me like a bolt of lightning. He was cutting the blot out of our precious new carpet. This carpet represented countless bake sales and fund-raisers.

Inter-county cooperation is rare in Western Kansas. Each county is its own fiefdom. In fact, most tiny little towns and hamlets have a tribal sense of self-preservation.

I wondered if this bishop could understand how difficult it had been to build this little four-county church. Agreeing on the location alone had required the diplomatic skills used to settle territory after World War I.

Now this self-righteous bastard was mutilating our carpet.

I usually know what to do. But thinking furiously, I realized it was too late. Too late. The damage had already been done. I stood rigidly unmoving. Tears trickled down my cheeks.

He finished his work, raised the stiletto again as though he were offering the elements, then wiped it and placed it back in the satchel. He knelt, picked up the piece of carpet, and handed it to me.

"Burn this."

My hands trembled as I received the remnant. Not trusting myself to speak I simply nodded.

He started toward the anteroom where Mary had fled. It was the only changing room we had. He was on my turf now.

"Sir, you can't go in there."

He whirled, his face no longer pale but angry, distorted.

"This was a sudden unattended death. There are things we must do. And besides, I don't think you would want to."

Dumb son-of-a-bitch. Stupid bastard. Was I going to have to draw him a picture? There are smells, fluids when someone dies. My voice did not shake.

He lowered his eyes and nodded his head again. Graciously. As though he were humoring me. He went to a far corner and removed all his vestments, carefully folding each piece. I began removing altar trappings.

He finished. Underneath his vestments he wore a black cassock. Strange, oddly formal attire.

His penetrating eyes scrutinized my tear-stained face. "This is just one death, Miss Albright." Then he swept out of the church without so much as another word and drove off in a white Camry.

Shocked, I watched from the doorway. He hadn't said goodbye, I'm sorry for your loss, or offered one speck of comfort. He hadn't even asked if I was all right.

I went out to my Tahoe to retrieve the basket I'd brought to gather up the linens. I went to the anteroom and looked around. The floor was untainted. Obviously Reverend Mary's layers of clothing and vestments had absorbed everything. I wanted to scrub the room clean, but could not until we learned the cause of death.

The room was barren. Windowless. A small battered mission style donated oak table was centered on the east wall. A calendar listing the church's seasons hung on a nail above it. There was a small wardrobe intended for spare robes in case the church experienced growth.

I called Sam. "I'll come back this evening after the picnic if we've heard from the coroner. And her car is still here."

"OK," he said. "We can store the car in back of the office."

I studied the anteroom one more time, then closed and locked the door. I picked up the basket of linens, walked outside, and secured the main door of the church.

I bowed my head in sorrow. Bishop Talesbury had not said one word, not one single solitary word over Mary Farnsworth's body. I started to drive off, then realized I had left the mutilated scrap of carpet inside.

When Talesbury had handed it to me, I had laid it on a piece of linen on a pew at the front of the church. I went back inside. I looked again at the mutilated sanctuary and picked up the jagged patch of blue carpet.

Worried that I had forgotten something else, I walked to the anteroom, tested the door to make sure I'd locked it, then left.

"Burn it," the Bishop had said. Well, I would have liked for him to use his head. This was Western Kansas, for god's sake. St. Helena, not Westminster Abby. Not high church. In fact, not proper in many ways.

The hardest part of my job in law enforcement is not working with the criminal element. It's working with ignorant people and that has nothing to do with their education.

One would think that this man would have a clue and consider our circumstances. Notice the absence of a baptismal font. We didn't even have an aumbry where the reserved sacrament was kept. No red light burning to indicate the presence of Christ. In fact this little church wouldn't have been built here at all if other denominations had given us permission to use their buildings.

In another Western Kansas county there's a beautiful little church that was once shared by the Methodists and the Episcopalians in the 1880s. It's located in Studley, named for Studley Park Royal in England. Western Kansas was once considered to be a grand place to send English remittance men and worrisome progeny. Kansas offered homestead land, theirs for the asking. A few got rich, learned to farm, and became Kansans. Which means proud of doing things the hard way.

But a much larger group who settled Studley had one hell of a good time. They had high tea, brought their English ways to America, and even rode to the hounds across the prairie. They substituted jack rabbits for foxes and quite a few sank into genteel drunken poverty and were called back by their outraged fathers. More than one poor aristocratic English woman lost her mind to the wind.

But since in this new century no denomination would let us share their building, we defiantly built our own wee St. Helena.

Nervously, I glanced at the bundle of carpets and linens. I had purchased a copy of the church Canons from Morehouse Publishing, but it hadn't shipped yet. I hoped there were instructions for handling this situation.

I believed under the circumstances it was proper to bury Him. It? Him? The carpet contained the blood of Christ. Had to be disposed of in a proper manner. Couldn't just heave the carpet into the trash for god's sake.

God's sake? Was I drifting into profanity?

Chapter Four

I topped the hill and came upon Fiene's Folly, our large three-story house rising like a white-walled castle on the plains. When I married Keith there was no question of where we would live, even though this house had been planned and decorated by his late wife.

Some brides are reluctant to live in a house that bears another woman's stamp, but I knew immediately it would be a colossal mistake to insist on moving elsewhere. It would have alienated Keith's grown children forever.

There is one room we avoid, of course: the one where Regina hanged herself. It was once her studio, where she painted, wept over her unhappy marriage, and stored all the trappings of her unfinished projects. I had decided immediately to banish every trace of this tragedy and transformed it into a spare bedroom with a sitting room. I hadn't even discussed it with Keith. Just did it. Nor did he comment on it afterwards.

The spare bedroom. That's what we call it. However, Josie is the only one who ever uses it, even when we are strapped for space during our huge family gatherings.

None of his children said a word about the redecorated studio. One of my stepdaughters is older than I, and if any one of my inherited brood would have spoken out, it would be she. Elizabeth.

For a brief period after last fall's tragedies, which we now simply refer to as "The Troubles," Elizabeth had actually been quite nice to me. But it hadn't lasted long. I don't like handling people and sometimes it takes all my energy to keep from slapping her.

The other children, Keith's daughters Bettina and Angela, and his son Tom, were only faintly disapproving of their father's remarriage, but there was nothing faint about Elizabeth.

To Elizabeth, her father marrying a woman twenty years younger had been absolutely unthinkable.

But not to us. Not to Keith and me. I loved my rock-solid, two-fisted husband. He was proud of my work as a historian and my contribution to the community. In fact, everything would have been nearly perfect if I hadn't decided to become a deputy sheriff so I could help solve a murder.

He didn't sign up for that.

My work load had increased since my promotion to undersheriff. A deputy is on call. The hours are flexible. Being an undersheriff is a real job requiring a set number of hours a week, even though it's not full time in Carlton County.

Keith thought he'd married a historian. Which I was. Am.

He still encourages my work at the historical society and tolerates my foray in law enforcement. But he worries. However, being either a sheriff or undersheriff in a small rural county mostly consists of boring routines.

Accepting my alleged promotion was a mistake. But it seemed like a good idea at the time and I thought I could handle it. The county commissioners wanted our county to have a more professional image. They were embarrassed by the blunders made last fall and increased our budget.

By now Sam had come to admire the fusion of my research techniques with police work. Truth was, I adored the old man and couldn't bear to refuse. But beneath the surface, both Sam and Keith believe in protecting the womenfolk: we should get in the lifeboats first.

A number of cars were parked close to the house and people started toward me before I could even manage to get my Tahoe in park. Through the involvement of EMT's and peripheral persons, information had infiltrated the picnic.

"Lottie, I'm so sorry. Do you know what happened?"

"What happened? Just what actually happened?"

"We won't know until the coroner gets back to us," I said. "And I'm sure he'll want to access Dr. Golbert's medical records."

"Well, you must have some idea." Inez Wilson spoke sharply.

Inez is our county health nurse. I thought a second before I replied, because whatever idea I put forth would be all over the county in an instant. In fact, since the residents of Carlton County had discovered Facebook, nothing was sacred.

"I suspect a heart attack, Inez. Heart attack or a stroke." In fact, I had no idea why Mary had died.

I wove in and out of the throng of people, and ran up the stairs to change into jeans. The weather was holding. Keith had started setting up tables and chairs early in the morning and those coming to our four-county celebration brought their favorite pot-luck dishes. I only had one goal now; to get the discussion about Mary's death over with and salvage what we could of the day for my niece's sake.

Josie stood beside the grill. She was a quick study. After her first disastrous visit to our farm, she'd figured out she had to leave her city clothes behind. I smiled at the label on her jeans. Two hundred dollars a pair, I would guess, and the dirt on them was not acquired by honest hard labor. The lightweight tan LL Bean pullover was just the right weight for the day.

Even though we're identical twins and people often can't tell us apart, I've always felt she is more attractive than I. We both have black hair and dark brown eyes. I lost ten pounds last fall, so if anything we look more alike than ever, with our model's slimness.

However, Josie really is more glamorous. Sometimes I envy her flawless grooming and regular facials. She is what I could look like if I gave a damn. Which I do, off and on.

She held her little Shih-Tzu, Tosca, and I laughed and rolled my eyes at all the admirers. Tosca was white and tan and her groomer had tied little ribbons in her hair and inserted spring flowers. Fake, of course, but then so was the dog. She wasn't worth much except looking adorable, and reminding everyone that the economy couldn't be all that grim if someone, somewhere, had the cash to pay for high-dollar doggie shampoos.

Keith was grilling hamburgers and couldn't leave his post, so I went over to see if I could lend a hand. He laid down his spatula and hugged me.

"You've heard?" I hugged him back.

"Yup. It's all folks have talked about. Hell of a thing to have happened."

I didn't respond. Just patted him on the shoulder, then started greeting relations. I gritted my teeth. Every last one of them had the same question.

"What happened?"

"We won't know for sure until the coroner gets done."

"But she was so young! And looked plenty fit enough."

"I know. But you can't always tell."

Edna Mavery came wobbling up. I'd privately labeled her the Bird Woman. In her late eighties she was incredibly frail with her arthritic joints jutting out like a baby bird's. Thank goodness she'd given up driving. Although her mind was still sharp, I couldn't imagine her having the strength to stomp on a brake pedal.

Her skin was as thin as tissue paper and her white hair was carefully rolled into sausage curls and covered with a nearly invisible net. Her dentures clicked faintly and an embroidered handkerchief peeked out of her floral-printed, pastel crepe dress.

Edna had declined sharply since I first met her. She lived in a little white house on the edge of Gateway City and for years when I drove past, I would see her out in her wonderful yard decorated with an eclectic assortment of rural art.

A couple of mornings I'd watched her start down the steps from the porch into her back yard carefully, deliberately placing one foot in front of the other.

Then when she was safely down, I thought she was going to jump and click her heels in anticipation of a day in her glorious old-fashioned flower garden filled with hollyhocks and sweet peas, pinks, Sweet William, and nasturtiums.

Edna, along with three others, was being honored today for her contribution of land encompassed by the forty acres on which we had built St. Helena. The titles regarding these parcels had been a first class mess. Some of the boundaries were inaccurate due to ancient county line disputes. There were casual undocumented sales, gentlemen's agreements, and careless abstract work by an inept clerk in the 1920s.

By the time we'd sorted out who owned what, the startled landowners were simply glad to get out of paying back taxes.

I went over to Edna. Her neighbor, Elmira Howarter, stood at her side, making sure she didn't fall.

"I'm so very happy to see you here today, Edna. You, too, Elmira. Are you still able to work in your wonderful garden? Would it help if Keith came over and helped till or are you going to have town boys do it?"

Tears filled Edna's eyes. "My hands won't work right anymore. Might be my last year." Her chin quivered.

"We heard about Mary Farnsworth," Elmira said. "The poor soul."

I sighed and resigned myself to discussing death every blessed moment the whole livelong day.

Edna clicked her dentures. "Lottie says she had a heart attack," Elmira said to Edna.

"No," I protested. "We won't know for sure until they complete the autopsy."

Edna eyes brimmed with tears again. "Well, I know. It's a heart attack all right. They say it can't be done, but I know better."

"What can't be done?"

"Giving someone a heart attack. You can. I know of another time."

The hair rose on my arm. Suddenly my stomach drew into a little knot. "What do you mean, Edna?"

Her voice quivered. Tears spilled over. "At the communion rail. When she spilled the wine. I think it's because of what that man said to her."

I closed my eyes and took a deep breath. "What did he say, Edna?"

"He said, 'I know who you are and I know what you've done.'"

Chapter Five

"The poor little thing. God rest her soul." Edna clamped hard on her dentures to still her trembling mouth. "That's when she gave a little yelp and dropped the wine. The Blood. I've only seen that once before. It's a mess when it happens, I tell you."

Incredulous, I stared at her for an instant, then turned to Elmira. I didn't want her to hear another word.

"Elmira, would you mind telling Keith that it's time to start? We've got a special table set aside for the land donors, so ask him to round up the other three and I'll help Edna get over there."

I led Edna over to a chair and eased her into it. "Just sit for a while, Edna. Catch your breath. You've had a shock."

Josie stood next to Keith and I caught her eye and beckoned for her to come over. "Something has come up. I need to stay right here with Edna for a bit. Please ask Keith to say grace. Then I'll say a few words thanking everyone who worked so hard and then we'll have Tammy stand and with any luck at all, we can focus on her confirmation."

Josie went back to Keith, leaving me to concentrate on Edna. I was in pure cop mode now. I didn't want to scare her, but I needed to follow up right away.

"Who was this man, Edna?"

"Don't know. Never saw him before in my life. But then, I didn't know most of the folks."

"What do you remember about him?"

"Nothing. He was just a man."

"Clothes? Age? Hair color?"

"It was Communion, Lottie. The Holy Eucharist. I try to keep my mind where it's supposed to be. On the Blood and Body of our Lord. Not on the people next to me. Shame on you!" She fished her handkerchief out of her purse and dabbed at her eyes and began to weep. "You're poking and prodding around at me like I'm on a witness stand."

Alarmed at the high color staining her parchment skin, I patted her hand. "I'm so sorry. I didn't mean you were supposed to remember everything. It's just that I'm surprised, that's all. Nobody else mentioned this."

She sniffed. "No reason why anyone would. Only reason I remember as much as I do is because of what happened. I do remember that the person on the other side of him had already gotten up to go back to their pew and I was still there because I have trouble getting up and down. But I can still kneel if I set my mind to it. I wanted to kneel." Her voice shook.

"Edna, thank you for mentioning this man. Anything at all you might remember could be important. Anything." I tried to keep my voice gentle, encouraging. I didn't want her to sull up. I waited. Carefully now, I asked, "Clothes? Anything at all? Hair?"

"Well, he was dressed normal. I would have noticed right off if he wasn't. It's a real caution nowadays how some of the young folks parade around half naked. Skinny little tops with shorts out of old jeans or those shameless skirts. No respect a'tall. Back in my day, the priest would have sent us right straight home."

Dressed normal? What was normal? I needed to know. "So he wasn't that sort of person?"

"Lawsey no, I'd of remembered if he was. Had on a tie and a jacket. No point in wearing a tie without a jacket."

"Is he here, Edna?" I held my breath. It would simply be too good to be true.

"No, I don't think so, but like I said, I just didn't pay any attention to the man after Reverend Mary dropped the chalice. You know what it was like."

I nodded. Dark confusion from that moment on.

"That bishop fellow, that person the Diocese sent out to give us a dressing down and remind us we're little better than no-count idol worshipping pagans out here, he sashayed back to the altar and made this show of re-consecrating wine. Most of us were watching him and trying to figure out what we were supposed to do."

"So this stranger went on back to his pew?"

"Yes, and I finally managed to get up so another person could take my place, and of course Reverend Mary hightailed it out of there to the changing room and the Lord High Executioner went back to serving the folks."

I remembered very little myself after Mary dropped the chalice.

"Anyways, I think that man gave her a heart attack," Edna said. "It can happen."

Elmira waved at us to come on over. I helped Edna stand up and walk over to the table where the other three land donors sat. We prayed. I spoke. My adorable niece blushed and smiled when the gathering applauded her confirmation.

Edna picked at her food, then stood and gripped her walker with her distorted arthritic hands and sobbed her way back to Elmira's car. I escaped to my kitchen.

Inside the house, I tried to still doubts popping up like mushrooms and apply a little logic. Reverend Mary had died in a windowless room locked from the inside. There could not possibly, by any stretch of the imagination, be any foul play involved. And despite Edna's insistence, one simply could not "give" a person a heart attack.

I poured a cup of coffee from my own personal pot. Keith wouldn't go near the "vile stuff" and neither would his daughters. Tough. If I liked it the consistency of motor oil, it was my privilege.

Jolted by caffeine, I made a gut decision that put things into play I couldn't call back. I picked up the phone and called Sheriff Sam Abbott.

"Sam, I know this sounds strange. Not just sounds like, *is* strange, actually. I want to treat the church like a crime scene and I want you to go over there by yourself. Just you. People will notice if I leave here. If you find anything, I'll come over in a flash. Not that there's likely anything to find. But Edna Mavery just told me something strange that I want to follow up on."

"You're not giving me much to go on, Lottie."

I told him what Edna had heard.

"And she's what? Eighty-eight? Eighty-nine?"

"Eighty-seven, I think, and I took that into consideration."

"She might have misunderstood or misheard period and displaced the sound. Could have been some kid in a pew smarting off or just whispering to a classmate. I'm pretty sure those very words were used in an old movie."

"I agree. I'll be honest Sam, I don't think there's any way in hell this was anything but a natural death, but I want you, not me, looking at it with fresh eyes."

There was a long pause followed by a groan. It was March Madness. I could just picture him in front of the television, the Sunday paper scattered around the recliner. Plenty of Budweiser in the fridge. Ready to cheer Kansas University through the second round of playoffs.

Sam's only son had been killed in Vietnam so he didn't have any family outlets. I hated to take this small pleasure away from him. Especially since I was the one officially on duty today.

But I could count on him being a pro. If he'd started drinking already, he would order me to go back over there in his place. Despite the fact that he was long past the age when most people retire, he is as effective as he looks. Hollywood couldn't have come up with a better model for the old time sheriff.

Sam's silver grey hair just touches his collar and his mustache is full and impressive. He has sharp clear eyes and an aristocratic Roman nose. With his square-shouldered military bearing, he looks the picture of wisdom and integrity. Which in fact, he is.

"I'm on my way."

"Sorry, Sam. Even though there's no way in hell…"

"This could be anything but natural causes," he said, finishing my sentence for me. "You would just feel better."

I laughed. "You've got it. Come by here first and pick up the key to the anteroom. Visit a little and grab a bit to eat so folks won't think there's anything wrong."

"Which of course, there isn't, which is why I'm on my way there."

Chapter Six

Twenty minutes later Sam drove into the yard. After he'd chatted up a few people and made a pass through the food tables, I called him into the kitchen. "Who's on dispatch today?"

"Betty Central."

"Damn it. I was hoping it was Troy." The new deputy, Troy Doyle, wasn't as nosy as Betty.

"Bad luck, but just in case, I have to check in as 'on duty.' I want it on record."

"Just in case," I muttered. Well, true, if he found anything wrong, he couldn't pretend he'd decided to go over there on a whim.

"I'll tell Betty I'm going to run by the church and make sure everything got locked up."

"OK. And make sure you double-check the anteroom. That's where we found the body. She was still in her vestments and wearing a dress and a cotton slip so they absorbed all the body fluids. I didn't see a trace of blood."

Through my window, I saw children dash in and out among the cedars. Getting filthy. Getting sticky. This should have been a fine day. "Sorry," I said again.

Sam nodded. "After I'm done, I'll pick up Betty and she can drive Mary's car back to the office."

"OK. After you look around I'll vacuum and clean. Maybe tomorrow. See what you think or find and the coroner rules."

And perhaps I would ask a priest to do whatever it is they do to chase out evil spirits, although I doubted that a full blown exorcism was called for.

"Try to calm down, Lottie. I'll take over duty today. You're off and I'm on."

He was back in a hour. "Nothing, Lottie. A few things left in the pews. Mostly just trash. Used Kleenexes, a couple of ball point pens, a pacifier, and a handkerchief with a crocheted edge. So we know nothing until we get the medical opinion."

"That's a relief. As for the pens and the hanky, I'll start a little lost and found box."

"She was a good woman," he said.

"The best. She will be sorely missed."

He slapped his hat on his head and started toward his car.

"Want me to take care of notifying her family?" I called after him.

He stopped. "Oh shit. No, the coroner will do it. Try to get on with what's left of the day. If you can."

I shuddered. I had a feeling our brave little church wasn't going to survive this tragic beginning. St. Helena was tainted. Invaded by a dark angel now hovering over the building and the congregation.

In fact, even if nothing else had happened, the ruinous sermon had set us up for failure. Western Kansans don't like to be scolded. We just don't. We don't like Eastern Kansans or outsiders coming in with high-faluting plans for our part of the state like we somehow lack the brains to manage on our own. The longer I live in Western Kansas, the more I become like the people who have always lived here.

After the long day finally ended I poured a merlot and joined Keith on the patio. Some of our relations were staying in the motel in town. Josie was staying at our house. Unaffected by our family's superstition about the spare bedroom, she'd retreated there about an hour ago trying to ward off a headache.

Keith reached for my hand and we both lay quietly side by side in the recliners on our patio. It was a rare warm evening for March but the weather likely wouldn't hold because it never did. There's a cedar windbreak on the north and west sides of our house. It's intended to thwart blowing dirt and snow, but tonight the thick trees felt oppressive.

Nothing bloomed. The branches of our cottonwood trees formed dark silhouettes. No stars twinkled through the smothering layers of soiled clouds. It was too early in the year for our buffalo grass to green up, so there was a sparse brown cast to our yard. Dried up. Like the whole miserable day. Even the cedars had the dry blue cast they have before they become fully green.

But it's comforting just to be next to Keith even when he doesn't say a word. I squeezed his hand. He's six foot two and big-boned. A lifetime of hard work has kept his body solid. He looks younger than fifty-eight. The back door slammed and Josie came out holding Tosca. She carefully set the little dog on the ground, and I decided a worthless little Shih-Tzu was exactly what I needed.

"Come to Aunt Lottie, sweetheart. Come over here."

Tosca looked at Josie as though she were asking permission. Josie laughed. "It's OK, baby. My sister needs a little therapy."

"Headache better?" Keith asked.

"No. I've given up on it, that's all. I'm too wired to sleep and that probably would do me the most good."

"I can't tell you how sorry I am that you had to go through this," I said. I was tempted to add "again" but Mary's death wasn't nearly as traumatic as last fall's ordeal because of her involvement as a consultant for Carlton County.

"It wasn't your fault, Lottie," she said quickly. Too quickly. Like whether it was my fault or not, the whole county was clearly crazy.

Keith beckoned toward an extra chair. "I would give up my recliner, you know. You don't have to wrestle me for it." He sighed. "It's been one hell of a day for all of us."

"Did Tammy get herself back together? I was so busy taking care of the stuff I needed to do with the body…" I stopped. That sounded cold. Real cold. I tried again. "…with Reverend Mary's body that I neglected all my duties as a hostess."

"That's understandable," Josie said. Then Tosca abandoned me, leaped down, and then onto my sister's lap as though she had coddled me long enough.

Keith got up and went into the house and came out with another bottle of wine and a bottle of his own home brew. "Don't know about you two but I need another round. At *least* one more. Then I want to hear about everything from beginning to end."

"I hardly know where to start." But Keith and I had reached an agreement. He wanted to be informed of everything going on connected to the sheriff's office. There's nothing illegal about telling a spouse everything, it's just that in the beginning, I didn't want to worry him. Secrecy had been a disaster.

In our new arrangement there would be no secrets on my part and in return he would not make sarcastic remarks or try to make me give up my badge. There were limits to the type of information available to historians. Now, as a law enforcement officer, I had access to detailed databases. It was the best of both worlds.

"I want to know about the whole day," he said. "What in the hell went on, exactly? People coming here from the church looked like they'd been at an execution even before word got around about the death."

"Lottie and I discovered the body and most folks had left by then," Josie began.

"But even if that hadn't happened, that asshole had no right to talk to us like we were worms," I said. "It's the sermon that started it all." I took a sip of wine.

"Lottie told you about the dropped chalice?"

"She did." It was too dark to see his eyes, but Keith is a devout Catholic and he understood the tragedy of the spilled Blood.

We both tried to reconstruct the morning. Each of us filling in details the other hadn't noticed.

"Did you see Tammy's face?" Josie asked.

"No. I was too preoccupied with worrying about Mary being stripped of her credentials." Then I told them about Bishop Talesbury's bizarre ritual after the service and his cutting around the blotch of wine.

"Jesus Christ," Keith muttered.

"Exactly."

He laughed. "And that carpet is where?"

"Still in my car. He told me to burn it, but I'll bet I can't do that just anywhere. Does your church have something special they use when things like this happen?"

He got up and switched on the circle of decorative pole lights surrounding the semi-circle of our patio. "Something isn't right here."

"What do you mean?" I asked. Having served on various parish committees throughout his life, Keith was well-grounded in the Catholic Church's canons.

"I mean something just isn't right."

"Well, I wouldn't know. I don't even know who to ask about some of the details. But until my copy of the Episcopal church's canons gets here, I'll do whatever your church says."

"OK. I'll dig out our canons tomorrow, but I've never heard of anyone cutting out the carpet."

This was beyond me. I hadn't even given the church, my faith, a thought for many years until last fall. After that life threatening experience, I'd resolved to get some of it back. I was paying for this effort with this ecclesiastical mess.

Tosca gave a little growl and leaped from Josie's lap. A rabbit darted into the hedges. Being considerably larger than the dog, the bunny was the only thing all day that gave us a reason to laugh.

"Yeah, Tosca. Atta girl."

"Oh lord," Josie laughed. "She's picking up bad habits and will start terrorizing our neighbors."

Tosca came charging back like she personally was responsible for banishing critters from our yard and leaped onto Josie's lap despite my attempts to lure her onto mine.

"Fickle," I teased. "Momma's girl."

A car turned up our lane. To our credit, none of us cussed, but we were clearly not in the mood for visitors. Even friends. We were a bottle away from getting a handle on the evening.

"Who is it," I asked.

"Can't tell from here," Keith said.

"Time for me to go to bed. Really." Josie got up and headed toward the screen door.

"Oh sit back down. Someone probably forgot something or it might be somebody needing directions."

But it was Sam.

Chapter Seven

He got right to the point. "The coroner can't find Mary Farnsworth's next of kin. He wants to notify them right away. He's also going to need instructions as to the disposition of the body."

"What about an autopsy?" Keith asked.

"Don't need their permission for that. That's standard procedure for an unattended death, but her people need to know."

"Her purse is still in my car," I said. "I was going to take it to the office tomorrow morning. I'll run get it." I rose and headed for the Tahoe and came back with her keys, her purse, her cell phone, and the small plastic bag she'd left on the table. "Couldn't Dr. Comstock find everything he needed online? There should have been emergency contact information."

"Not according to Comstock. He supposed I'd gotten in touch with the family, and I thought he was on top of it, so this is a royal screw-up. Just awful." His face tightened.

I tried to think. I hadn't been around Mary all that much, but when I was she hadn't mentioned family. I always remember when persons do. Part of my work at the historical society is to record family histories, so I have a second antenna out for these stories. Of course, there wasn't any reason for her to talk about her family. When I was in her office, it was usually an emergency. Some kid needing foster care immediately.

"She's the only supervisory person out here. There's no boss to call. Except on a state level and those offices won't be open until tomorrow morning. In fact, I think she just kept a skeleton support staff after the budget cuts."

"Beer, Sam?" Keith asked. "Might as well while you get this sorted out."

"Can't. Not till midnight. Then I get to turn this whole mess over to your wife. For twenty-four hours. Day was ruined anyway. KU got shut out of the playoffs."

"Sorry you had to drive all the way out here," I said. "You could have called."

"Did. You didn't hear."

"Sorry again. We can't hear the house phone outside unless I plug in an extension and since you were on duty I didn't bother."

My cell phone didn't work at the farm. We finally got a new tower outside of Gateway City, then an ice storm took it out. Our region was next in line for repairs but technicians were in short supply.

"Figured you would know right off who to get in touch with, Lottie." It was a rather unreasonable, but mild reproach. I was used to it.

"You can't just let her lie there," Josie said, her voice sharp. "This will be a terrible shock to someone."

Sam reached for his pipe and gave her a sour look.

"I don't know a thing about her family," I said, "but there's got to be some information in her purse."

First I flipped open the contact list on her cell phone to see if there was an ICE, In Case of Emergency, listing. There wasn't. Then I started through her wallet, but the only identification was a single credit card and her driver's license.

"I would have sent these with you when you came over earlier, but I assumed since she was a state employee there would be information on the computer. I guess on a local level, her paperwork would be at her office in Copeland County."

"Her house is in Bidwell County," Sam said.

I checked the address book on her cell phone for any listings under Farnsworth, then "mom" and other likely nicknames and drew a blank there too. I went through the purse again. It contained some cosmetics in a cheap plastic pouch, a checkbook, a mending kit from a hotel, tissues, and Wal-Mart receipts.

I dumped the contents of the plastic sack on the patio table. As I had first thought, she'd obviously planned to deliver these things after the service because she had a little hand drawn map enclosed and each item was listed on the back: aspirins for the Caldwell baby, a diabetic kit for Bertha Summers, wound dressings for Jim McAvoy, and antibiotic salve for Irma Johnson.

"Sam, I'll take her keys and go over to Copeland County right away and get her personnel file from the office. Then I'll call her people. Want to ride along, Josie?"

She got up and followed me into the house. "I thought you weren't on duty."

"I'm not." I glanced at the clock. Nine-thirty. I had time to drive over and back before I had to check in. "I'm going over there as Mary's friend. That way we won't have to arouse Betty's curiosity by Sam's going off duty and me going on early. We've already made one switch today."

Sam continued to visit with Keith and would until I got back. No doubt he planned to accept Keith's offer of home brew the moment I took over. But he couldn't have known it was like moonshine; it varied considerably from bottle to bottle.

Josie was solemn on the ride over to Copeland County. Drained. She had left Tosca with Keith. Her hands were tucked under her armpits like they were chilled. I turned on my scanner.

"I can't imagine having to go one hundred miles for an autopsy. What does law enforcement do out here if there's been foul play?"

"If it's obviously that, we notify the KBI immediately and they send an agent to witness the autopsy."

"And if it's not obvious?"

"You watch too many crime shows."

She didn't laugh.

I used OnStar to call Dr. Joel Comstock, our district coroner, and told him we would have contact information to him soon.

◇◇◇

It was fully dark when we arrived in Dunkirk. The street was deserted. The town was smaller than Gateway by about six hundred persons. Even though Gateway City was the Carlton County seat and our population was only two thousand five hundred we were a metropolis compared to Dunkirk, the county seat of Copeland.

Retail businesses have a hell of a time in both towns and most of them double up. Our computer guru sold an assortment of essential office products, vitamins, Malaluka Oil, and his mother-in-law's crocheted doilies.

Hardly any of our stores would have been considered normal in a large city.

Mary Farnsworth monitored six counties. Her caseload was staggering. Her part-time staff consisted of a secretary and two women who investigated "situations." The sign on her blond brick office read "Northwest Kansas Social Services."

We parked in front and Josie came in with me. I flipped on the light and we winced when the cheap fluorescent bulb stabilized. Everything was in its place. Neat, but dreary. Low budget and no hope for improvement. Kansas was operating on a shoestring.

"Aren't there privacy issues here?" Josie asked. "Don't you need some kind of official paperwork?"

"Nope. I'm just doing what any friend would do. There's no crime involved and no suspects so I don't need a warrant. I'm just trying to figure out how to get in touch with that poor woman's family. As a friend."

"Still. It's wrong to look at her clients' personal records."

"That's why I won't. But I don't need the law to tell me that." A row of mismatched file cabinets stood along one wall. Two of them were locked. I looked through the key ring. "I'll bet that's what these little keys are for. With luck, all the personnel files, past and present, will be in one of these two-drawer files."

But they weren't. I found minutes of board meetings, old ledgers, budget sheets for the state, copies of compliance reports, pages of statistics, and government rules and regulations. "They have to be in one of these locked drawers."

"That's good. She was a careful person, then," Josie said.

I unlocked the drawer and opened it. "Look at these files. She's even got me beat. Color-coded and every label bolded and in caps."

"No personnel files," Josie said. "But there's no good reason to keep them in the top drawer. That's something she wouldn't check every day."

We worked our way down and found a file labeled "Employees" in the bottom drawer of the cabinet closest to the wall. I pulled it out and placed it on Mary's desk. I flipped through the sheets. A total of eleven men and seven women had been employed by her office during the past nineteen years.

Some had left to find work that paid more. A couple files contained notes in Mary's large extroverted handwriting that they were going to get more schooling. These were followed by exclamation marks and one even had a smiley face.

I paused. Mary was very much involved in the lives of people, whether clients or employees. I winked back tears and looked at Josie. She squeezed my shoulder.

"Life's a bitch, sometimes," she said softly.

I started to complete her sentence "and then you die," but couldn't bear to inject any humor into this day's events. I reached for a Kleenex sprouting from the box on the desk, glanced around the office, and was struck by a detail I hadn't noticed before. There were no pictures of her with family.

None.

No picture of her period.

There were enormous collages of kids she'd helped or placed in homes. But no photo of her with persons wearing dated clothing suggesting her own childhood. There were 4-H pictures, pictures of multi-county events, pictures of fair exhibits, but no pictures of adults who might be her relation. Slowly, I went from grouping to grouping.

Granted she would usually be the one taking the photos, but some little kid would always be pestering her to have their photo with her for the scrapbook. For that matter, where were the photos of her at church events in her role as an Episcopal priest?

"This is starting to weird me out," I said, calling Josie's attention to the omission.

She stared. "It is strange. Let's go through the files again. We only looked at the files labeled 'employees' before. That's where I keep my own personal records, but maybe she files it somewhere else."

"OK. But I don't see how we could have missed anything."

"We must have," she insisted. "It's part of government compliance. And she has to have her fingerprints on file with the state."

"Maybe not." I said. "I'll check with Sam, but she came here nineteen years ago. I doubt if that rule was in place then."

"There has to be a specific form submitted," Josie said. "She can't have waltzed into here like a little Jayhawk and started a government-funded mental health service."

"No, but she could have faked compliance," I said. "Not that I suspect her of doing anything that wasn't one hundred percent on the up and up."

There was no knock.

He was just there. Bursting through the door. A flashlight in one hand and his other hand on his gun.

Irwin Deal, sheriff of Copeland County.

Chapter Eight

I knew this man and I didn't like him. It's not reasonable to judge someone by his eyes, but in his case I can't help myself. His are black and flat and dead. Like dry olives. Without sheen or expression. When one can see his belt buckle, it's large and shiny, but it's usually obscured by his large belly.

He had slipped into office after the old sheriff retired. Once in, he had been fanatically proud of the honor. He invariably introduced himself as the High Sheriff of Copeland County. His snickering constituents usually referred to him as "The Mighty High Sheriff."

At that time I did not think he was evil. Just stupid. I had never said so out loud to anyone, but I am free to think whatever I like. I've heard his questions at district training sessions and listened to the complaints of his victims. He was a mean petty bastard who forgets our motto is "to protect and serve." He thinks it is and should be "capture and accuse."

He doesn't like me either.

Yet for all his comical inept braggadocio, there is a dark streak to this man. He reminded me of high school bullies who could explode when pushed too far. It was evident in the sudden flush of his face, and his over-the-top bursts of profanity. When one mistake compounded the next, Irwin didn't have sense enough to stop. He doggedly pushed on until he became embroiled in messes God couldn't fix.

Small counties work around such persons. Large cities work around them. Whole countries work around them. There's a certain delicacy to sheriffing in a small town. We're more inclined to load drunks in our squad cars and drive them home. What's required is a little judgment.

One night Deal had pulled over a load of high school boys who were celebrating the fact that Oren Pinnaker had just learned he was a National Merit Semi-Finalist. Oren was driving and John Chauncey had an open container of 3.2 beer in the back seat.

Deal gave Oren a breath test and when it came up clean, Deal arrested him for contributing to the delinquency of a minor. It was ridiculous of course, but Oren was jailed overnight. All charges were dropped and Deal was reprimanded by the judge, but the arrest was all it took to ruin Oren's chances of being accepted at Brown.

Colleges don't take kindly to students lying about the "have you ever been arrested?" question on their form. Nor do they give students a chance to explain the circumstances. After multiple rejections from Ivy League schools, Oren bitterly stopped applying for scholarships. His family was desperately poor, so he found work on a construction crew and after two years finally acquired enough money for tuition at a third-rate school.

"Hold it right there," Deal yelled.

"Good evening, Sheriff Deal." I kept my voice even, pleasant.

"Lottie Albright? Deputy Lottie Albright?"

"Undersheriff, actually. And you are not seeing double. This is my twin sister, Josie."

"You ladies are under arrest for breaking and entering."

I tried not to laugh. Even Irwin could not be that stupid. But the excited flicker in his little black eyes said he was.

"Sheriff Deal, we came over to try to find out who to notify about Reverend Mary Farnsworth's death." Inside, I seethed. Josie kept still and nervously eyed the gun which he put back in his holster.

"You have the right to remain silent," he said stiffly.

Unbelievable. Absolutely unbelievable.

Triumphantly, he finished reading us our rights.

"Irwin, I came over here as a friend of Mary Farnsworth. Sam Abbott sent me. But even if that were not the case, I'd like to remind you that I'm an officer of the law and could just as easily have come in that capacity to investigate her death."

"Hell you could. Not without my permission. You don't have the authority. She died in my county. My jurisdiction."

"You're crazy," I blurted, then thought, and shut up. We had built the church on the corner of four counties for the sake of unity, and not given any consideration to the other implications. St. Helena would be exempt from paying real estate tax, and after a brief squabble over its description in a brochure, law enforcement problems hadn't crossed my mind.

I had simply assumed Mary's death was in my bailiwick.

I glanced at Josie. She was regal, icy. Stone cold furious. I knew this although her face was still. Totally without expression. The quiet of a clinical psychologist required to stifle emotion in front of a psychotic client capable of violence. I closed my eyes. Deal would be extremely sorry for this stupid move.

But Josie's retribution would be in the future. This was now. He had not given us a choice. He was the sheriff in this town, this county, right here and now. We could not stop him from arresting us, but I could break the bastard's balls tomorrow.

"I get one phone call," I said.

"And I get one too," Josie added.

"We need a moment to talk about this," I said.

He looked unsure. I took Josie's arm and we marched into the ladies restroom, knowing Deal wouldn't follow us simply because the sign said "women."

"I can't believe this shit," Josie said. "Why in god's name you would want to live out here in this dogpatch piece of…"

"Shut up," I snapped. "Don't start any of that. We've got to use our heads. He will hold us to that one phone call and we need to make it count."

"Mine is going to be to Harold," she said.

I laughed. "Perfect. Just absolutely totally perfect." Harold Sider was a retired FBI agent and a lawyer to boot. He was a registered consultant in my county as was Josie. Harold would blaze right out here with enough authority to banish Irwin into outer space.

"And you? You'll be calling Sam, of course."

"Actually, no. He and Keith are probably still outside trading bullshit. I can't take a chance that they'll hear the phone. I'm going to call our dispatcher, Betty Central, and ask her to page Sam and get ahold of Troy Doyle and ask him to drive out to our farm. Betty will make sure they get the message. And I'll have her double check to make sure you get through to Harold." I fished in my purse for a notebook.

"I have Harold on speed-dial," she said.

"Wait. Let's make a list. Make sure we think of everything beforehand. Betty's a pain, like plugging into Twitter. This will be all over the state in a flash. However, she has her virtues, and will do everything we ask. She's like a rat terrier worrying a mouse."

We meekly walked into the main office. Deal nodded toward the telephone. He leaned against the wall, standing on one leg, his other shoe cocked against the cheap paneling, his arms folded across his chest, faking a Hollywood law officer stance.

Casual, casual, but his eyes gleamed with malice. "Phone's right there." He nodded toward it. "You each get one."

"Why Sheriff Deal, that would be illegal. I can't use Mary's funds to pay for this kind of call." Honey dripped from my tongue. "I know you want to do this right." I stuck out my wrists.

His face darkened. "Don't think that's necessary," he mumbled.

"No, I understand that you want to do everything just right." Behind me, Josie snorted. "I know you'll want us to make that call from your jail."

He frowned as though sensing some kind of a trap. Then he manned up and told me to get a move on. My sister, too.

"One moment sheriff," Josie said. "I have my cell phone with me. Let me see if I can make my call from here." She pulled it from the side pocket attached to her purse.

I looked at her hard to warn her not to waste her time, then I realized from the dull red gleam on her Blackberry, she'd activated the video function.

"Darn," she said. "My reception is no good here either." She tucked the phone into the breast pocket slit on her pullover with the lens facing out.

"Just don't hurt me." I turned back to Deal and stuck my wrists out once more. Maybe I would get the academy award. "Just don't do anything to hurt us. We'll come along quietly."

He blinked, sensing he was losing control of something he couldn't put a name to. Mutely, Josie stuck her arms out too.

Uncertain now, he hesitated before he got a grip on himself and snapped on the handcuffs.

It was like shooting fish in a barrel. We headed for the door, Deal trailing unhappily behind.

The jail was empty.

"We get our calls now," I snapped, knowing Josie was still recording. "You stopped us before, but it's the law."

Like fish in a barrel. We would probably both go to hell.

"Didn't try to stop…" he protested, confused. "Just call, damn it."

"We're entitled to privacy and I'll use Josie's phone."

Betty Central gasped with delight at the sheer importance of being charged with such a critical mission. "I'll get Troy right in here and go out to the farm myself."

"OK. And let Sam know we couldn't find information about Mary Farnsworth's family or her personal life. He'll have to send someone to her house and that's in Bidwell County. Next, Josie's going to call you. Separately. She's standing right here. She'll tell you how to reach Harold Sider. But before she does, hang up. I'm going to send you a video. Take it with you to show Sam and Keith and make sure you send it on to Harold. Then post it on YouTube."

Josie gave her Harold's work phone, home phone, cell phone and email address. Then we both obediently marched off to our cells.

Chapter Nine

Sam and Keith burst through the front door together. They shouted, raged. But Deal had passed the Rubicon. He could not turn us loose until the following morning even though by this time he'd undoubtedly figured out he'd made a serious mistake. Sheriffs can't simply change their mind once a criminal has been booked.

I hoped Keith would shut up, but of course, he didn't. When he started cussing Deal in earnest, Sam intervened. "Outside, Fiene."

When they came back inside Keith was silent.

"You've made a bad mistake here, Deal," Sam said. "And Keith's going to be outside all night long. I guess I don't have to tell you nothing had better happen to those two women."

"You can't talk to me like I'm some kind of a goddamn pervert, Abbott."

"Just telling you. Keith is going to be sitting outside the door."

"I can arrest him for loitering."

"Why don't you. That's a great idea."

"Oh go to hell. All of you. Wish I'd never heard of any of you. I have a notion to just turn those crazy women loose."

We could hear every word. I turned to Josie. "He can't. He's gone too far. He has to follow due process."

"Can't leave them alone either," Sam said. "What if they're suicidal?"

"Don't have no one else to call," Deal mumbled. "What if something else comes up?"

"Little late to think about that."

"Won't get no sleep with a homicidal maniac outside my office with a shotgun."

"Oh you'll sleep all right," Sam said. "That's when I'd be worried if I were you. Keith is an excellent marksman. Not that you have to be with a shotgun."

"He can't do this. Can't threaten an officer of the law." Deal's voice tightened.

"Course not," Sam said. "And he didn't. And won't. And there's no law that says a man can't have a nice little rifle or shotgun in his own gun rack in his own pickup. As a matter of fact, I recall that's one of the issues you ran on. The right to carry fire arms. Second amendment and all that."

We took turns dozing and were fully awake when we heard the outside door open shortly after sunrise. We heard Keith, Sam, Harold Sider, and other voices I didn't recognize. Deal came back to the cell, looking like he hadn't slept a wink. "Your lawyer is here, then we're all going over to the courthouse." He stalked off.

"Harold can represent us both," Josie said. "There's no reason to split this case. Unless you plan to turn on me." I was too tired to smile.

But when Harold Sider came back to our cell, he looked worried and even more rumpled than usual after an all-night drive from Manhattan. His soft brown eyes appraised us like we were a couple of teens who couldn't assess consequences.

"Now will you ladies tell me what's going on and how in the hell you managed to get yourselves into such a mess?"

We both started talking at once, and if it wasn't for Mary's death it might have been funny, but all of a sudden it wasn't. The fact remained that Mary Farnsworth's family had not been notified.

One look at Josie's face told me that despite our previous night's baiting of Sheriff Deal, she wasn't taking any of this in stride. She is a clinical psychologist with a lucrative practice and a part-time professor at Kansas State University. Harold began teaching there, too, after he retired from the FBI, but he focuses on forensic anthropology.

Josie could not afford to just shake hands with Deal when this was over and say "no harm done." And I knew it wasn't in her from a personal psychological stand-point either.

Only fools crossed Josie.

Harold took notes, nodded, then said, "We are pleading not guilty to the charge of breaking and entering, of course. I'll move to dismiss all charges and the only words I want to hear from you two are 'not guilty.' Got that? Nothing else."

We nodded in unison.

Magistrate Judge Willard Clawson had already gotten wind of what would take place today. Instead of his usual striped polo shirt and jeans he wore a blue button-down oxford with a limp knit tie and khakis. Normally there was a stack of Farm Journals and weed control bulletins on his desk.

He was my friend. There aren't many Democrats in Western Kansas and we tend to bond.

The Copeland County attorney, Fred Baker, stared at the floor, cleared his throat, and then announced the charges. But he couldn't look the judge in the eye. There were a number of persons observing the proceedings, all strangers to me. Some had notebooks. Others merely watched.

Harold moved to drop the charges immediately, and explained the circumstances; that I was the undersheriff of Carlton County and that Josie was a consultant for the KBI as well as the Carlton County sheriff's department. Judge Clawson knew all that, of course. Then he threw everything out and gave Deal the dressing down of his life.

Deal's face grew redder with each passing word. But instead of the county attorney trying to interrupt the judge's tirade, Fred just stood there and let Clawson go on and on.

When the judge finished, Harold walked over to Deal and slapped a paper into his hand.

"You've been served," he said.

Chapter Ten

Sam drove back to our farm in Keith's pickup, and Keith, Harold, Josie, and I went in the Tahoe.

"So just what was in that paper?" Josie asked. "I thought Deal was going to have a stroke."

"Charges I'm filing against him," Harold said. They include false arrest, malicious prosecution, defamation of character, and obstructing a police officer."

I was too tired to laugh. I noted my husband's tense posture, his firm grip on the steering wheel like he was driving on ice.

"Who were those people in the courtroom?" I asked

"Concerned citizens," Keith said. "Very concerned. They are organizing a recall election to kick Deal out of office. They don't like what's happened to you and your sister. It was the last straw."

"But how would they know?" I was dumbfounded.

"Seems there was this video someone put up on YouTube. Put up there by someone not too terribly bright. Someone not exactly known for assessing long range consequences. Someone who has a gift for bear-baiting. Someone who doesn't have the sense God gave a green goose."

My face flamed. I said nothing.

◇◇◇

Josie packed and I watched.

"I'm so sorry this happened," I began. "I'm just glad you'll be back home safe and sound."

She zipped her carry-on, then looked at me hard. "I'll be back during Spring Break," she said. "Next week. I'm not letting this go. This man besmirched my reputation."

I closed my eyes and pressed my fingers against the bridge of my nose. *Besmirched.* Now that was a word. I wanted to put this behind us and focus on Mary Farnsworth.

But Josie was out for blood now.

"But why? What can you do?"

"I'm going to help with the recall election."

We loaded her Mercedes and strapped Tosca into her cushioned elevated doggie safety seat which was designed to let her sleep or peer out. I leaned through the window and kissed them both goodbye while Keith watched, his hands shoved in his pockets.

"Sure you're going to be OK to drive? You've had a hell of a night. And morning," he added gloomily. "Might as well stay an extra day and get your bearings."

"I'm fine. Harold is going to be right behind me."

"I'd feel better if you would ride with him," Keith persisted, "and leave your car here since you're short on sleep. You'll be back out in another week."

She looked at me and winked. Harold had been up all night too, but then he was a man. She turned back to Keith. "I'm fine," she said softly. "Really."

◇◇◇

Keith milled around the kitchen. I could feel his eyes on me, hear his unspoken thoughts. Knew he was biting his tongue to keep from reminding me that he made a wonderful living and even if every crop on our farm failed and all our cattle died, he could do right well as a full-time veterinarian.

So why in god's name would a woman with a PhD want to tackle the work and humiliation that went with being a law enforcement officer in a poor county in Western Kansas? Yadda, yadda, yadda. I knew it all by heart. And I wished he would shut up, even though he hadn't said anything.

Besides, I had work to do. I called Sam. "Still no information about Mary's family?"

"No. The Bidwell County sheriff went over everything in her house with a fine-toothed comb. There's nothing there."

"Sam, that doesn't sound right. Are you sure? There should be some old Christmas cards with return addresses. Something.

"Smith swears there wasn't."

"Did she own or rent?"

"Rented. It's a little bungalow. Plenty nice enough. Neat as a pin. But nineteen years without buying? Just throwing money down the drain?"

"I don't see how any woman could live in a house for nineteen years without having some evidence of family around. Are you sure this man did a thorough job? Would a woman know of more places to look? Should I volunteer to double check?"

"It wouldn't hurt, but I've known Scott Smith for years and I don't think he would overlook anything. He's a good man. He says she didn't even subscribe to magazines or buy books. Everything she read she checked out of the library."

After we hung up, I headed for the stairs, then paused and listened to Keith's guitar coming from the family room. He softened his powerful bass, but there was no mistaking his sorrowful mood as he strummed and softly sang "Knoxville Girl." An ancient little ditty with at least a thousand verses about a man yearning to murder a woman.

When we were first married, I'd thought his selections were conscious, but I'd come to know he was innocent. Unaware of how clearly his choice of songs reflected his state of mind. That he didn't know this about himself fascinated me because he was highly intelligent. But Josie had noticed it right away.

I wanted to break his guitar over his head. He was searching for the right words to take me on when he finished playing. To let me know he was worried.

Silently, I went to the doorway and watched. His hands are large and thick-fingered. I don't understand how they can be capable of such dexterity. His jaw is square with a slight cleft. He's the first man women notice when they step into a room.

The family was deeply damaged by Regina's suicide. Keith most of all, though we never discuss it. He had thought it his duty to make that vain self-centered woman happy. Intellectually, he knows it doesn't work that way. But when we were first married and I would come home from the historical society joyful over discovering an obscure historical document, there was a look in his eyes that can only be described as relief.

Then seven years later, I introduced the mother of all double binds: he hated my foray into law enforcement, but feels duty bound to support me if it makes me happy. But when situations might lead to physical danger, it's painful to watch Keith struggle.

Deep down, he would like me barefoot and pregnant. Metaphorically, that is, because I never have been either—pregnant, anyway. By choice.

Starting a family was a big decision when one's husband is twenty years older and I have a stepdaughter older than I. And although we've been married seven years now, I'm still the wicked stepmother to Elizabeth.

For a brief period after I had responded courageously during last fall's crisis dealing with an elusive criminal, I had hoped our truce, her admiration would last. But it was a shadow victory, fraught with problems.

I sighed. I wasn't being fair to Keith. He was worried about the video riling people up, and his lovely old-fashioned protective instincts were the traits I loved the most. He wouldn't be the same person without them.

When he reached the verse, "Oh, Willie dear, don't kill me here, I'm unprepared to die," I smiled and walked over and gave him a hug. "I'm going to catch up on my sleep. I'm done in."

He said nothing. Just stood and wrapped his arms around me. I buried my face against his broad chest and he kissed the top of my head. I left and started up the stairs.

The phone rang. Keith answered, then called up to me. "It's Sam." He came up the stairs with the handset.

"Lottie we've got a serious problem," Sam said. "Mary did not die of a heart attack."

Chapter Eleven

Time seemed suspended. "Well, what then?"

"The district coroner doesn't know. They don't have the resources to find out."

"Please, please tell me they didn't use embalming fluids before they discovered this."

"They didn't. The KBI is taking her to Topeka immediately. Her family couldn't claim the body anyway now until the pathology department figures out the cause of death."

"I looked through her purse again to see if we overlooked something the first time. There were no hidden pockets."

"Did you wear gloves?"

"No. By now we have about a jillion fingerprints on everything anyway. I went through the checkbook again to see if there were slips of paper between the pages. The Wal-Mart receipts were for groceries. There was nothing unusual in the cosmetic bag and the mending kit came from a Super Eight."

He sighed. "I feel like a fool."

"I'll call you right back. I want to take another look at that bag of supplies she was going to take to persons around here." In fact, tired as I was, I knew I wouldn't be able to sleep until I checked out an idea. Maybe she hadn't planned to distribute everything. Perhaps some item was for her personal use.

But if so, why would the items be labeled with the names of persons living in this county?

I hung up and went to our home office and took the plastic sack out of the cupboard. Keith watched from the doorway. "I want to look at the diabetic kit."

"Wait." He went into the kitchen and came back with a pair of disposable latex gloves from the box he kept for professional use when clients brought small animals over to the house.

"Thanks. But, it's a little late for that." Yet Sam also had commented on fingerprint contamination, so I supposed it wouldn't hurt. I slipped them on, then reached for the diabetic kit labeled Bertha Summers. I unzipped the little case holding testing strips, the lancing pen, and the monitor. I pushed the memory function.

Nothing. No thirty day history or fourteen day history. I checked the code on the testing strip vial. The monitor code had not been set yet. Everything looked brand new. Even so, we would check all of Mary's medical records.

I sighed and zipped it back up. If she had been a diabetic, perhaps there had been an insulin screw-up. An overdose or underdose.

"Something?" Keith asked.

"Nothing. I thought maybe Mary was a diabetic and she was in some kind of a medical state because of that. It would have made it simpler."

"That's because you don't want to consider murder," he said flatly.

He was right. I wanted a simple solution. Most of all, I wanted one quickly.

I put the kit back in the bag, pulled off the gloves, and stood.

"Your instincts were sound," he said. "Turn the bag over to the KBI. Might be something in that salve, or the aspirin, or hiding in that roll of bandages."

I looked at him sharply. He was not kidding. "You're right. I'll call Sam back and tell him the KBI needs to look at these things too."

Wearily, I dialed Sam and told him that Mary didn't appear to be a diabetic, but of course we needed to check it out with her doctor.

Just in case.

◇◇◇

I woke up six hours later and took a warm shower. Keith had coffee waiting and had rightly decided that a big breakfast made more sense than a lunch.

"Oh honey, you didn't have to wait around for me to wake up."

"I had office work to take care of. So say thank you and sit down."

"Thank you," I smiled. My stomach wasn't up to bacon, eggs, and toast, but I faked it. And I expected to be grilled. For a take-charge person, my job had to be pure torture to him. But I kept my side of the bargain now by telling him everything.

As I ate, I went over everything I knew.

"There have to be employment records. Her W-4 should be on file along with everyone else's."

"Well it wasn't. And none of this makes sense. A normal healthy human being doesn't simply drop dead. And what do you think about Edna's saying that a stranger gave Mary a heart attack?"

Keith didn't like to stray over to a medical doctor's territory. As a veterinarian he usually stuck to his area of expertise, but he read and studied a great deal. "I've read that a sudden shock can cause an episode, but you said there wasn't any sign of a heart attack."

I nibbled on a strip of bacon and thought about Mary dropping the chalice. "As to the stranger, everyone was a stranger to most of us. Then afterwards, we all just wanted to get the hell out of there."

"So you have a body, no way to notify anybody, and no cause of death."

"Right. That's about it."

"I'd start with the family issue first. There's got to be something somewhere that will let us know who she is."

I smiled at the "us."

"Did you check her phone logs?"

"Yes. It was all business or local calls. Nothing there. Pizza Hut, dry cleaners, places like that."

"You said absolutely no one got near the body?"

"That's one of the few things I'm sure of. No one got in or out of that room. It was in full view of the entire congregation until the end of the service. There's simply no way someone could have taken something out after she died either, because everyone left except me and Bishop Talesbury, and I'm the only one with a key to that room. It was unlocked during the service and after she ran there she locked it from the inside. She died without a soul going near her."

"Then she had to die of a natural cause. They simply haven't found it yet."

"They'd better."

"Face it, Lottie. There are really only two other possibilities. Suicide or homicide."

"If it were suicide or a homicide, there had to be a method, a means. We've got nothing."

"Don't want to piss you off, sweetheart, but is there any chance at all that someone came in after you left?"

"Oh, don't worry about upsetting me. The only thing that's bothering me right now is figuring out how this woman died. Believe me, if you or anyone else has a bright idea, I want to hear about it."

He rose and walked over and kissed my cheek and squeezed my shoulder before he picked up our coffee cups and carried them to the sink. "Well, one thing's for damn sure, Mary Farnsworth didn't just suddenly materialize out of thin air. There has to be some record of who hired her and when."

Sam looked up from his desk when I came through the door.

"Anything?"

"No, I'm tracking down the state agency that would have hired someone—what? Nineteen years ago?"

I shrugged. "Don't ask me. She's been here ever since I moved to the county and you've been here forever." Sam was one of those perpetual sheriffs that are simply reelected every four years in Kansas. Long hours and low pay doesn't attract very many candidates.

"Can't remember when she came," Sam said. "I'll tackle the government and why don't you start on when and how she became an Episcopal priest."

"OK. Couldn't have been before the mid-eighties because there was a lot of division over the whole question of admitting women to the priesthood. It was a flaming mess. Worse by far than the knock down drag-out over gays right now."

"And you were in diapers and remember all that?"

I smiled. "Not that young." Josie and I will be thirty-nine this fall. "Research, Sam. Last winter I finished an article for *Kansas History* tracing the introduction of liturgical religions on the plains."

He reached for his pipe, tamped it, added tobacco, and eventually coaxed it back to life. "Learn anything at all that might have some bearing on this case?"

"Not that I can see. But some things are really peculiar. Bishop Talesbury is a dead ringer for a Catholic bishop in the 1880s."

"Who wouldn't have had any off-spring."

"Right. Theoretically. But the resemblance is creepy. Just plain eerie."

"Can't see where that would have any bearing on this investigation."

"It doesn't," I said, slapping my knees. I rose and started toward my little cubicle of an office. "It should be possible to trace Mary through Diocesan records. The Episcopal Church in America has one of the most stringent vetting processes in the world for ordaining clergy. They look at everything from intention to psychological soundness. So there have to be detailed records at the Diocesan office, even if she was a Canon Nine priest."

"Which is?" Sam drummed his fingers on his desk, as he thoughtfully pulled on his pipe.

"One who is not seminary trained and only administers the sacraments. That Canon was eliminated in 2003, but priests ordained before that time retained their status. They have to earn a living another way and are sometimes sent to places where congregations are struggling and only have enough money to keep the lights on."

"A tentmaker priest then," Sam said.

He surprised me sometimes. "Exactly."

Sam had finally developed respect for my historical methods. I was tempted to launch into a spiel about Catholic monks forced to serve communicants on the frontier, but I didn't dare get started on that subject when I need to spend every second on Mary's death.

"What was the title of your article, Lottie?" he asked as he began dialing the phone.

"To Hell or to Kansas."

He laughed.

Chapter Twelve

I had never met the office manager at the Diocesan headquarters but she recognized my name.

"Yes, Miss Albright, I imagine you're calling about scheduling St. Helena's consecration ceremony."

She hadn't heard! "Actually, no…"

"Rest assured that it's on the top of Bishop Rice's list. Now let me see what we can work out."

When I could get a word in edgewise, I told her the very bad news.

Silence. Then, "Where can you be reached?"

I gave her my number.

"I'll call you right back."

But the return call came immediately from the bishop, the Right Reverend James P. Rice. He didn't bother with so much as a "Hello, how are you."

"Miss Albright, is this your idea of a joke?"

Why would I be joking? I was so rattled I hardly knew what to say. "I can assure you, sir, that this death is no joke."

"I'm not disputing the fact of a death," he said, softening his tone.

"I'm simply trying to find her family, sir, and I knew the Diocesan office would have a record. Perhaps you haven't heard all of the details? She died in our little church during my niece's confirmation service."

A long pause before Bishop Rice replied, then he spoke carefully. "The church we're trying to schedule for consecration later this year? A young woman's confirmation without my permission?"

I froze, overcome with a feeling that something was going on that made no sense.

Even though I had never met this bishop I had heard wonderful things about him. As a lapsed Episcopalian I knew there had been a lot of changes in the church, and my opinion about religion had changed dramatically since I was young and rebellious. I wanted to go back to the church. If I could have even a fraction of what Keith had through Catholicism, I would be happy.

The Bishop and I were both speechless.

"Let me make sure you understand why I asked if this was some kind of a joke," he persisted. "Your niece was supposedly confirmed in an unconsecrated church by a bishop I've never heard of? Assisted by a female priest I've never met?"

Edna Mavery was right. It was possible for a heart to stop beating. Just from hearing words.

"I don't know what to say," I finally managed as mine restarted.

"Needless to say, I don't either."

"I'll come there. Right away. Do you have time this afternoon?" I glanced at the clock. "Around four?"

"Yes."

His "yes" sounded more like a command than assent.

I usually spent Monday afternoons at the courthouse putting together family stories for the county history book. I called Margaret Atkinson, the office manager, and asked her to see if William Webster could man the office. Both persons had just barely approved of me before I took the deputy sheriff job. It's hard telling what they thought of my becoming an undersheriff.

"Sam, I'm heading to Salina," I said breezing past his door. "Gotta hurry to make it there by four. The Bishop wants to talk to me about Mary Farnsworth. And a number of other things.

I'll call Keith on the way." He was on the phone and wiggled his fingers at me to indicate he'd heard.

Salina was generally considered the historical division between Eastern and Western Kansas although I consider Hays to be the philosophical place where we ripped the sheet. Nevertheless, the split has been stark since the 1880s with jokes like "There's no Sunday west of Junction City and no God west of Salina."

There was some basis for truth to that. I've never studied a region so grounded in self-reliance. Although most of the settlers who rushed to Western Kansas when the Homestead Act opened up free lands were from the Midwest, it was the New Englanders who most often stayed. Proud stubborn S.O.Bs. Or Volga Germans like my husband's ancestors who rejoiced in hardship and proving how tough they were.

I would like to have a nickel for every time I've heard someone say "God helps them that helps themselves" out here.

◇◇◇

Bishop Rice was a tall thin man with a regal air and a reputation for having a wicked sense of humor. There wasn't a trace of that present when he came to the reception room after the secretary announced my arrival.

"Bishop Rice," I murmured, my mouth dry.

"Miss Albright, come in. I'm sorry we're not meeting under different circumstances. I've read several of your publications with a great deal of interest."

"Frankly, I'm surprised. Sometimes I think journal articles are the dullest reading material in the world."

"Well, yours aren't," he said kindly.

I looked at the wide range of titles in his ceiling to floor bookcases. The usual predicable tomes by theologians. Plenty of philosophy and classical fiction and much to my surprise, a large number of contemporary mysteries. Some were hard-boiled police procedurals. I smiled at the shelf of old-time westerns. He was not a squeamish man and certainly not a snob.

His lips lifted in an amused smile as he followed my gaze. "Well, do you approve?"

"Sorry, sir. I didn't mean to be that obvious. I'm always interested in what people read."

There was a quick flash in his unwavering green eyes. He'd caught me in a lie. I was sizing him up and he knew it. But through his reaction, he'd cleared up my first question. I could trust this man. He wouldn't tolerate the slightest bit of dishonesty.

"I hardly know where to start," I said.

"That makes two of us." He gestured toward a chair opposite his desk, and sat in the large wine leather one behind it. He templed his fingers under his chin and prepared to listen. "Why don't you begin by telling me all the steps that led up to this tragedy, then your involvement both as an Episcopalian and as a law enforcement officer."

"All right." It took a while and he interrupted me often and took notes on a legal pad. I included the account of Josie's and my night in the jail, and ended with the information that Mary had not died of a heart attack.

When I finished, he swiveled his chair toward the window and looked at a squirrel leaping along the branches of a greening elm. Then he turned back toward me.

"Needless to say, I've simply never come across anything like this before. But you should understand that as far as the Diocese is concerned, there's no Mary Farnsworth, your niece has not been confirmed, your church has not been consecrated, and furthermore, I've never heard of the Right Reverend Ignatius P. Talesbury."

I swallowed and tried to take it all in.

"So let's start with what we do know, if anything. Your little group of four counties had approval to build St. Helena. And you obviously understood that permission depended on every last bit of it being donated. That was one of the conditions." He looked at me closely to see if I acknowledged the importance of not depending on the Diocese to fund anything in this economy.

"Yes. And it was on donated land with donated materials. The inside is nothing to brag about, but we'll take care of that in no time with silent auctions. Bake sales, the usual."

"Here's the second condition. Before I can consecrate a church I must make sure the land on which it is erected has been secured for ownership. That was the reason for delay. I wasn't fully satisfied about land ownership."

"Well…those forty acres were a problem, but the alleged owners…"

"Alleged, Miss Albright?"

"It was the best we could do, sir."

"Being satisfied with paperwork is part of my job description."

"Sir, I'll give you all the abstract information. Ownership of all the land around is clear and easily traceable. It's only these forty acres that seem to have risen up from Middle Earth. It's funny, but one of the land owners of an adjacent field said it has always been a family tradition not to farm those particular ten acres on the edge of his property. He didn't know why."

"And the other owners or alleged owners?"

I smiled. "When we pointed out the legal mess, that's all it took. Two of the other land donors, used their acres for pasture and one of them doesn't run cattle anymore. The Carlton County donor was a widow, Edna Mavery, who thought all her land had been sold when she moved to town. They were all glad to sign over their acres for our little church."

He sighed. "I come from Dallas. It's hard for me to get used to these little churches out in the middle of nowhere. They're all over. And all denominations. When I first came here, I thought they were abandoned buildings. They are, but parishioners won't let them die."

"We made a terrible mistake having St. Helena straddle four counties. From every angle. It's a legal nightmare because no one knows which county has jurisdiction." I gave him more details about Josie and my encounter with Sheriff Deal and our wild night in the Copeland County jail.

"Can Sheriff Deal do that?" He was clearly amazed.

"Technically, yes. So he did."

"You a coffee drinker?"

"Sir, I am. Black."

He nodded, walked over to a little inset sink and mini-bar, and flipped up a louvered cover anchored to an upper cabinet. Filling cheery mugs sporting the Episcopal church symbol, he handed one to me before he sat back down.

"All right, let's move to what you do have some answers to and work our way up to this fake Bishop. To begin with, why did your niece want to be confirmed in St. Helena? Isn't she from Junction City?"

"She is. And of course, there's an Episcopal Church there. It's where she received all her preparation for confirmation. My uncle, Frank Clements, my mother's brother, used to go on the wheat harvest in Western Kansas when he was in high school and he just fell in love with the High Plains."

He held up his palm to stop me while he made a few notes. "Go on."

"Uncle Frank heard about this church and called me, asking if Keith and I would host a family reunion if Tammy could be confirmed out here. We're overdue for one. A lot of my folks have never met Keith, my husband. So naturally we said yes and we thought it would get our little church off to a great beginning if we included the whole congregation."

"My next question has to do with Mary Farnsworth," he said. "I don't know who she is."

"Apparently, I don't know either. That's one of the reasons I came in person. I have too many questions myself for you to handle with a phone call."

"Our office doesn't have one iota of information about this woman."

"I thought I knew Mary well. She's been in the area a long time." I explained her unselfish service as a social worker. Her long days. "But it turns out we didn't know a thing about her."

He thrummed his pencil on his desk, then laced it back and forth between his fingers like he was handling a baton. "Are you sure she's a priest?"

"I've been thinking about that. I have no proof, but yes, I'm sure. Different persons have mentioned her being at little house churches in Northwest Kansas. No big deal. Not unusual out here. Several families just want to receive communion. A coffee table substitutes for an altar."

"There's no reason I can think of why someone would want to fake being a priest," he said flatly.

"None," I agreed. "No money or prestige out here. Back East, maybe, but not here."

"There's no record of this woman in the Diocese records. She had to have been ordained somewhere else and if she came here nineteen years ago, it would have been in a firestorm of controversy. A lot of people left the church over the ordination of women."

"Could she have used a different name?"

"Not if she were ordained in this Diocese. I've traced every woman processed here. They are all either alive and well or dead and buried."

"So she entered the priesthood before she came here."

"Yes. And I'm inclined to agree with you. I believe she was a bona fide priest. Especially if she was involved with house churches. Parishioners who are devout enough to organize one usually know ritual backwards and forwards. I'll see what I can find out. Which brings us to…"

"Which brings us to the Grand Poo-Pah himself," I said. "Why would anyone try to impersonate a Bishop?"

"Can't come up with an answer for that one either. I know for a fact Mary Farnsworth wasn't ordained in this Diocese. And I believe she either changed her name or was simply using an assumed one. But this bishop fellow…" His voice trailed off.

"I know this sounds like a cliché, but you'd really have to have been there." I launched into all the gory details of the savage sermon, the people's reaction and the awful finale of the man cutting a circle out of the carpet.

"He's not an Episcopal priest," Rice instantly put his hands on his desk, shoved to his feet and began pacing. "He's Catholic. An old, old-line Catholic. Haven't heard of anyone doing that for years. He's ultra conservative. They did that back in the 1800s."

I was relieved to know my own denomination didn't cut out carpet for burning.

"Who invited this man into my Diocese to begin with? Visiting clergy have to be cleared by me."

"A Mrs. Mabel Sidwell. She said it would be just fine and I didn't know any better."

"Maybe not, but something's rotten in Denmark, all right, Miss Albright."

"Worst of all, we're not one bit closer to finding this poor woman's family." Actually, there was something worse. The mystery man's comments that caused Mary to drop the chalice. But until I checked with Sam, I thought it prudent to withhold that detail.

My cell phone rang. I flipped up the carrier on my purse and looked at the display. Sam.

"Excuse me, but it's Sheriff Sam Abbot. I have to take this." Bishop Rice rose and gestured toward a door. "If you need privacy."

"Hello Sam. One moment. It's not necessary for you to leave, sir."

Then blood thrummed in my ears as I listened. Bishop Rice watched and grew very still. I have the kind of complexion that visibly loses color. I could feel it happening now.

"My god, Sam. I'm telling you that's impossible. No, nothing here. Nothing at all. Bishop Rice checked the files. Is there anything else I should do while I'm here in his office? Or should I head back home?"

Sam told me to take my time. I hung up the phone and squared my shoulders.

"Bishop Rice. Sir, it is my sad duty to inform you that Reverend Mary Farnsworth was murdered."

Chapter Thirteen

The drive back to Western Kansas gave me time to think. I put in a classical CD, all instrumental, not wanting to be distracted by words from any wailing vocalist down on life. I was already filled with sorrow.

Facts and puzzles chased through my mind like leaping squirrels. Sam had stated flatly in his no-nonsense, no-argument tone of voice, that Mary Farnsworth had been poisoned. That was a fact. The KBI said so. The bureau had moved Mary's body to the state headquarters in Topeka to do a sophisticated screening.

Fact two was there was no way in hell anyone could have murdered that woman. No way in or out of that door after she dropped the chalice. Besides, the anteroom was right off the sanctuary. Anyone coming or going would have been in full view of the congregation.

My OnStar phone rang in. Sam again.

"The KBI wants to process that chalice, Lottie, and when I told them about the carpet they want to look at that too. I just hope to hell you haven't burned it yet."

"I haven't. And I haven't actually washed the chalice. I'm supposed to wipe it with a special cloth. But the KBI is barking up the wrong tree."

"Maybe so, but they want to cover all the bases."

"OK, but believe me, no one could possibly have put anything in the wine during the service. I'll explain this to you when I get back home."

"Keith says he's looked all over your house and nothing is there from the service."

"It's still in my car. The chalice, the linens, the carpet. Everything."

"OK. Terrific. Turn around and take everything to Topeka. I'll let them know you are coming."

"But what about the chain of custody?"

"They'll just state that they received it from you. None of us suspected any of that stuff might contain clues to a murder."

"I'm on my way." I hung up and turned around at the nearest gas station. Even though everyone apparently assumed that something happened during the service, I knew it wasn't possible. Our church has a common chalice. The Bishop is the first person to partake of the Body and the Blood. The second person is the priest, and then the choir members and lay readers, followed by the congregation. Even though we had no choir and Mary had doubled as a lay reader, none of the communicants had keeled over. No one could do a bait and switch with everyone in the church looking on.

The stark fact was that Mary's poisoning occurred after she fled from the sanctuary. I had been nearly back to my seat when I heard her scream. She was fine until some stranger played bloody hell with the service.

Edna had said the precise words were "I know who you are and I know what you've done."

I knew who Mary Farnsworth was too, and I knew what she'd done. She was an unselfish brown wren of a woman who built nests and nourished little birds. She found homes for babies, the abused, orphans, or children who would be better off as orphans rather than remain with their parents.

There wasn't a mean bone in her body and no signs of a double life. No reason on God's green earth why anyone would want to kill her. I winked back tears. Keith worried about my job because he didn't want me to come to any harm. He wanted to take care of me. I thought I loved my job because of the dose of real world existence. But today I hated it too. I hadn't signed up for murders.

I went through layers of security before I could hand over the collection of items, and then I had to write out a formal statement. Despite exhaustion and coming down from a coffee high, it wasn't hard to organize my thoughts.

I covered every detail I could think of. I included Edna's account of the missing communicant and suggested someone question her. Perhaps someone skilled in hypnotic techniques would pull more information from her. As for myself, I had not been aware of this man as I was too upset by the vicious sermon.

The agent in charge, Frank Dimon read my entire statement. "If you don't mind, Miss Albright, we have a few more questions. Especially about church procedure."

"This wasn't typical," I said. "I don't want you to think this was the way things are usually done."

"What do you mean?"

I explained that an established church would have a formal Altar Guild who understood the importance of their work. "Yesterday, I found rules for Altar Guilds on-line. I was woefully ignorant of the proper procedures. There's even a special way to launder the linen. Even the purificater used to wipe the chalice has to be rinsed before laundering and the water poured into a special sink called a piscina with a pipe draining directly into the earth."

To the officer's credit, he did not smile or indicate disrespect, but I thought it sounded crazy. Like we were some kind of fanatical cult instead of members of one of the first denominations on the American shores. Many of the founding fathers had been Church of England, and the Episcopal Church in America was still part of the Anglican Communion even if some faction was always raising hell.

Frankly I didn't give a damn what Agent Dimon thought of our church. All I cared about was finding a Sleep Inn where there was good lighting the whole width of the bed so I could read a little before I went to sleep. Because I had no intention of driving back home until I got some rest.

I stood. "I'll call back with my motel number. I'll leave around eight tomorrow morning so let me know if you have more questions."

I swung by Wal-Mart to pick up toothpaste, a toothbrush, a few cosmetics, deodorant, a nightshirt, and Loren Estleman's latest mystery. At home everything was prepacked into a tote. I kept supplies of my favorite toiletries so I could go anywhere, anytime, at a moment's notice. But today, I hadn't planned to drive on in to Topeka. I had intended to talk with the bishop and go straight home.

After taking a long shower and washing my hair, I thought questions would still be banging around in my brain. But when I settled down to read, I was a goner. I woke up about two to use the bathroom and saw that I hadn't even managed to turn off the lights. Since I hadn't asked for a wake-up call, I slept until nine and then I felt like I'd been beaten.

No room service here. There was a café across the street and I was starving. I threw everything into the Wal-Mart shopping bag and slid the heavy brocade drapes open to let in sunlight before I called the KBI to see if they needed anything before I headed back.

"As a matter of fact, we do have some issues," Agent Dimon said. "It's about the service at your church."

Inside, I groaned, but I wanted them to have some respect for the Western third of the state and I couldn't expect that if I acted like some wimpy woman who crème-puffed out over having to work a few extra hours.

"Certainly, I'll swing by as soon as I've had breakfast."

Agent Dimon gestured to a chair directly opposite him. At least we had some privacy even though his office was sparse, almost monk-like.

He did not waste time on small talk, and reminded me of the serious, bleak man who played Hotch on *Criminal Minds*.

"Would you please go through every step of what occurs with the wine and the wafers."

"I'll be glad to but you're looking for clues in the wrong place. Probably because it's been done so often on TV and in books, where someone slips poison into the communion wine."

Again, I explained why this was not a possibility because the Bishop sipped first, then Reverend Mary, then the remainder of the congregation.

"It's sort of like the dog that didn't bark," he said.

"Exactly." I was relieved he understood. "Only in this case, there's all the people who were not poisoned. That's my point exactly. It would be impossible for the suspect to poison one person without poisoning them all."

He took extensive notes and his eyebrows rose over the locked anteroom. "We'll know more when we're sure what poison was used. In the meantime, we're going to find out where Mary Farnsworth came from and needless to say we need to know more about that mysterious bishop. And we want to interrogate the woman who heard the man say words that apparently set this whole episode off."

"Edna Mavery? I wish she didn't have to be involved. She was extremely upset."

"Has to be done. You know that."

"Of course. Just go easy. Don't badger her." We didn't need another death in Carlton County and Edna looked like a heavy breeze would blow her into Kingdom Come.

Chapter Fourteen

On the way home, I replayed everything, sure of only a few things. The KBI would soon know the chalice had not been tainted, the carpet just contained cheap wine, and none of the gathered linens had absorbed even a trace of poison.

Then my mind rebelled against the next confusing fact. Mary had been poisoned. The KBI said so, and the most likely suspect was a man who got had gotten away. A man no one remembered except a very timid little old lady. If only the bishop…

I was a hundred miles from home when Sam called.

"Just thought you might like to know right away, Lottie, the test on the carpet, the chalice, and the linens were all negative. Just plain old cheap wine there."

"I knew that, but at least now they know that, too. So we've made some progress."

"Not really. Doesn't account for the poison. We still have over a hundred witnesses that no one went into that windowless room."

"Oh, it's worse than that, Sam. Bishop Rice says he can't find Mary Farnsworth in any records and no information at all about Bishop Talesbury."

He said nothing.

"I can see how Reverend Mary might have slipped under the radar, but not Talesbury. Any new developments on Deal's recall election?"

He snorted. "Are you kidding? It's the talk of Northwest Kansas. You wouldn't believe the folks coming forward. There's no question but that he's out the door. The no-good son-of-a-bitch will be lucky if he doesn't end up in jail."

"Goody."

"He's gearing up to make trouble, Lottie. Just feel like you need a heads up. Deal is related to nearly a third of Copeland County and those inbred cretins are tight. They look out for each other. Circle the wagons right off the bat. And you are still an outsider."

I sighed. I had lived in Western Kansas going on eight years this fall, but would be considered an interloper until the day I died.

"Heard from your sister yet?"

"No, but she's coming out here over Spring Break. She didn't take well to being arrested and fingerprinted."

◇◇◇

I swung up our lane late afternoon. Keith's Suburban wasn't there, which was just as well. I couldn't stand the thought of answering any more questions or having to reassure him that I was fine. Perfectly fine.

He'd left a note on the counter explaining that the Holder's cattle had gotten out and one had been struck by a passing pickup. He was going to see if the steer was just bruised or had to be slaughtered. "Love you," he'd added. "Don't wait supper. Be home as soon as I can."

Exhausted, I headed for the deep leather chair and ottoman that was my home turf. I read and dozed there, and did my best thinking. I managed to think all of three minutes before I fell sound asleep again. The night in the Copeland County jail and the drive across Kansas had worn me down. A single night's sleep in a motel certainly wasn't enough to restore my energy.

A sound woke me up and I started awake to see Keith tip-toeing across the floor. "I'm awake," I mumbled.

"No you're not," He crossed over to my chair, scooped me up, and sat back down cradling me in his lap. I lay quietly against his big chest.

"Just hold me," If we were in bed, I'd be asking him to cover me all up, without any part of me sticking out from under his body, so no one could find me or get me.

A fine brave mindset indeed for an undersheriff. He laughed, recognizing my intentions as I snuggled closer and closer.

We're both early risers, but I was up first the next morning and called up the stairs when breakfast was ready. I fixed a western omelet and ladled hash browns out of the skillet, then poured orange juice, and buttered toast before placing the slices on one of our cheery Fiestaware plates. He bounded down the stairs, kissed me good morning, then ate like a professional wrestler as usual.

A deceptive morning. A normal morning. An all's right with the world morning. There should be a law against such a morning. A law against such a belief in sanitized security that allows us to believe that if we are good people and do our best and try to love our neighbors then everything will be fine. Absolutely fine.

But that's the kind of people we were. Me, because Josie and I were to the manor born, with the kind of bright optimism that comes with wealth. And Keith, because he had risen up from sheer force of will. He could, by God, simply make things go his way.

So we spoke of normal things. Spring things. Gaily joking about it being the time of year when the tumbleweeds come and beat my tulips to death. His eyes shone at the prospect of lambing time for some of our neighbors. Our stubborn buffalo grass would soon be greening up.

"I'm going into the courthouse today. I didn't see yesterday's mail?" A question, not a statement.

"Damn. I forgot. I'll get it right now." He headed out the door. Our mailbox at the end of our lane was assembled from yard art and featured a cowboy with a rifle slung over his shoulder cradling the mailbox under one arm.

I went back upstairs to make the bed and put on make-up. "Lottie!" Keith bellowed at the bottom of the stairs. "You need to read this. Right now."

I bounded down the stairs.

"What?"

Silently, he handed me a folded piece of paper. It did not have a stamp or postmark. Someone had put it directly into the box. It had been printed off a computer onto the kind of white paper nearly everyone bought from Wal-Mart. I read the blunt message.

"You have no business trying to get rid of Sheriff Deal. He's a fine man. He has a family. Cease and desist or you'll be sorry. P.S. We mean business."

I looked up. "Deal's relation, no doubt."

"Those people can be nasty, Lottie. Just because they're dumb, doesn't mean they're not dangerous." He slapped a rolled magazine against his thigh. He brushed a lock of his hair from his forehead and reread the letter. "Can't tell if this is intended for you, me, or both of us."

I shrugged. "I'm not going to let it bother me." I turned and started back up the stairs.

"Wait a minute. We need to talk."

I came back down.

He waved the letter. "This is the last straw."

"Keith, it's not that big a deal."

"I've been mulling things over ever since Irwin threw you and Josie in jail. We always end up making fun of the bastard and leaving it at that. That was one of the reasons I was so upset over the YouTube video. It diminished him to some kind of harmless buffoon. He's not."

The morning sun streamed through the window, highlighting his light brown hair.

"I thought you were mad simply because we did it."

"I was. Still am. But mainly because you didn't seem to understand that it's a mistake to cross that family."

"Listen! He crossed me first."

He held up his palm gesturing me to stop. "I don't want to get into an argument about that video."

"Good."

"It's time we started taking that man seriously. I'm going to put an end to this."

"How? This isn't the Wild West, you know."

"I'm going to help Josie and get behind the recall election one hundred percent. We're going to put that whole ignorant clan in their place."

"OK." This was clearly a pronouncement. A decision he'd come to before the "last straw" letter came. He had no intention of talking it over with me. I smiled at the image of Keith and Josie working together. Superman and Wonder Woman on the High Plains.

The phone rang. I sighed and went into the kitchen to answer it. Sam again. I listened as Keith watched my face.

"Trouble?" he asked when I hung up.

"You could call it that, but it might be a blessing. Troy called in sick again today, and I think Sam is getting ready to fire him. He's simply not working out. He wanted the job, or at least the badge. Just the badge probably. Without all the piss-ant duties that go with it."

Keith smiled.

"Now I'll have to sheriff again this afternoon and I wanted to spend the whole day at the historical society. I have a whole stack of family histories piled up, and we have to get new pages to the printer by Friday."

On the drive into town I went over all the events of the past two days. Absolutely nothing made sense. Not Mary Farnsworth's death, nor the appearance of the mystery bishop, if he really was a bishop. In fact, the only thing that seemed comprehensible was the letter. It was a good old fashioned real world petty threat.

I could handle that.

Chapter Fifteen

The next morning I was able to work at the historical society, and had appointments with three persons. Helping two of them organize their family stories would be a welcome diversion. However, the third person was Edna Mavery and I hoped she had recovered from being so close to such a grim event. If she were still tear-prone I couldn't guarantee that I would keep myself together either.

My office is inside the Carlton County courthouse in what can only be described as an old vault. The room is narrow and the ceiling is laced with old pipes. It is painted institutional green and the floor is covered with yellowing tiles, many of which have corners torn off to reveal the black tar paper underneath. Unsanitary, depressing, and trippable.

I could afford to repair and redecorate the whole place. For that matter, I could afford to build a decent office somewhere outside the courthouse, but I was in a battle to the death with the county commissioners. They refused to grant one penny for "expendables" and I kept submitting the same budget requests year after year. The county benefitted plenty from the plethora of electronics I had brought in to use. All I asked was that they do right by their responsibility to keep the place up.

The first person to walk through the door was Chip Ferguson, an ancient cowboy so thin I'd considered the possibility that he might be anorexic. The old bachelor wobbled a little when I rose to shake his hand.

"Miss Lottie." He touched the brim of his hat. His pearl-buttoned western shirt was clean, but frayed. He surveyed the pictures hanging on the walls. A can of Scholl chewing tobacco left a white outline on the back pocket of his faded jeans. His straggly little beard did nothing to improve his appearance. He handed me five pages written on lined tablet paper.

I was thrilled that all kinds of persons were contributing their family stories. Some counties used county history mills with fill-in-the-blanks forms to create standardized stories. The responses usually came from affluent established families. But in Carlton County we used a home-grown format exclusively. All the fillers and illustrations came from our own residents. The pages were sprinkled with clippings from old newspapers.

To my amazement, quite a number of spinsters and old bachelors like Chip came forward. It was as though they were eager to leave a written record since they had no family to bear witness to their lives.

I glanced at the pages. "Would you mind staying for about ten minutes, Chip? While I look this over? I may have questions."

"No, ma'am."

I went to the copy machine and made a working copy of his story. Once in a while something came in that was highly unusual and this was one of those times.

There was no white space on his pages. Absolutely none. No space between the lines, no margins, and his handwriting was tiny. This man was either very rich or very poor. He did not come to town often and the heels of his boots were lop-sided and practically worn off.

I wrote "working copy" at the top with a red ink pen. This was an instance when the paper, the manner and size of writing, said as much about the person as the writing itself. I was not an expert in handwriting analysis, but sometimes the evidence was very, very obvious.

His first sentence was about money. His first dollar. And the rest of the copy followed the same theme. It was hard to read because of the crowding. He sat stiffly, his hat balanced on his knee, his mouth a thin line. I usually have tremendous sympathy for a person's struggles and emotions. It's an instant insight into their souls and I expected to pick up on this man's loneliness and despair.

But as I read the totally objective account of how he had deposited the original dollar here, then there, then bought sheep, then land, then gold, and as I kept glancing at his face, I realized he was a predator. He would never ever allow anything to come between him and his money. Certainly not a wife and family. Suddenly chilled, I laid down the story.

"Very impressive," I said carefully. There was no doubt in my mind that he was the wealthiest man in Carlton County and with this story, he intended to announce that fact for the first time. I did not make the mistake of trying to draw him into conversation.

"Thank you so very much," I said, rising. "No questions on my part. Your accomplishments are quite amazing."

He nodded. Clapped his hat back on his head, turned, then paused in the doorway, as though he wanted me to know something, then changed his mind and started down the hall. A small boy slammed into him.

"Jimmy! How many times have I told you not to run. Apologize to that nice man this very minute."

He refused. Head bowed in shame, hot tears trickled down his flushed cheeks. He put his hand inside his mother's and she gave him a tug. "Right now, Jimmy."

The boy looked up and up and up. "A cowboy," he marveled. "A real cowboy."

She tugged on his hand again.

"Say it, Jimmy."

"I'm sorry, mister cowboy." He stared in wonder as though Chip had just stepped out of an old TV western. "Can I ride your horse?"

"Jimmy! Please excuse his manners."

"No harm done, partner," Chip straightened to his full height, tugged on his hat and nodded to Myrna Bedsloe and walked on down the hall. But not before I had seen the momentary proud softening in his eyes when he'd looked down at the boy.

Myrna was my next appointment and she came in with her usual entourage. A little boy clung to her skirt, she carried another, and little Jimmy followed. All three were adorable in matching outfits, and they all had her bright red hair and hazel eyes.

"That man? Was he Chip Ferguson?"

"Yes." I was surprised by her interest.

"He tried raising sheep about five years ago, but got out of it. I wondered why he quit."

And I wondered why she cared. Myrna talked non-stop while I made working copies of her husband's story that started with his grandparents and ended with the birth of their own children. They were the least likely family I knew to have skeletons dangling from trees.

"I guess my own family's story is sort of dull," she said. "But we've just always had good luck. We've been blessed." The boy she held tugged at her hair, and she pulled his hand away and nuzzled his neck until he giggled. "You're a blessing. Yes you are, even when you're full of the devil."

"Candy?" I mouthed, not wanting to suggest it if she didn't allow sweets between meals.

"What about it, boys? Think you've been good enough to pick out a sucker?"

"Yes," they both chorused together.

I opened my desk drawer and pulled out an assortment of Tootsie Pops. They said "thank you" with a little prompting and waved goodbye as I watched them walk down the hallway.

If only there were more people like Myrna in the world. "All blessings and good luck," she'd said. No problems. And she'd meant it. I could see it in her happy face and those of her kids. "No problems."

The truth of the matter was that she had been taking care of her husband's mother ever since they were married. A nasty old woman with Alzheimer's who could aggravate a saint. Her husband was a broody man who second-guessed every decision they made on the farm.

If he'd planted wheat, he immediately regretted that it wasn't milo. If he borrowed operating money, he wished he'd skimmed by and done without fancy fertilizer. I knew this because he managed to find time to come to the coffee shop every day and complain about himself. Not about God, or the world, but himself. And of course every word he uttered was transcribed, verbatim, into the town gossip mill. Twitter had nothing on the speed of our town's information network.

"Well, I'm a dumb son-of-a-bitch," he'd begin, according to the husband of my office manager, Margaret Atkinson "They ought to take a rope and hang someone as dumb as me." Then he would launch into his latest farm decision, his antenna aquiver for opinions, to tell him if he'd made a mistake or had lucked out.

Myrna held his world together.

This woman swore she had a blessed life. But she worked like a galley slave and most people knew it. No one would be able to keep up that kind of existence forever.

I watched her cheerfully herd her sons down the stairs, and stood there for a moment, thinking about the two persons who had just dropped off stories. Chip would be shocked that I considered him as ruthless as any Mafia don and Myrna would be really shocked to know I saw her as teetering on the edge of tragedy.

Margaret came in and picked up a pile of newspapers she would scan for clippings in her home. "So what did Myrna have to say?"

"Not much. She changed Tim's family story. Again."

"That's what? The third time?"

"Uh-huh. Until it goes into print, or I've done some work on it, I guess it doesn't matter."

"Changing that story should come natural to her." Margaret said. "Considering the front she puts up about her husband."

I didn't reply, because I didn't want Margaret to get started on Myrna. My office manager can be a dreadfully unkind person, but she was often right. She simply looked for the worst in people, and of course it's always there.

"Folks think Tim depends on her, but that's not so. Myrna needs to be married to a weak man so she can be the star. She needs to hear 'ain't that pitiful. She's little better than an indentured servant. Just think what she might have been.'"

Margaret left with the papers. I hoped she was wrong. But there was something unnerving about Myrna's relentless cheerfulness.

Chapter Sixteen

Was Margaret right? I knew how easy it is to read into other persons' lives complications based on our own. My own curiously difficult marriage that only Keith and I understand, or think we do, sometimes causes me to look at situations with rose-colored glasses.

Strangers. We were all strangers to each other and ourselves, I thought savagely as I stared at my face in the mirror. I dug out a brush and unpinned my chignon, attacked my thick black hair, then braided it while I focused on the collection of strangers besides my immediate family who were driving me crazy: the Reverend Mary Farnsworth, Bishop Ignatius P. Talesbury, and an unidentified man who had triggered a series of events that had set the Kansas Bureau of Investigation reeling.

Edna Mavery was my last appointment of the morning. She had asked for personal help with her story because she had trouble grasping a pen.

Her old rheumy eyes were wet when she came through the door. Alarmed, I rose and squeezed her hand as I put my arm around her shoulder and ushered her over to a chair.

"Edna, you didn't have to come in today," I said gently. "We can postpone this. Give yourself a little more time."

"Don't need no more time. Can't get that poor woman's face out of my mind. She was the sweetest person." Her eyes brimmed again.

"Yes, she was."

"Have you found that man yet?"

"No, I'm sorry to say that no one remembers a thing about him. Not a thing. But let's get on with your story." I spoke quickly, suddenly realizing that very few people knew Mary Farnsworth had been murdered instead of having a heart attack. There certainly was no need to burden this poor woman with that information.

"Do you mind if I record all this?"

"No," she sniffed. "I'm just sorry you're going to have to go to all this trouble just because my hands won't work right."

"Nonsense. I write about thirty-five percent of the stories."

"I can't dig and pull weeds anymore. Could last year. Now my son in Wichita takes care of all my bills. My social security, everything, goes through some kind of a fancy on-line bank. But as long as I have my little house, I do OK."

It was a good arrangement, but I doubted it would last much longer. She was simply too frail to keep living by herself. Just months away from falls, missed steps, leaving pots on the stove too long.

A fight loomed, and I had met Stuart Mavery. He was a conscientious man, a CPA. He understood the importance of keeping his mother in her own home in charge of her own beloved garden as long as possible. But the time was coming.

I switched on the recorder.

"I was born in Iowa. There was three of us girls and two boys."

I paused the tape, checked the spelling of names and listed them on my pad.

"I was not the wild one. Gerta was."

The phone rang. I dealt with a couple of printing problems before we continued. It was close to noon and Edna's ride would soon be here to pick her up and take her back to the house. She had finished high school, then married a farmer her parents had more or less selected for her.

"I wanted to teach, but my parents thought I ought to grab Henry when I could. We had two children. A son and a daughter.

They was just darling. Henry turned out to be…not the person we thought he was. Mean. Mean to his stock. Mean to me. And mean to the children.

Shocked, I paused the tape. Her chin quivered and her mouth tightened. She clenched her teeth to keep her dentures from clicking.

This was a clean-up story. One that persons told me behind the scenes. The kinds of stories that never made it into the books. County history articles and family stories were not intended to embarrass anyone and they were not supposed to get the historical society sued for libel either.

"I did everything I could to keep my children happy. Made little treats, looked after their clothes. Once when they was just little, Oliver found a little nest of field mice. The mother mouse got plowed under and he took them home and Mary Claire tried to feed them with an eye dropper. I knew Henry would beat the boy half to death. He was that kind of man. Course we couldn't keep the mice. No one in their right mind lets them get started."

I took notes, but I still did not turn on the tape. Tears streamed down her parchment cheeks. I reached for a box of Kleenexes and handed it to her.

"Freezing is the easiest way to die. I read that in the *Reader's Digest*." She dabbed at her tears. "So I put each little mouse in a section of an ice cube tray and froze them. I thawed them out before the children came home from school and told the kids it was awful hard to keep wild things alive."

I laid down my pen. At the historical society, I hear my share of strange stories, but this one was right up there.

"It saved the children from a beating. We gave them a nice little funeral before their dad got in from the field, and they didn't have to think of their mother as a mouse murderer."

Just then the phone rang. The caller ID displayed Josie's number. Edna's ride knocked on the door and she struggled out of her seat. We weren't finished and it was hard telling when I could lure her in again.

"Josie, let me call you back." I hung up and helped Edna into her coat.

"I'm sorry we had to cut this short," I said. "I'm free next week if you can come in then. Or shall I come to your house?"

"No need. Nothing more to tell. I came to Kansas and married Archie, Stuart's dad. He died fifteen years ago." Her mouth quivered again. "I get up every morning and go to bed every night."

Her depression was worse than I thought. "Well, if there's anything you want to add, let me know." I said this knowing there was no way she could unless someone brought her in here again. Those hands, those poor old arthritic hands certainly couldn't handle a telephone.

After I saw her out the door, I called Josie back.

"I'm just checking to see if there's anything you want me to bring there from civilization," she said.

I groaned. She would be in Carlton County in another week. It was quite clear she had no intention of cancelling the trip and Keith certainly hadn't mellowed.

I took a deep breath. "Josie, there's something you should know."

"In the interests of full transparency," she chided.

"Something like that. Anyway, yesterday morning, someone…"

"Left a note in your mailbox."

"Yes. How could you possibly know that?"

"Well, my darling brother-in-law told me so."

"You've been talking to Keith?"

"Every day. We are coordinating the recall election. For Sheriff Deal," she prompted. "Lottie, are you there?"

"Are you two nuts? Coordinating? Like heading it? I thought you and Keith were merely going to help out Copeland County residents. You barely survived this county last year and you're going against a man who has more crazy relations than a dictator in a third world country."

"Didn't you tell me just a couple of days ago that we needed to do something about this man?" No mistaking the frost in her voice. I was not up to a little mini-analysis session. I headed her off.

"Yes, but I meant quietly behind the scenes, not setting the whole Fiene family against the Deals. Or perhaps I should say Deals and Albrights."

"Well, get over it, Lottie. I'm not going to let this go. I'm going to nail that bastard's hide to the wall."

She would too.

Chapter Seventeen

My afternoon at the sheriff's department was uneventful. Like the job was supposed to be. I checked some of the databases I didn't have access to on my home computer, but could not find any records on Talesbury.

Betty Central would relieve me at five. I spent my time compiling a list of expenses and composing the weekly report for the *Gateway Gazette*. It was worded as though offenders were anonymous, but there wasn't a person in town who didn't know exactly who had committed an offense within minutes of the occurrence.

Sam had once threatened to send all our forms directly down to the boys at the coffee shop and save our office the work of filling them out.

About three Bishop Rice called.

"I've got some good news and some bad news," he announced.

I laughed. "Is there any other kind?"

"The good news is the bad news, actually. The Right Reverend Ignatius P. Talesbury is really and truly a bishop."

"So that means Tammy is really and truly confirmed."

"Yes, possibly."

"Possibly?"

"There are circumstances regarding Talesbury that are a bit peculiar."

"That doesn't surprise me. Has he been defrocked? Just released from the pen?"

"No, no, nothing like that, and I didn't mean to give that impression. He was ordained in Africa many years ago."

"Africa?"

"Yes, his father, John Talesbury was in the Peace Corps there in the 1960s. He fell in love with another volunteer who was actually from Western Kansas. Someplace around where you built your little church."

"Another small world story." I emptied a box of thumbtacks and starting sorting them by color as I listened.

"Yes, but it's complicated."

I smiled weakly, full to the brim with daily complications.

"The father was Catholic, and mother Episcopalian. In fact, she descended from an Englishman who settled in Kansas."

"I know a lot about these settlements," I said. "They tried to recreate the Church of England on the High Plains. I'm working on an article about them, but go on about Talesbury."

"Of course the mother had to agree to raise the child Catholic."

"I knew it! Or rather, you're the one who said Talesbury was Catholic right off the bat."

"Not only that, but being raised in the Church abroad explains why the ways you described were old, old rituals. That is often the case in other parts of the world. He may have even been raised hearing the Latin Mass long after it was discontinued over here."

"So their son became a priest?"

"Yes, and went to a very strict seminary."

"Obviously. But I want to know how he became an Episcopalian."

He sighed. "The usual way, naturally. He met a woman, left the priesthood, and of course, our church welcomed him with open arms. Better to marry than to burn, not everyone has the gift of celibacy. Yadda, yadda."

"As in St. Paul. How to keep from going to hell. Etcetera, etcetera. "

"Yes, well."

"Did the marriage take?"

"No. As you can imagine from what you've said about him and according to some letters from parishioners I had faxed to me, he was a very rigid man." He sighed. "Some priests carry a token stole everywhere in case unexpected circumstances call for vested rites."

"Rigidity is often a disguise. Please don't tell me he's some kind of pervert. Or a thief." Although our denomination hasn't been plagued with the massive sex scandals devastating our Roman counterparts, we've had our share of sticky-fingered clerics.

"No. He has an absolutely stellar ethical background in one sense of the word. In fact, that seems to be the problem. He has no tolerance for human fallibility. It's a despicable mindset. He's supposed to be the mediator between the people and our Lord. Instead he's refused communion to an appalling number of persons if he's heard about a whiff of scandal."

"He can't do that," I said. "It's one of the things that can get an Episcopal priest in deep trouble."

"Exactly. And that's just what happened."

"And the Diocese kicked him out?"

There was a long silence on the other end. "Miss Albright, actually we have another way of referring to this procedure. It's called a statement of disassociation."

I stirred my little pile of thumbtacks and messed them up again. "So that makes him what?" I asked. "Exactly what is he now? What is his position or status within the church?"

"Well." I could visualize this elegant man's face struggling against the impropriety of making light of Bishop Talesbury's unexpected appearance in our little corner of the world and his sense of humor that appreciated irony. "Well, this makes him an ex-Catholic priest who married, became an Episcopal priest, then a bishop in a little country in Africa we know very little about."

"And then he came over to America where he went over like a lead balloon."

"Exactly. And then he went back to Africa to a region where he was appreciated."

"But why did he come to America?"

"That's one of the few things I do understand. Anyone who had a lick of sense got out of Africa in the nineties. Did you see the movie, *Hotel Rwanda*?"

"Yes. Massive killings. Massacres and governments changing every little whip stitch. There wouldn't have been any problem getting over here, since his parents were American citizens. Even if he was born in Africa."

"There was no problem with any of his papers."

"And his wife? Was there a problem with her credentials?"

"What wife? As one might imagine, the marriage didn't last any time at all."

"Was she an American?"

"No, Afrikaner."

"So, he migrated to America alone?"

"Yes. No children. Oddly enough, African bishops and the Episcopal Church are often linked in the news lately. Many conservative American congregations who object to the ordination of gays find ardent supporters in African bishops who are all too happy to come here and perform sacramental duties."

"I'm aware of the controversy."

"That's too lengthy a topic to go into over the phone," he said, "but I was quite vexed to learn that it was an African bishop making this end run into my Diocese."

"Thank you, sir. I still have some questions, but you've cleared up a lot of them."

"Glad to talk to you. Let me know if you need more information."

"I will. Again, thanks." I was tempted to tell him about the results of Mary's autopsy, but Sam had become a stickler about protocol since last fall, and I supposed I should wait until we knew the method used to murder.

We said our goodbyes and I started to hang up, then I wanted to get in one last question.

"Sir, Talesbury's parents. You said the mother had come from around here. What was her maiden name?"

"Deal."

Chapter Eighteen

I do my best thinking on the drive home between the sheriff's office and our farm, Fiene's Folly. So named because our house is very extravagant for Western Kansas: multi-storied with many frou-frous. Actually, it's smaller than a number of the Tudor or contemporary homes that family corporation farmers built in a fit of euphoria during spikes in wheat or cattle prices.

Deal.

That one word had cleared up a number of mysteries. Talesbury was a Deal on his mother's side. And even if he had not been trained in Africa, it explained his mean little mind. No matter what their occupation, a Deal was always a Deal.

Keith was coming from the west and he honked and waved giving me first dibs on pulling up the lane. He parked his Suburban beside my Tahoe, and rolled down the window. "Want to go out for a bite to eat before I put this up for the night?"

"Great. Let's." I pushed the remote and drove into my side of the garage, parked, then flew up the stairs to strip out of my sheriff's shirt into a blue and black striped T-shirt and a black fleece jacket. The jeans would stay, of course. There was little reason to wear anything else anywhere at any time.

When I wanted to put on the dog, as I did now and then, I went back to visit the urban scene with Josie. Plus my husband could look like a million bucks when he chose to do so. And he did so choose. I saw to that even if it were only an appearance at one of Josie's charity functions. Usually for battered women. Black tie. Expensive.

I would like to say these events were primarily attended by pampered married couples and women whose idea of trauma was choosing the right nail polish. But Josie had set me straight on that. The jewels, the expensive hair-dos, the European vacations, the cars, were often facades for hiding patterns of cruelty that curled my hair.

Families, relationships, are the same everywhere. Happiness in those least likely. Devotion, devastation, cruelty, all those traipsing down Thoreau's path of quiet desperation.

Keith was going through the mail when I came down the stairs. "Boy oh boy, do I ever need this."

"Thought so," he said, as we swayed into a kiss that came dangerously close to derailing the night out. "Gonna ply you with likker."

"When has that ever been necessary?"

I loved these evenings even though the Broken Pony was a dive. The lower part of the walls were corrugated steel like that used in stock tanks, and the upper section sported old paper bags slit open and pasted into a rustic collage. Naked single bulbs hung from the ceiling and the floor was bare concrete.

There were rumors that the owners intended to paint it someday in a mottled brown that emulated upscale places in Denver, but I doubted it. There was no need. It was the closest place to go outside of the Moose Lodge in Gettysburg and that was a forty mile drive.

They served wonderful prime rib, even if their idea of scotch and soda was a sinus clearing double jolt of some concoction that came from god only knew where. In fact, I suspected it was residue from our local ethanol plant. But anything was better than Keith's home brew.

Brenda Gold waved us toward a table where menus were stuffed into a plexiglass stand adjacent to paper napkins. The placemats had connect the dots drawings and a little word game along with a large picture to color.

She did not offer us any Crayolas. She silently slammed our drinks down on the pocked, cigarette-burned, chipped, Formica-topped table. She stood before us and waited for our order, then stamped off as though we'd affronted her when we asked for prime rib and baked potatoes.

A fight with her husband again.

We'd learned not to take this erratic service personally. I didn't mind. In fact, it was infinitely preferable to evenings when the two of them were getting along and I was bombarded with complaints about her "cretin neighbor who turned on his screeching woodworking tools night and day and if I didn't do something about it she was going to kill him herself."

Keith winked and walked over to the jukebox. I sipped my scotch and studied his broad back, knowing exactly what he would select: one of the few old country classics listed.

I smiled as Kitty Wells launched into her reply to the "Wild Side of Life." I was ridiculously happy. These evenings began with good talk and ended with good sex. And while we were here, I would tell him every last detail of this incredible tangle of persons involved in Mary Farnsworth's murder.

And he would treat me like an adult law enforcement officer instead of some beautiful wild animal in a nature conservatory needing protection from predators.

God bless scotch. All it took was a couple of swigs and I bravely launched in to "there's a few things you need to know."

His eyes narrowed. "She was murdered."

I checked myself before I murmured, "Maybe."

She was, and I needed to face that.

"Yes."

"I thought you said there's no way someone could have put poison in the wine without everyone being poisoned."

"There wasn't, Keith. There just wasn't. And besides, all the tests run on the residue in the chalice and on the carpet were negative."

"So what then? How?"

"Don't know." Our salads came. We were quiet for a couple of minutes. "Oh and the bishop called." I told him about Talesbury's background.

"I think we should start writing soap operas," he said. "Sort of a rural husband and wife team."

"They would be an instant hit."

My cell phone rang. I glanced at the ID. Betty Central. I considered letting it go to voice mail, but didn't.

"He didn't show up," she said happily, loving to be the bearer of bad news.

"Who?"

"Troy. The new deputy. He's supposed to be on duty, but he didn't show up."

"Is he alive?"

"Sort of. When he didn't answer the phone after three separate tries, I sent one of his neighbors over to check. He was there watching *American Idol* with his girl friend. Bertha said they were already three sheets in the wind," she added triumphantly. "So I decided to call you. Sam is plumb tuckered out. So I called you first."

In fact, Sam and I had agreed on new rules. One of us was to be on duty at all times. When that proved nearly impossible, we'd wrung enough money out of the commissioners for a part time deputy.

Troy was fired. Right this instant. I called him and told him so and managed to keep my voice steady. He was too drunk to ask why.

I could have wept, but I didn't. My lovely evening gone. And I hadn't even gotten laid yet.

"I've got to work," I said simply. The façade, the little lie I assumed in the presence of my husband when I first became a deputy sheriff slipped back into place. Despite my pledge to be honest at all times. My heart ached with disappointment but I wanted him to see me as a professional.

He sighed and examined his hands. Whatever he yearned to say, he kept to himself. He rose and headed toward the cash register. I followed. He paid for uneaten steaks, knowing that Brenda would raise hell if he didn't. It would be all over town the next day that Keith Fiene and his high-falauting city wife walked away. Just walked away from a bill.

The Suburban was cold and so was Keith.

"You going to be all right?" he asked as he parked in front of the office and let me out.

"Yes. I didn't even get to have a full drink and all I have to do is sit here because the chances of something coming up is…"

"Remote? Shit!"

"Damn it."

"And by the way, I hate to challenge your notion of just how fine you are, but I think I should point out that you don't have a car here."

"Uh-oh."

"Got you covered. I'll take Betty out to the house with me and she can bring your Tahoe back."

"OK. She was supposed to go off duty when Troy got here, but I suppose she won't mind a bit of overtime. I'm sorry."

He said nothing and drove away.

I threw my purse into a corner, then remembered I didn't have my gun there and called Keith on his cell and asked Betty to pick it up before she came back. I went to the closet where I kept an extra shirt and changed into it.

We have a cot set up and a little mini-fridge. I was starving since we had left the Broken Pony before we were served. I opened the fridge and took out a withered apple and checked out the half-loaf of old bread for mold. It looked iffy, so I threw it away and settled for cheese and crackers and brewed a bracing pot of coffee.

Betty came bouncing through the front door, gave me my gun, and gleefully announced that Keith didn't seem like himself and she hoped nothing was wrong between us. She hopefully scanned my face for some trace of affirmation.

"Everything is fine," I said brightly. "He just had a hard day. Some kid's 4-H lamb died." A bald-faced lie, but she deserved it.

Her face fell. "I'll be off then. Call me if something comes up."

"Will do." She didn't live far from the jail and one of her very few virtues was that she woke instantly and relished the idea of being called in when something happened. Which it rarely did.

She left. I found one of Sam's old paperback westerns and settled down to a long still night in Western Kansas. I couldn't concentrate on my book and ended up pacing back and forth. I laid down and tried to sleep, but it was fitful. I jerked awake about one. The wind had come up. I looked at the deserted street.

Dead tumbleweeds that had piled up against the grain elevator last fall were making their escape. Bugs zoomed around the street lights which barely illuminated the few scattered cars.

Suddenly the electricity snapped off and I felt my way toward Sam's desk. I opened the top drawer where he kept a flashlight. We had one land line phone that didn't depend on electricity so folks could call in a 9-1-1. There were no street lights.

Nothing to do but go back to sleep now. Literally nothing. No reading. No watching the cheap portable black and white TV. It usually had miserable reception under the best of circumstances, so even if the electricity was on, there was little point in firing it up.

I winked back tears. My wonderful evening ruined for nothing. I couldn't even make lists. Lists help, no matter what Josie thinks of them. A crash. I jumped, then peered out the window. A tin bucket dislodged by the wind ricocheted down the street, joining the tumbleweeds in a wayward journey.

Women had gone crazy on the prairie years ago. I've often thought about what it must have felt like to sit in a one-room soddy with a passel of kids when the wind was blowing. How did they stand it when the wind rounded the corners with an eerie whistling sound? A teasing sound. If it blew long enough and hard enough to dry out precious banks of overturned sod, it could strip the topsoil little by little and layer by layer and blow the seed right out of the ground.

Even when I couldn't hear it, the air was charged inside my own tight house with good windows. Static electricity hung in the air and we might as well have been living in a mental institution that applied electroshock therapy.

I went to the cot and stretched out on the thin mattress. I pressed my fingers against my temples, hoping I could ward off a headache.

Deprived of light, too exhausted to sleep, I was forced to face facts I had been evading. I wasn't able to manage these two part-time jobs. Part-time jobs have a way of morphing into full-time. I couldn't keep up our household either. It showed and I knew Keith hated it, although he never complained and pitched in whenever he could.

I felt guilty wherever I worked. I was behind on the county history books. Sam and I were run ragged when anything came up that drew us out of our daily routine. On the home front, I could barely manage to keep up with the laundry and daily chores.

Unless I made some changes, my overworked life was not a temporary condition. I was sinking into a bog. *But I can still reason*, I thought. I punched my pillow. Time to climb out of the quicksand.

We needed a reliable deputy, and I would find a weekly housekeeper. Someone who would run errands.

I absolutely would not reduce the hours our historical society was open. Perhaps I could tickle Margaret into organizing a search for more volunteers. Perhaps if I gave her more authority to boss to people around, she would be flattered. And perhaps pigs would fly.

When the thrill of planning concrete action wore off, I began to cry. Why not? I was safe here. Not likely that someone would come in or call or even need me. The only person who needed me was home alone in our lovely king-sized bed.

And I was here alone on a lumpy cot.

Chapter Nineteen

Josie's Mercedes pulled into the yard two days later. It was piled with suitcases and boxes. Tosca yipped disdainfully at our two sheep dogs as the car sailed past. She was buckled into her special seat and sported special riding attire.

Josie parked and rubbed the small of her back as she climbed out from behind the wheel.

"My God, my God. Why hast thou forsaken me?"

I laughed. "Oh come on now. The drive across Kansas isn't all that bad."

"It is. And it gets worse every time. Even Tosca seems to know what she's in for."

Keith came out of the house, opened the door on the passenger side and undid Tosca's seat belt. "Come on girl. Let's get some water."

Tosca scrambled out and Keith hugged Josie. Just last fall it would have been unthinkable. Back then, they both prickled up when they were around each other.

"Good to see you, sis. Despite the circumstances."

She laughed. "And how is my campaign buddy?"

"Making progress. I go out and talk to people just about every night. We've already got a lot of signatures on the recall petition."

"Good. And I've thought of a great slogan," Josie said. "Time for a New Deal."

Keith whacked his forehead with the palm of his hand and groaned. "New Deal has been done, I think."

"You don't like it? Really?" Her eyes were wide open. Innocent.

"I can top that," I said. "How about No Deal."

"And we are the Dealbreakers," Keith chimed in.

"Perfect. Now let's get her luggage inside the house." Josie and I happily headed up the stairs for the "spare bedroom," in fact, a private suite.

"You look drawn," she said, putting her suitcase on the floor. "What's happening here now?"

I sighed. "Lots. Get settled in and I'll tell you everything." I wanted her to hear my version before she heard Keith's analysis.

She fished in her purse for her cigarettes and a lighter. We had an agreement. Actually, she had an agreement, and I didn't know for sure how it had happened. I could bitch, scold, and throw all kinds of fits, but the truth was, my work brought me in contact with all kinds of persons. And if I was judgmental about their smoking it would hamper a lot of conversations. People smoked when they were nervous or happy or depressed and especially when they wanted to tell me something about their family.

And as far as the second hand smoke factor, once I'd inhaled a lung-full of dust and been caught in the drift from a crop-duster it seemed foolish to make a fuss.

"You're going to die." I said anyway.

She smiled. "Eventually, yes. Still sort things?"

"That's not the same," I protested, firmly suppressing the image of thumbtacks. I hurried toward the doorway. "I'll get your luggage, and put the finishing touches on supper."

She blew a smoke ring and looked amused. Too late, I remembered I had said "supper" instead of "dinner."

It was too windy and chilly to sit outside on the patio. But Keith had installed a fire-pit in our screened-in porch on the east side of the house. It functioned as a morning room and partial greenhouse. On days when I couldn't bear the futility of trying to grow flowers on the plains, I fled to this room. It was private and green and lovely.

"You were going to catch me up?" Josie said.

"Yes, but you and Keith go first. Just where are you in the grand campaign to oust Sheriff Deal?"

"It's not going to be a grand campaign," Keith said. "It's going to be sneaky and underhanded and a *fait accompli* before the S.O.B. gets word of it. It's the only way it will work. The last thing we want is to get that whole clan riled up."

"But he'll know who's behind it."

"Of course. Eventually. And then all hell will break loose. That's why we've got to get all the signatures first."

"I agree, Lottie," Josie added quickly. "He's told me a lot about these people. They sound sadistic."

"They are. It's a harsh word, but they are." My stomach muscles tightened. It was the truth. They were simply mean people. I'd known when Josie decided to take them on, that it would mean trouble.

Josie never backed down.

Gloomily, I sipped the very good scotch she had brought with her. I raised the glass and eyed the contents back-lit against the flickering fire and tried to remember just how I'd gotten into such a mess. For the hundredth time since I'd become a law enforcement officer I went over the toll it was taking on my personal life.

I always came full circle back to the beginning. It was all my fault. I had volunteered for the job to have access to information so I could solve a murder. And I'd stayed because I felt I was doing a good job with a position in the community no one else wanted. Or at least no one who was actually worth a damn. Too many Troys wanted to carry a gun and too many Deals did too.

This county deserved better.

"When we go inside where I can spread a map on the table, I'll show you where I've been, and we can divide up the remaining territory," Keith said.

I glanced at him and then Josie. They had obviously been talking a lot. It was a welcome event. When they'd first met, Josie could barely manage to be civil to my husband. It was as though she regarded him as the incredible hulk and not remotely worthy of marrying her sister.

"And am I going to have a part in this grand scheme?"

"No," they said together and immediately.

"Sorry. You just can't do this, honey," Keith said. "Josie and I have talked and it would be disastrous if a sheriff from Carlton County got involved."

"I need to be the resident bastard," Josie said. "You would be an unnecessary complication."

I couldn't think fast enough to decide if they were right.

"Remember, Deal threw us in jail maintaining we didn't have the right to investigate Mary Farnsworth's death. Now murder."

"Murder?" I looked at Keith. How did she know that?

He looked sheepish. "Josie had to know what she was getting into. I couldn't just let her come out here without knowing a thing."

"Right."

"There's a murder involved here. A murderer running around. Someone killed a fine woman. You two were just trying to find some information so you could notify the family when Deal jumped you."

"He wasn't totally off-base," I said. "I've given this a lot of thought. If it were my county I would have questioned anyone I saw in a county office after dark. After a death."

"I know that," Keith said. "You might have questioned them, but you wouldn't have thrown the sheriff from another county in jail."

"No, there is that. But that's Deal for you."

"You still haven't told me about the rogue bishop," Josie said.

I laughed. "Rogue bishop just about sums it up." I told them about Talesbury's background.

Having adopted Keith, Tosca slept on his lap emitting soft yips from time to time as he stroked her coat. Tonight she had soft yellow bows in her twin tufts of hair. Little yellow flowers were anchored in the ribbons.

Keith smiled down at her. "Spoiled rotten, aren't you sweetheart? Like two women I could name, but won't, because they would take my head off."

Josie smiled and blew a smoke ring. It was good. Mellow sitting here in the fading light with my two favorite persons in the world. Trading ideas, sipping good liquor, talking, united in purpose, exchanging gentle banter.

"Oh and there's something else," I looked at Keith. "Even you don't know this because I didn't have time to tell you before I went to work the other night. Bishop Talesbury is connected to folks out here."

"So that's how he came to preside over Tammy's confirmation," Keith said. "I've been wondering about that. He's an odd duck to just show up out of nowhere."

"You're not going to believe this." Tosca lifted her head and studied me with interest. "Talesbury's mother was actually from Western Kansas. In fact, her maiden name was Deal. He's related to the Deals."

Keith exploded. "Jesus H. Christ." Tosca yelped and ran trembling to Josie. "Do you mean to tell me that bishop is a Deal?"

"Well, yes. Way back. But chances are he's never met any of these Deals."

Josie studied my husband. Studied this man whom she no doubt had regarded as a great logical stabilizer, the arbitrator of everything reasonable and sensible in the family. I didn't know whether to be embarrassed or appalled that she was being exposed to his other side.

He slammed his fist into his open palm.

"This changes everything. What if a Deal was involved in this murder? Josie, you should rethink getting involved in the recall election. If there's a chance someone could get hurt, this kind of business is best left to the menfolks."

My heart sank. I was too stunned to laugh, and the look on my sister's face was beyond offended. Way, way past offended.

She was looking at him like a bug under a microscope. A smile twitched at the corner of her mouth and a look of infinite tenderness crept over her face.

Go figure.

In an instant, I knew she would take a bullet for Keith, but she would not stop organizing the recall election.

We are identical twins and it's not reasonable for me to view Josie as prettier or smarter, but from time to time I feel like Cinderella's ugly step-sister and right now was just such a moment. If she'd said "Oh, Rhett," and begged him to carry her up the stairs and ravish her, I wouldn't have been surprised.

She looked incredibly lovely in the fading light. Her dark eyes widened at the force of this man she couldn't have.

He was mine.

She knew that.

"I'll be fine, Keith." Her voice was firm, closing any further discussion.

We all stood and went inside.

Chapter Twenty

The next morning we acted as though nothing had changed. Keith and Josie agreed on territories and he circled houses that belonged to Deals, their relations, or dyed-in-the wool supporters.

"Just remember we've got to get this done fast, before Deal's family launches a counter-campaign. And if you don't mind, Josie, I don't think your showing up in a Mercedes is a good idea."

"Gotcha. Do you have something else I can drive?"

"My pickup."

"Good."

"You're going to play this straight, aren't you?" I asked. "Not pretend you're me?"

"The thought never entered my mind."

"In fact, that's going to be part of her pitch," Keith said. "That she was just visiting and is a KBI consultant and a psychologist and Deal was so dumb that he just arrested her out of the blue without trying to find out a thing about her background."

"You know this just might work."

"Oh it will," Josie said. "We secretly freelance as political consultants."

"Don't want you to feel left out, Lottie," Keith said. "But you've got to keep your nose out of this."

I laughed. "All right. It's not like I don't have anything else to do. I'm very, very behind. In fact, I've decided I need more help than just cleaning ladies coming in once a month. I'm going to find someone willing to clean every week and run errands and catch up on laundry."

"Great," Keith beamed. "That's great."

I smiled at the relief on his face.

"And a cook?" Josie asked. "Please tell me you're adding a cook."

"Not a chance," Keith said. "Then we'd have to show up on time for meals. It doesn't work that way out here. It would create more stress, not less. I can't come in from the field to please some woman wanting to show off her cooking."

Josie rolled her eyes.

"It might take me a while to find someone. Then I'll look for a competent deputy. I haven't had a normal day at the historical society in ages."

"Is there such a thing as a normal day out here?"

"Not really, but there are a few bright spots. Edna Mavery's son called. She's the one who claimed the man kneeling next to her gave Mary the heart attack."

They both looked at me expectantly. "Did she remember something else?" Josie asked.

"Nothing like that. Stuart just said that his mother perked right up after last week's taping session. She'd stopped dwelling on the murder. He wanted me to know it had been very good for her and wondered if I could work something out so she'd continue."

"Great. But won't managing technology be difficult for her?"

"Yes, but I'll take an old cassette player over to her house. We have one here with large buttons, and I'll pre-load the tapes. All she'll have to do is press start and stop."

Tosca yipped and wagged her tail, sensing that Josie was about to leave. Keith looked at her solemnly, his hands shoved into his pockets. I knew what was bothering him and took over.

"Why don't I take Tosca with me? It won't look good to knock on people's doors carrying a little dog. You might as well be driving the Mercedes." I didn't add that Tosca's sessions at the groomer were more expensive than a visit to the dentist for most families.

"All right. Can we all meet for lunch?"

"You and Keith just go on without me. After I go to Edna's, I've got to run over to Myrna Bedsloe's. She made some changes to her story and can't bring it in because her mother-in-law is having a bad day."

"She can't just email it?"

"No. I don't think they even have a computer yet. They've had a hard time and her husband prides himself on doing without."

"Don't the kids need one for school work?"

"Not yet. I think the oldest started kindergarten last fall. The others are still little."

"Others?"

"Yes, she has four."

"So this is a mother taking care of an older woman with Alzheimer's and she has four little kids besides?"

"Yes. And she cooks great meals and makes all their clothes and works like a galley slave."

"And her husband?"

"Her husband is another story. Then after I finish at Myrna's, I need to make two more personal calls before I can settle in and begin editing. So I'll see you after work."

I scooped up Tosca and waved goodbye. I got her car seat from Josie's Mercedes and might as well have been caring for an infant by the time I got her strapped in.

Somewhere along the line, I'd started talking to Tosca. She was a great comfort. Her dark eyes tracked me and she'd even started yipping at all the right places.

My Tahoe jolted through a large pothole and Tosca yelped in protest.

"Sorry, sweetheart." I reached over and petted her. "Budget cuts. Our roads are the pits." The day was grey with a touch of fog, and overcast with deceitful little clouds slinking past like guilty dirty dogs with tell-tale feathers hanging from their mouths. Teasing us with the promise of rain, then snatching it back.

The clouds bounded and ricocheted against other clouds, then gathered strength for another run at a patch of blue. Dust rolled behind us. It got worse as I drove into the Bedsloes' farmyard.

Myrna wore two baby monitors around her neck as she swept the porch. I carried Tosca, knowing the kids would dive for her with disastrous results.

"Hi, Lottie," Myrna called cheerfully. "Come in, come in." Tosca trembled, but she didn't have to worry, I wasn't about to set her down.

Inside, Myrna's house was cool and spotless. Her mother-in-law sat in a rocking chair humming some tune I didn't recognize. She wore a fleecy, flowery pink sweat-suit with a kitten appliquéd on the front. Her feet were shoved into bunny slippers and around her neck she wore a device that communicated with one of her daughter-in-law's monitors.

I closed my eyes, wondering how Myrna stood her life. Soup simmered on the stove. In the corner was a patchwork quilt in a large free-standing hoop.

And in the coffee shop sat her no-count, good-for-nothing husband complaining to the boys about his sorry lot in life.

"You'll just have to excuse the way things look," she said gesturing around the immaculate room. "I'm late getting things done. Mom had the runs last night and we didn't get much sleep. Did we, honey bunch?" She cooed cheerfully to the little boy balanced on her hip as she nuzzled his neck. "No, we didn't." He gasped and laughed as she made slurping sounds against his skin. "Going to eat you up. Yes I am. Can you stay, Lottie? Would you like some coffee?"

"No, I can't. Really. I'm too far behind. I'll just pick up the story you want me to use and go on. I want to include it in the pages we send to the printer this week."

"Let me get it. I've got it all ready to go." She carefully set her youngest down on the floor. He began to wail. The old woman started screaming and Tosca commenced to bark. My mind went south. I had to get out of there.

"Thank you," I said when she handed me the pages. "I'll send you the proof pages from the printer and you can look them over before they are set in stone."

"Wonderful." She picked up the little boy. He stopped crying. She walked over to the old woman, patted her hair, and handed her a soft Raggedy Ann doll and she stopped screaming. I petted Tosca and she quieted right down.

I left, feeling like a fugitive from an old nursery rhyme about driving a pig to market.

The faint fog had lifted but the wind had increased. When I reached Edna's house I was anxious to deliver the tape recorder and get to my office. I hate being outside on windy days.

Edna did not come to the door when I knocked. I tried again. I was scared silly. Then I heard a faint shuffling. I waited. The knob turned and she reached for the hook and loop catch on her screen door. She was dressed in a front-snapped, flowered, seersucker duster. She looked at me blankly. Her eyes were red.

Crying again. She was obviously depressed. I made a mental note to call her son.

"Lottie! What brings you here?"

"I've brought you a gift." She stared. "It's a tape recorder. It's a present from Stuart. So you can go right on recording all your memories without having to find someone to drive you to the courthouse." There was a spark of interest in her eyes. "Let me set it up and show you how to use it."

She stepped aside. I walked over to the table at the end of her little dining room/living room combination that was typical of a 1920s house. Beyond was a galley kitchen with a single row of cabinets. A rose frieze sofa and large chair sporting intricately crocheted doilies took up most of the living room. I put the recorder next to her neatly arranged clutter: stacked newspapers, magazines, letters, and assorted appeals for money from charitable organizations.

I looked for an electrical outlet. Luckily there was one within reach of the plug. "Now don't feel you must do this, Edna," I said. "I don't want you to feel pressured."

"I don't mind." She stared at the machine. "In fact, I've thought of a lot of things since I started talking to you the other day. Things people should know about."

"Great." That was often the case. If I could just get people started, all kinds of memories started pouring out. And with some persons there was something easier about oral histories. Especially those struck by the English teacher syndrome when they picked up a pen or pencil. They started worrying about grammar and worst of all, about sounding smart.

The great diaries and journals were written by persons blithely unaware of the importance of their entries. But our society has changed. Now even written letters, let alone journals, are rare. Emails and texting has replaced neighboring and personal contact. Clearly, Edna was going to be the type of person who lost all trace of self-consciousness when she started talking.

"I want to be sure you know how to use this. Just talk. Never mind the order. You can either do it chronologically or by topic. It's your choice. I'll pull your family story out of it later. You can look it over before I finalize it for the family history book. But in the meantime, just talk."

"Well land's sake. It will be nice to have something to do on days when I can't get outside."

"It's all important, Edna. Everything. All the details. What it was like to have women over to quilt. Barn raisings. Everything."

"I didn't get out much. Henry didn't like it."

"That's all right. We're interested in a lot longer stories than the ones in our books."

"I wasn't nobody important."

I hugged her. "You've always been somebody. Now sit down and let's have a go at working the buttons."

She lowered herself into the chair and suspiciously eyed the recorder.

"Press here to start recording. Then just talk. When you're done, press the red button to stop. You can do this as long or as little as you like. Anytime, day or night. And when the cassette won't go anymore, just call me. Don't try to do anything else. I don't want you accidentally erasing anything."

"What if I've still got something to say?"

"I'll bring you more cassettes." I patted her hand and headed toward the door. "Bye now. Don't bother to get up. I've got to run. I've got Josie's little dog in the car. And she's not known for her patience."

I left cheered, feeling like I had done a good deed. A lonely old woman who had gotten caught up in a bizarre and terrifying experience now had something else to think about.

Tosca eyed me with disapproval as I opened the door to the Tahoe. "Oh come on," I said merrily. "I rolled the window down so you had fresh air. And you don't need someone paying attention to you every minute of the day." She yipped. I drove to the courthouse.

◇◇◇

Margaret looked tired. It had been a long week for her because of the hours I was spending at the sheriff's office.

She rose when I walked in. "Hello, my name is Margaret Atkinson, and you are?"

"Oh come on. It hasn't been that bad."

"Plenty bad enough. You'd better be glad it's me instead of William here. He's been on a real tear."

I sighed. William Webster was my most irritating and reliable volunteer. With impeccable integrity as he frequently reminded me. Very frequently. As though I lacked this virtue. Totally.

We had to call on him often lately. Much too often. He and Margaret were unpaid volunteers and they both had had a fit when I began "sheriffing".

I was the only person on God's green earth who approved of my new job. Keith worried about it. Josie thought I was a certifiable lunatic for taking it. Even Sam Abbot would have preferred someone huskier with fewer brains.

"Well William can relax. My latest crisis is…" My voice trailed off before I said "over." I couldn't guarantee that. Besides, there was still a whole catalogue of unanswered questions. "My latest crisis," I finished gamely, "will just have to wait until I'm caught up here."

Margaret had enough sense not to reply, but rolled her eyes. She stared at Tosca who returned her gaze. I could swear the little dog sniffed. As though she were nobility confronting a commoner.

"And just what is that?"

I seethed. But actually Tosca had started it. "Oh this is Josie's little dog, Tosca. I'm dog-sitting today." I refrained from explaining that my sister was out running around with my husband collecting signatures to oust the sheriff in the neighboring county.

"I'm allergic to dogs," Margaret said. She sneezed and her eyes began to water. "Did you know medical research has established the fact that even if a little animal runs through a room once it takes five months to get rid of the dander?"

I suspected that was a lie, but I couldn't afford to rub Margaret the wrong way. "OK. I'll call Sam and see if I can drop her off at the office."

"And if there is an emergency?"

"He can lock her up in one of the cells."

Chapter Twenty-One

By the time I collected Tosca and headed home, the wind had begun blowing in savage intermittent gusts that slammed the side of my Tahoe.

Keith and Josie were sitting at the kitchen table eating the casserole I'd left in the refrigerator with instructions for baking.

"See you found everything OK," I said.

"Yes, and it's a good thing," Keith said. "No eating outside for this jolly little band of workers. Pull up a chair, honey. We've left plenty for you."

"OK. I'm starved." I put an ample serving of hamburger casserole on my plate, ladled green salad onto one side, and dipped up plenty of green beans. "Well, did you make any progress?"

Keith smiled. "That's an understatement. I've never seen so many persons on such a rant. The majority hate Irwin Deal."

"I got the same reaction," Josie said. "Although mine was a little more complicated because I had to convince everyone I wasn't you. But after they got started it was amazing. And some of their feelings go way back."

"People don't get over slights out here. In fact, some of these quarrels go back to the nineteenth century."

"Wow. If ever a psychologist was needed."

"Maybe. But they won't go, I can assure you."

"I'm going to watch the Royals get smacked," Keith said, "unless you have other plans for the TV."

"Masochist," Josie taunted.

I smiled. "We just need the DVD player. We'll go upstairs to the sitting room. Josie brought some opera videos. *Tosca*," I teased, knowing how much he disliked that one.

"Goodbye for sure then. See you much, much later."

I ate quickly, rinsed the dishes, and put them in the dishwasher. Josie and I happily headed up the stairs and plopped down in recliners. Soon we were lost in the ultimate drama, our favorite opera, *Tosca,* the inspiration for her little dog's name.

The powerful voices filled the room. We forwarded through the intermission and didn't talk again until after the final scene, which always made me cry. Josie dabbed at her eyes and as usual, I bawled outright. Tosca had been betrayed. She trusted the wrong person and her mistake had caused her lover to be executed by a firing squad. Then she killed herself.

Betrayal, betrayal. Condemned by everyone since the beginning of time.

"Didn't you bring anything a little happier?"

"No, come to think of it."

"Tomorrow night let's see what Keith ordered from Netflix. Likely old westerns or World War Two movies."

"Have you stopped watching opera, Lottie?"

"Not exactly. But I can't get Keith interested. I record some of them that are broadcast through PBS and then just watch them by myself."

"We used to love to do that together."

The phone rang. It was Sam. "Can you come in? A guy hit a deer with his pickup and I'm on my way over there."

Damn, damn, damn. It served me right for firing Troy before we had a replacement.

"Of course. I'll be right in."

"Trouble?" Josie asked.

"Nothing major, but Sam has to inspect a wreck. So I have to man the phone, just in case."

"OK. I'm about ready to turn in. Keith and I had a long day."

"I did too. In fact, it feels like two days. I'll be back as soon as Sam returns. You'll probably be asleep so I'll see you tomorrow morning."

I went upstairs to tell Keith I was leaving. I leaned over just as he leaped to his feet and cheered for a very rare Royals home run.

"You're the only one I know of that thinks this team will improve."

He dropped down and pulled me across his lap. "Take it back, witch, before you put a curse on them." He lightly slapped my butt as I pretended to wriggle away.

"It's true and you know it." I sat up and kissed his cheek. "Let me go, brute. I've got to go to work."

"Again? I thought Sam was on duty tonight."

"He was. Is. He got called out and that leaves me."

"Haven't found anyone to take Troy's place?"

"Nope. At least no one that's worth a damn."

He pressed his hands against my face and pulled me toward him. "Just be careful, sweetheart. You still don't know what's going on with all this craziness. And Mary's being poisoned changes everything."

"I know that. I'll come straight home after Sam gets back."

Clusters of millers circled and batted against the street lights lining main street. When I got out of the Tahoe, I held onto the door to keep it from being snatched forward by the wind. I closed it and went inside. Sometimes I liked being in the jail at night without Sam around. It gave me a chance to go through old files without arousing his curiosity.

Sam never said anything, but I could feel him watching my every move. I had the authority to look through them, but I would have been hard pressed to come up with a rational explanation for following up on my hunches.

Tonight however, I wanted to check specific information. I was puzzled by Keith's reaction when he learned that our visiting bishop was a Deal. The family couldn't be that bad and the Fienes were certainly not exempt from carrying ancient grudges.

I set to work. I was wrong. The Deals were that bad. When they came over to Carlton County at least. Then after Irwin was elected sheriff they seemed content to aggravate the citizens of Copeland County. Records and charges dried up like magic. Clearly they found Irwin much more accommodating than Sam Abbott. The files on the Deals had begun with Sheriff Melvin Dixon when jurisdiction among unorganized counties often overlapped. Then I realized the really old information would be back in my historical society records. Crimes would be listed on ruled pages.

Sam had an entire hanging folder just for this family. I skimmed Dixon's neat handwriting. James Deal arrested for dragging a dog behind a car. Note at the bottom of the file that the charges had been dismissed because the plaintiff had explained that he was not being cruel.

In fact, just the opposite. He was breaking the dog of chasing cars and from getting killed. He did this by attaching a gunny sack to the bumper and the dog was supposed to attack the sack and be dragged a couple of feet and the dog would learn its lesson and never chase cars again. But dad gum it, in this case, he'd stopped and the dumb dog hadn't learned a dad gum thing and when he started up again he just honest to god hadn't noticed he was dragging the dog until Sheriff Dixon pulled him over.

But Sheriff Dixon had written "like hell" at the bottom of the file. Another note that Deal hadn't even been fined.

Another charge; the local doctor reported the same Deal to the sheriff for spousal abuse. But old "dad-gum-it" had wriggled out of that one too. Another accusation six weeks later. This time the doctor had included pictures: broken ribs, old bruises-some yellowing, some fresh, a black eye, a broken nose, far too many to have come from a single incident.

Jimmy claimed the little woman was getting careless. Going through the change. She backed him up. Saying she found it hard to concentrate sometimes. Hormones.

Classic case of an abused wife too frightened to defend herself. In this case Dixon had written "evil bastard" at the bottom of the file.

Then a bigger folder on when the woman had died. She'd been six months pregnant. *So much for going through the change,* I thought, glancing at the previous entry. Then she'd had a miscarriage and simply bled to death.

It happened far too often in the 1920s. Wintertime. No way to get to town. Phones only worked about half the time. But this time, the doctor had accused him of murder. The sheriff's report was handwritten and the crossed-out replaced words were a story in themselves. They were heavy, jagged. The hand of an angry man. Dixon wanted a record of all this. Wanted people to know what was going on in the neighboring county.

Charges dismissed for lack of evidence.

This time Sheriff Dixon's notes were lengthy.

"I tried to tell the judge that the doctor said this woman had been beaten. She'd been pregnant all right. I've no doubt she bled to death. When I went out to the house, I asked him where the baby was. He said there wasn't a baby. Just a blob. And he'd buried it. He 'didn't exactly remember where.'"

Just a blob. It probably was, considering the abuse suffered by its mother. And of course he'd just dug a hole and buried it. That's what people did back in those days. A small farm out in the country. Wasn't like there was a bevy of nurses in a fancy hospital with a tradition of grieving rituals. No different than women on the trail who had to abandon small babies.

But who was this judge that would ignore such a clear pattern of evil? Sheriff Dixon's narrative continued.

"Naturally, his cousin, Christopher Deal, decided to drop the case for lack of evidence."

His cousin! I was beginning to understand Keith's explosion and his saying I didn't understand who I was challenging.

There were more folders in the Deal family file and other ones I was curious about. I glanced at the clock. 10:30. Past time for Sam to be back. I rose, paced back and forth, then went to the broom closet and grabbed a dusting cloth and a can of Lemon Pledge and started spraying our desks. A little cleaning would give me something to think about besides crooked judges and a family who seemed to be as populous as tumbleweeds.

I wanted Josie to go home. Where she was safe. I scolded myself for being more like my husband every day. Wanting everyone where I could control what happened to them.

A thunk outside. I peered out the glass in the front door. A wood planter had blown over. The shallow-rooted dried little fir pointed due north like the needle on a compass. Nothing loose left for the wind to blow away, I decided. But perhaps a storm was brewing.

Maybe. Even though I'd lived in Western Kansas for eight years I still couldn't tell the difference between signs of sure enough storms and clouds that were just kidding.

But clouds could be motionless, as innocent as a bowl of marshmellows, and there would be an ominous feel to the air. When this occurred I was jumpy and couldn't concentrate. I started at sounds. Snapped at Keith if he was unfortunate enough to be working inside and just generally acted like a first-class bitch.

I stood by the window and saw headlights approach. A rack of lights on top. Sam. I put up the Pledge and made sure the file was closed and peered out the glass pane of the front door.

Then a car sped up the side street and made a right turn toward the jail. A man leaned out and I dove for the floor. Gunshots shattered the front window. Too stunned to move, I stared at the shards of glass lying all around.

The driver raced away. I got to my feet and went to the door and waved at Sam to let him know I was all right. Sam accelerated right after the car. But I could have told him that his old pickup was no match for whatever the men were driving. He might as well have given chase in a horse and buggy.

About five minutes later Sam came back. He rushed through the door, where I waited, my gun drawn and both a shotgun and rifle leaning against the desk.

"Are you hurt?"

"I'm fine. He just shot out the window. Who were they?"

"Don't know. I was coming from the east and the driver blew right past me at the intersection going north. Then I saw the other man leaning out the window and realized he'd taken a shot at you. Saw you wave so I knew he'd missed. I didn't even manage to get a license plate."

"Everyone knows my Tahoe even if I don't have lights on top. And this is the sheriff's office! They had to know I was here." Shaken, I sat down. "But they only aimed at the windows. They wanted to scare me. And did."

I held out my hands and watched the tremors like they belonged to someone foreign. Sam stared and I tucked them under my thighs.

"Goddamn Lottie. Goddamn it all to hell. What have you gotten yourself into this time?"

Furious, I jumped to my feet. "I have not gotten myself into anything. When some homicidal maniac goes on a rampage, it's not my fault."

"Shit." He took off his hat and ran his hand over his thinning hair. "Goddamn, Lottie. I didn't mean it that way. I mean… well, goddamn it, it's just that…"

"I'm going home. I was supposed to stay here until you got back. You're back and I'm out of here." I shrugged on my jacket, grabbed my purse, and left.

◇◇◇

The lights were all on when I got back to the farm. Keith met me at the door. Josie stood behind him in a chenille bathrobe. Her hair was down. She had obviously been in bed.

"So Sam called?" I came through the mud room.

"Yes." Keith reached for me and pressed me against his solid body. I closed my eyes.

Josie went to the kitchen and walked over to the stove. "I'll heat milk for cocoa. I think we need it to steady our nerves."

Tears filled my eyes. "That bigoted old bastard blamed me because someone tried to shoot me," I whispered to my husband. "Blamed me! Like I had brought this all on myself."

He stroked my hair and kissed my forehead. "Want a real drink? Or tea? Or Josie's cocoa?"

"Not a drink. The cocoa. Better for my stomach."

We sat around the table and I began trembling again. Keith was oddly quiet while I told them both every last detail.

"And you don't have a clue as to who it was?"

"None. It all happened so fast. After I realized I'd been shot at, I got up and ran for my guns."

"And if Sam hadn't come along, they would have been through that door in a second," Keith said. His voice was flat, harsh. "And it's hard telling what might have happened."

"They were aiming at the window. They used a shotgun, not a rifle. Maybe they just wanted to scare me."

A sharp look. That's all it took for me to close my mouth. They might have been capable of more. I might be wrong and Keith might be right.

"OK you two," he said. "Here's the way it's going to be. I don't care how liberated you think you are. I don't care how competent or how brave or anything else. You don't have the right to deprive me or your families or all your people or your community or anyone else of your life. Your *life*. This is your life we're talking about here. Your *life*. Don't either one of you get that? Josie, you nearly got yourself killed last fall, and Lottie you're coming in at a close second."

Keith had been a captain in the Army. He was used to giving orders. Having people snap to.

"Josie, I want you and Tosca gone the first thing in the morning. If you're in good enough shape to drive. If not, I'll drive you myself and take a bus back."

Josie said nothing. I didn't either.

"And you, Lottie. It's time to call a halt to this whole charade. Sam's pissed as hell and I am too. You're going to resign first thing in the morning. In fact, I'll go with you."

I said nothing. Knowing the reason he wanted to go with me was because he didn't trust me to do it on my own.

It dawned on me that he couldn't be with us both simultaneously.

He'd thought of that too. "We'll all go to the sheriff's office tomorrow morning before I head out with Josie."

We said nothing.

He wrung his hands, stared at his white knuckles, clasped them, and leaned forward, his forearms on the table, the tendons in his neck taut, his mouth a straight line.

"Goddamn, Lottie honey, I'm sorry that it has to be this way." His voice softened. "I know how much this job means to you, sweetheart. Really, I do."

I said nothing. We said nothing.

"And I know we've had this discussion before." He turned to my sister. "Josie, I'm sorry to sound like the kind of man who orders women around. Lottie can tell you I'm not that way."

Oh god, I groaned inwardly. Deeper and deeper and deeper, with no concept at all of the depth of the pit he was digging.

Josie, my twin, my best friend, my other heart. We didn't need speech or signals. We just knew.

She turned to me. "Can you keep Tosca again for me tomorrow? I still have a couple of sections to cover."

My heart thumped. "Yes. But we're going to have to make different arrangements when I'm working at the historical society. Margaret doesn't like her. But I'll be on duty tomorrow anyway, so Sam can get some rest."

Keith jumped to his feet. He looked hard at me and then Josie. Then he swept his mug off the table. It crashed into little pieces on the tile floor.

Face flushed, he stomped up the stairs.

Chapter Twenty-Two

When he was out of sight, I took a couple of sips of cocoa but my mouth trembled. I reached for a napkin and wiped tears from my eyes.

"He does have a point, you know," I said.

"Yes, he does. But tonight he's pure reaction. Not thinking about the larger picture. Your resigning as undersheriff won't solve the problem."

"Someone wants to scare me. I think."

"But why? There has to be a reason."

I pressed my fingers to the bridge of my nose and closed my eyes. "I don't know. I guess to stop me from doing something. The most obvious would be to stop circulating the petition to recall Sheriff Deal."

"But you're not doing the circulating. It's Keith and I."

"Anyone who knows Keith well, knows the quickest way to get to him is through me."

"I agree, but we don't want to fix on the petition before we consider other motives. Someone may want you to stop delving into Mary Farnsworth's murder."

"I can't think of any reason why anyone would want to stop me from doing that."

"I can. The murderer."

We stared at each other.

"Just to make sure we've covered all the bases, are you working on someone's story at the historical society with something hidden? Again?" she added. "We know where that can lead."

"None relating to Mary."

"I'm going up to bed."

"Me too."

I slipped out of my clothes and pulled on a nightgown. I glanced at the dark motionless shape of my husband's body, on his side, back toward me, feigning sleep. I sighed. This was going to be another difficult time in our marriage.

The phone woke me up about fifteen minutes before my alarm went off the next morning.

"Morning, Lottie."

"Sam." I sat upright. "Has something else happened?"

"Nope and nothing else is going to either. Not to you, at least. I'm going on duty today so you can recuperate from last night."

"I'm fine." Or would be if a couple of men would stop trying to take care of me. "Just fine. Really."

"Maybe so, but I might as well be here worrying about you as home worrying about you."

"All right. I'll be at the historical society. Call if something comes up."

I got up and went out to the balcony to check the weather. It's the very first thing we do in the morning in Western Kansas. Our whole day is determined by the weather. The outside temperature gauge said 48, but that could change. No wind, so I didn't have to worry about power lines snapping. In fact, with any luck at all, I might be able to get in a decent day's work.

I dressed in my best khaki pants and pulled on a coral lightweight cotton turtleneck and twisted my hair into a French roll. A little make-up, a little attention to my eyelashes and I looked like a casual competent professional woman on top of her game. In fact, I was surprised at how well I felt.

Keith was gone. Josie sat at the table half listening to the morning news.

"What time did Keith leave?"

"I don't know. He was gone before I got downstairs."

"Well."

"Yes. Well."

I scrambled a couple of eggs, grabbed a slice of toast, and carried the plate to the table. She did not expect me to talk before I got coffeed up.

"About Tosca," I said. "No one boards dogs around here. I've been trying to think of someone she can stay with while I'm at work and you're out running around."

"No need. I have her little kennel with me. She can just stay in it and I'll leave a note for Keith to take care of her when he comes back."

"If he comes back."

"Oh come on. He's a big boy. He'll get over it."

"I know. And he does mean well. Really."

"I know that too. He's a smart man. After he's had a chance to think he'll know that whoever took a shot at you last night was probably some of Deal's relations and we can't just quit. We've got to get that man out of office."

"Something has to be done about that whole family. This chain has to be broken." I told her about the files, the crimes that had been overlooked in the twenties.

"That's a long time ago. Are you saying 'bad seed'? That some families have murderous hearts?"

"That's your territory." I picked up my keys and headed out the door. Then I paused and looked back at her. "I'm afraid you won't be safe driving up to folks' houses. I don't know what we were thinking."

"Don't worry. This morning I'm going to businesses. I'll talk to the owners when there aren't any customers around."

"That should be doable. No customers around is a fact of life out here."

Mrs. Rodney Howarter came in about ten o'clock. She lived next door to Edna and brought her tapes.

"So soon? I expected these to last her for a couple of weeks."

"You've given her a new lease on life. She says she wants to get all kinds of things off her chest."

"Well, they say confession is good for the soul." I doubted that my little mouse murderer had many sins on her conscience, but I was glad she was enjoying the project. "Here. Take her two more. Do you know how to insert the cassettes?"

"Yes. And she nearly talked me to death when I went over. I give her the morning paper when I'm done with it."

Elmira Howarter wore blue polyester pants with a coordinating long-sleeved multi-colored top. She always looked neat and put together. Her sharp eyes behind her thick glasses didn't miss much. Edna was lucky to have Elmira checking on her. A kind woman, she was an informal cheer committee of one to a number of elderly neighbors.

"Is she doing all right?" I knew full well it was all over town that Edna was the last person to receive communion from that poor preacher woman who had just dropped dead. No wonder it had just about put Edna under, too.

"Yes, really well considering the shock."

She didn't linger. I composed an ad for a housekeeper, and another for a deputy. I put everything away, and headed down the street for the sheriff's office so Sam could check the copy for our newest help-wanted ad.

We had set up a makeshift desk for Troy. Mostly to make him feel official. It was scarred green metal and I think Sam had found it at a used office supply store. One of the drawers didn't work and the top was chipped. It took up too much room and I wanted Sam to haul it off to the landfill.

I breezed through the front door.

Sitting at Troy's desk wearing a shiny deputy badge pinned to a dark blue shirt with a pistol strapped to his side and a Stetson pushed back on head without a trace of a smile was Keith.

My husband, Keith Fiene.

Chapter Twenty-Three

"You absolutely, positively cannot, cannot do this."

"I can. All it takes is a sheriff's signature to appoint a deputy. I would like to remind you that this is how you got to be one."

"We should have discussed this. Talked about it."

"I would like to remind you that you didn't talk a damn thing over with me when you became one."

"That's different." But I flushed, knowing it wasn't. He'd learned the hard way, through the coffee shop, that I had become a deputy sheriff without so much as my saying "boo" to him. Because I was afraid he wouldn't like it. Make a fuss.

All this was going through my mind, but if someone had taken my temperature, it would have been dangerously high.

"Keith, you can't do this."

"I can and I will."

His eyes, his mouth, his muscles, everything about him did not show a bit of humor. He was dead serious. There wasn't a trace of spite. He wasn't a petty man. But I simply couldn't imagine a worse situation. It would be like Godzilla and Tyrannosaurus Rex working together. He watched my face but refused to smile, nor did his eyes soften. A rock. A mountain. Unmoving.

Speechless, I whirled around and left. On the way home I pounded the steering wheel and began to cry. Blinded by tears, I pulled over to the side of the road. How could Sam do this to me? How could Keith do this to me? I tried to get a grip on myself, but failed. I sobbed and hiccupped, then blew my nose and drove on home.

Once there, I headed for my leather chair and curled into a sodden lump. Hating Keith, Sam, God, Western Kansas, the impossible collection of quarrelsome people out here, my Dogpatch existence, the rabbits that devoured my tulips, the wind, the goddamn wind, and wildly yearning for civilization—something pretty—I cried until there were no tears left.

I dozed and woke with a start when Josie came through the door.

"What's wrong, Lottie?" By her tone I knew she thought something had happened to Keith. Not yet, I thought, but something would. And soon. Very, very soon.

I shoved my quilt from across my face. "My husband is now my new deputy sheriff. And they didn't even to bother to talk it over with me first."

I couldn't look at her face. If she thought this was funny, she would quickly join my list. She sat Tosca on the floor and the little dog immediately sprang into my chair, reached for my face and began licking my tears. I pushed her down onto my lap and began petting her.

"I'll make some tea," Josie said. "Then we'll talk."

I was past the hiccupping stage. Josie came back with a steaming cup of chamomile, handed it to me, then went into the family room and put on a soothing symphony. She had more sense than to choose anything country that would accentuate my sense of tragedy. She came back and lit a candle. The tea, the music, the scent of lavender began to sooth me. She sat down in the chair Keith usually used and leaned forward.

"Don't even think of playing shrink with me!"

"OK. How about playing grown-up?" She pulled out her cigarettes and lighter and eyed me coldly.

"That's not fair." I sat bolt up-right. "So not fair. I have a right to…to…take umbrage at the arrogant son-of-a-bitches… goddamn high-handed dismissal of my abilities like I'm some kind of a teenage dilettante trying out new adventures."

"No one sees you as messing around, Lottie. I haven't heard Keith accusing you of that. And I suspect Sam doesn't feel that way either or he wouldn't have promoted you to undersheriff."

I sipped my tea.

"And as to Sam and Keith not talking to you about it in advance, I would like to remind you that Keith was absolutely furious when you took your deputy job without so much as a word to him."

"That's different. It would have been like asking for his permission."

"Oh, Christ." She blew a smoke ring and called to Tosca, who immediately jumped from my lap. They both haughtily left the room. Too mad to cry, I got up and went outside and started pulling weeds from my neglected pitiful little patch of tulips and jonquils. I threw a rock at a bunny peeping out of the cedars. Then I went inside and laid out some hamburger patties for supper. I fixed a large salad and stemmed strawberries, mixed a passable shortcake and whipped some cream.

That evening, from our bedroom, I heard Keith's Suburban pull into the drive. He whistled as he came into the kitchen. After I judged enough time had passed for him and Josie to have eaten, I went downstairs.

I paused at the bottom of the steps. Keith and Josie were playing music in the family room. Although her best instrument is the piano, she plays the violin beautifully and Keith was on his guitar. Their laughter pealed through the air, then I heard Keith gently instructing her on some of the finer points of bluegrass. At first, Josie had been condescending in adapting to this genre. She was strictly classical, but to her credit, she was beginning to understand. Surprisingly, she noticed the parallel between bluegrass ballads and opera. "It's all high melodrama," she had said.

Tonight the two of them were playing an early George Jones recording, "White Lightning." Josie abandoned the frenetic violin accompaniment and I saw her double over with laugher. "I can't keep up. I can't."

"Sure you can. Here I'll show you."

He went over and took the violin from her and she stood by his side as he demonstrated the difficult fret work. An orphaned feeling swept over me. Not as strong as envy of their easy camaraderie, but lonely, left out.

I could be standing there, appreciating his wonderful music, enjoying being the focus of his attention.

If I weren't married to the bastard.

I stomped outside and lined up beer cans on the fence lining the back of my garden. I paced off twenty-five yards, the maximum sensible distance for self-defense although I was a crack shot and sure of my accuracy at thirty-five. Most real world shooting was a lot closer.

I sent the cans reeling one by one. Between shots, I heard the back door open. I turned. Keith came out and sat on a chair at the edge of the patio. He watched silently as I continued my assault on the beer cans. I heard the door open and close again, and turned back to my practice. Then he stood by my side holding the .345 magnum he'd had in his holster at the sheriff's office.

In his other hand was a sack of cans. Wordlessly, he walked over to the fence and lined them up. I shot first. He shot second. I looked at him hard and we coldly continued alternating down the line. The moon went behind the clouds and a sudden splotch of light caught my eye. Josie had come out on her upstairs balcony to watch. Her form was as black as a specter with only the tip of her cigarette breaking the dark.

My hand and wrist was tiring from the weight. His wasn't, but he finally missed.

"Rifles?" he said.

I shook my head. No comparison there. He would win hands down. I glanced at the balcony. Josie had gone inside. I started to tremble. I carefully laid my gun down on the nearest patio table and covered my face with my hands. He set his gun beside mine and reached for me.

"Bastard," I whispered as I buried my face in his chest.

"I know," he murmured. He kissed me and then walked off and left me alone.

He's a seasoned husband and knows many things from having had two wives.

I arranged pillows in a patio recliner and watched the moon for hours. I watched the rabbits play in the moonlight and heard frogs set up a dreadful clamor from our pond. I pondered reality. Facts. Between fitful dozing.

There was no changing this man. And I knew good and well he had not done this to spite me or because he thought I was incompetent. I thought about different stances and attitudes because at thirty-eight, I knew it was possible to simply adopt a different attitude. A nice trick, which had come to me late, but it was possible. My options were not pretty.

I could continue to rage and pout, thwart Keith at every turn and make his life miserable, try for a cutsie husband and wife combo, a kind of Mr. and Mrs. Smith, or act coldly professional toward my brand new deputy when we were working together.

I settled on the last option.

Chapter Twenty-Four

The next morning there was a note from Keith by the coffeepot, where I would be most likely to see it immediately:

Sam's on duty. I'm at Henselys checking one of their horses. Call if you need me.

The phone rang. I groaned, hoping it wasn't Sam. I had dozed off in the recliner on the patio and hadn't moved inside until the wee hours of the morning so I was stiff and still tired. But it was Harold Sider. For Josie.

I called up the stairs and she took it on the extension. When she came down, her lips were in a straight line.

"We've screwed up," she said. "All of us. Harold called Keith to go over some of the charges filed against Deal and Keith told him about the recall petition. Harold is furious."

"Why?"

"He says that only three people can carry it, the signatures all have to be witnessed by those three, and the three have to be citizens in the county of the person they are trying to run off."

Stunned, I sat down. "Oh boy. So the signatures of everyone you've coaxed into signing will no longer be valid."

"No, according to Harold. And he does know what's legal, Lottie."

"How did this happen?"

"We googled 'Kansas Recall Petition' and downloaded the forms. But Harold says we obviously missed the part about the three sponsors having to be registered voters of that particular county." Still in her robe she poured a cup of coffee. She patted her pockets, hoping for a stray pack of cigarettes and finding none, she headed for the stairs. "And he says we also missed the line that it was highly recommended that we seek legal advice first."

◇◇◇

Sam looked up for only a second when I came in. I stood in front of his desk until he was forced to give me his full attention. "Sorry," he said. "I've been looking at all our notes about Mary Farnsworth and I'll be damned if I can find any motive at all for murder. She was as pure as the driven snow. I would swear to it."

"Any leads yet on the missing man?"

"None," He sighed and pushed his hat back on his head and reached for the pipe lying in the ashtray. His shirt, like most he wore, was pocked with little burn holes.

I cleared my throat. He had to know. "Sam there's been a complication." I told him about the error Josie and Keith had made in obtaining signatures for the petition.

He laid down his pipe, lowered his head, and squeezed his temples with his palms as though to ward off future headaches. "Oh goddamn it all to hell. We're going to have to call every single one of those persons that have signed and tell them that there's been a royal screw-up. The best we can hope for is that the Deals won't find out who signed and retaliate."

"But what can they do?" It was a foolish thing to say. By all the incidents in the file, I knew it was plenty. Everything from vandalism to lethal word of mouth against a business.

"Keith wasn't going to be able to keep circulating the petition anyway, since he's now a deputy. I guess the only bright side is that he and Josie had just gotten started. If there is a bright side." He picked up a stack of papers and tried to align them.

"I don't think there's been a bright side to anything from the moment of our first church service at that church."

"Josie up?"

"Yes."

"Tell her to fax me those petitions. I'll give them all a heads up right away."

"Sam, you shouldn't have to do this."

"Shouldn't ever have happened in the first place."

I swallowed, well aware of his flash of regret that he'd ever hired me, let alone promoted me.

I suppressed the urge to apologize, and called Josie, told her what Sam wanted, made sure she knew how to use the fax in our home office, and gave her the fax number at the sheriff's office. "I'll be at the historical society," I said, leaving Sam to his misery. Worse, leaving him to cope with the fury of the betrayed citizens of Copeland County.

One of the advantages of my work at the historical society is that I'm my own boss and can choose among tasks. There's a category of work that I can do when I'm technically brain dead. Due to the combination of pent-up worry and anxiety over the bewildering events of the past week I looked forward to a Dumb Day. When I could catch up on donkey work. Transcribing tapes certainly fell in that category.

I put on headphones, scooted the telephone over so I could see the call light if it rang, slipped one of Edna's tapes into a player and adjusted the volume. We had discovered early on that voice recognition software did not work well with the variety of voices and old terms and usages by persons long ago.

In fact, sometimes it was difficult to decipher hand written terms. I'd struggled with "inst." in old letters and finally learned it meant "in the present month." Many other old documents contained strange characters.

Edna's voice was clear and her narrative contained precious details. She explained the process for separating cream. Women studies scholars would love her passionate explanation about the importance of "egg money," which most women used to fund little expenses. Given what she had said earlier, I was surprised her husband "let her" keep it. Then she said:

My husband never liked chickens so he didn't bother to go out to the chicken coop. I did all the work and the children helped me. Henry didn't know how many laying hens I had. He thought I had about thirty, but I really had about fifty, and I gave Henry most of the money. I kept some back so the kids would have decent clothes and for little school expenses. My little chicks came through the mail every spring and now when I can't get out in my garden, I think about the happiest times in my life and I would give anything to go back to those days and my joy at receiving those flats of fluffy yellow chicks.

I paused for a moment to catch up with the typing. I also made a note to see if baby chicks were still shipped live through the postal service. It had been a huge issue after 9/11 when flights were shut down and so many animals died in cargo planes. I frowned, aware of the sad undertone in Edna's story. Her accumulation of little deceptions. From the mouse murder to concealing egg money. It was a miserable way to live.

There were three more tapes to go. However, I was interrupted by a call from Keith. "Just wanted you to know that all hell is breaking loose, Lottie. News about the petition is all over town and Deal is leading a crusade to have Josie and me thrown in jail."

"For what?"

"Malicious mischief. And worse, he's vowed to make trouble for every person, every business, that signed the recall petition."

"It won't work. He's going to cause more trouble for himself. And if he's smart, he would be looking ahead to the next regular election which will be in just another year. I'm sure people will oust him then."

"I'm not. Think about it. He has a lot of family and a lot of supporters. And from the calls we're getting people are scared. Not about physical danger, but economic retaliation. Hell, most of these poor bastards with retail businesses can't afford to miss a single sale."

When I hung up I poked the caller list and saw that he had called from the sheriff's office, not from home. I poured a cup of coffee and walked outside to the corridor and stared out the exterior glass double doors.

Jonquils lined the walkways and only the cottonwood trees were withholding their buds. When driving to the office, I'd noticed a few lawn items on the sidewalk in front of the hardware store and there was a sign promising 20% off of garden hoses. Someone around this town believed in spring.

I walked back to my desk and forgetting that Josie was out of range, I called her cell. I was sent to voice mail so I dialed our house phone, but she didn't pick up.

She would be livid over Deal's retaliation. Certainly, she wouldn't go home to Manhattan. I took a chance that she was on her laptop and emailed her that we had managed to rile up all of Copeland County. I got an IM back:

It's not that I don't want to leave this miserable hellhole. But I will not be run off. Besides, Harold and I are working on something. He has an idea.

I groaned, wrote that I had to get back to work, and signed off. I couldn't stand anymore bright ideas.

I resumed work with Edna's tapes. Her memories were not chronological and she flitted from topic to topic and dipped into times before her marriage. Much to my delight, she had included every last detail of preparing for box suppers.

Young girls would put a meal for two in a decorated box. The boxes were auctioned off at a community event, usually connected with a school fund-raising, and young unmarried men would bid on the boxes and the privilege of eating with the girl.

Although it was disguised as random and anonymous, naturally most of the bidders knew which blushing damsel had prepared which box. In some cases, it was the community's first clue to budding romances and sometimes, it was a young lady's first indication of a potential suitor:

I had told Buddy Astor which box was mine. We was already sweet on each other. He was…

She broke off. Somehow I knew what would be coming next. It did:

Buddy went up to one dollar and fifty cents. It was a lot. A fortune and he was just starting to work his folk's hard-scrabble farm. Everyone there knew what it meant. We had just started making eyes at each other, but I knew, knew if he was willing to pay that kind of money, the next step was keeping company.

Then Henry stood up and bid two dollars. Just like that. I looked at Buddy and he looked like he was about to pass out. He didn't have that kind of money and the next bid would have to be fifty cents higher. So Henry won the box. And me. We didn't have much to say but he didn't seem to mind. I was real pretty back then.

After that, my folks never let up. Henry already had a fine start. Three hundred acres and a team of work horses and a pair of matched mules and thirty pigs. From then on, Buddy acted like I was just a passing whim. He just plumb gave up. Looked right past me when I saw him on the street.

So I showed him. Me and Henry got engaged and then got married.

She could have talked to Buddy. Poor timid girl who became a poor timid woman, never standing up to her husband.

Margaret would be here at one o'clock. We closed during the noon hour. I put away all of my equipment and decided to go back to the farm as apparently it would not be necessary to take a shift at the sheriff's office.

An old hymn, "Sweet Hour of Prayer," echoed through my mind as I drove toward home. It wouldn't hurt me to try a little solitude. Silence.

I drove out of my way and headed for St. Helena.

But when I approached I saw a white Camry parked in front of the church.

Bishop Talesbury.

This man had no business here. I parked at the outer edge of the parking lot. I considered calling Sam to inform him that there might be a "situation" and then remembered it was Keith who had called to tell me about Deal's threats. I wasn't ready to cope with my husband's paranoia about my well-being.

Since I hadn't planned to work at the sheriff's office today, I didn't have my .38 with me. It's bad form for an editor to be locked and loaded when persons come in to submit their family history. But I always had a gun in my purse.

I quietly shut the car door and dug out my little Airweight, just in case. I walked toward the front door, then soundlessly pulled it open and peered inside. My eyes struggled to adapt to the semi-dark interior.

There was no sign of Talesbury. The anteroom door was closed and only I had the key, but it was the only place where he could be. Then I heard a sound directly in front of the altar. A moan. I looked down the aisle and saw Talesbury lying full-length face-down on the carpet with his arms out-stretched. Stunned, I started to rush toward him, then stopped, realizing the groans were in Latin. He was not injured, but prostrate before the Lord.

He heard me, slowly rose to his feet, turned, and his hollow-eyed gaze met my own shocked eyes. He wore a cassock and looked ghastly. Otherworldly. Guilty. Like he had been caught in an unclean act.

Profoundly ashamed, I put my gun back in my purse. "Sir, I am so sorry. I did not mean to intrude."

He had already pulled himself back together. The moment of vulnerability passed. "Miss Albright," he said in acknowledgement, with a slight nod of his head. He walked toward me without a trace of friendliness, clearly heading for the door.

When we were adjacent, I stopped him. "Bishop Talesbury. I have a few questions about Mary Farnsworth's death. The KBI does too. We haven't known where you were staying. We don't have a phone number where we can get ahold of you."

He stood motionless, not volunteering a thing. I dug out a little notebook. "We need to know where we can contact you. Where are you staying?"

"With my nephew, Sheriff Irwin Deal."

I can't assume a poker face at will, like Josie. But I did a pretty good job. And I certainly didn't yield to the desire to slap him. Resenting his arrogant distance, next I went for the information that plagued me the most.

My heart pounded. "Sir, did you know Mary Farnsworth?"

He stiffened, lost even more color from his blue lips, and stared straight ahead.

"Yes, I knew Mary Farnsworth," he said softly.

He swept out the door.

Chapter Twenty-Five

Dazed, I drove home. I couldn't think straight. In fact, I was too bewildered to think at all. All I could manage was a merry-go-round of questions and fragmented facts. I'd already reviewed them endlessly, but they kept circling around in my mind.

The decision to build St. Helena on the corner of four counties was innocent, but stupid. My original assumption that Reverend Mary had died a natural death was understandable, but stupid. As a historian I knew better than to make assumptions about anything. And I was certainly stupid to have assumed there was no connection between Talesbury and Reverend Mary.

And it was beyond stupid to hope Josie would simply go back to Manhattan.

The KBI, everyone, needed know about this immediately. When I arrived home and went inside, Josie was waiting.

Simultaneously, we started to speak, "I've got news…"

She laughed. "You go first," I said.

"Harold thinks Mary may have been in a witness protection program."

Dumbfounded, I set my purse on the kitchen table. "My news trumps yours," I said. "I think." I tried to process Harold's idea. It would make sense. Then I told Josie about the episode with Talesbury at the church.

"If she was in the program, it would explain why she was so jittery during the procession," she said. "Her nerves went beyond uneasiness over Talesbury's overbearing ways."

"We've got to find out what their connection was."

"That shouldn't be hard to do," she said. "Just haul him in and ask him."

"I can't because of this quarrel over jurisdiction. Not with Sheriff Deal insisting the murder took place in his county."

"But the KBI will have authority."

"Yes." Then I thought again about Talesbury's strange comment the day of the service that "this was just one death."

While Josie phoned Harold with the latest developments, I went upstairs and changed into old jeans and went outside to pull weeds from around my hyacinths. I removed thatch to give my summer daylilies a chance if they chose to make an appearance and the rabbits weren't plotting against them.

My mind cleared enough to gain some objectivity. I straightened and rubbed my back. The smell of earth, the growing pile of weeds, the small patches of green promising the arrival of spring restored my perspective.

I went inside and made a glass of ice tea and sat at the kitchen table. Josie came into the kitchen.

"Want some?" She shook her head and lit a cigarette. Tosca came in and looked at her first and then me as though trying to decide when one of us had the greatest need.

Josie went to the patio doors and gazed outside. I followed and saw a platoon of rabbits springing out of my windbreak. Undoubtedly setting up their next assault.

"Is Harold making any progress?"

"No, it's way too soon, but he's less sure about the witness protection program being a possibility after I told him about the Talesbury connection."

"I feel like I'm walking across land mines."

"You are," she said flatly. "But for now, it's as dangerous to start back as it was to begin all this in the first place." She went to the window, then back again. Edgy, touchy, not like herself.

"Storm coming up," I said. She studied the clear blue sky. Only a few stray clouds floated serenely toward the east. I laughed. "It's the electricity in the air. It gets under your skin. Makes you crazy. That's why you can't settle down."

"There's nothing wrong with me." There clearly was and Tosca thought so too. She lay stretched out with her head on her paws, anxiously watching Josie's every move.

"It's not just the weather," she said. "I've collected all the local papers in every town I've visited. And there's so many things I don't understand. Some of the issues that I haven't even heard about sound like a matter of life and death out here."

"Like what?"

"Wind. Wind energy. Wind farms. What do people have against wind farms out here for heaven's sake? It would boost local economies, it's green, and it's so logical. This has to be one of the best places in the world to harness the wind."

"People are fighting it tooth and toenail in the Flint Hills, aren't they?" She had to be aware of the controversy there. Manhattan was in the heart of this treasured area. The Kansas Flint Hills region extends from near Nebraska down into Oklahoma. It's the last large expanse of tallgrass prairie in the nation.

Keith has long envied the ranchers lucky enough to own land there. The lush grass, whose roots reach down on limestone and chert, contains calcium and minerals and produces some of the finest beef in the world.

"The Flint Hills are a different matter altogether," she insisted.

"Many farmers feel the same way about the land out here. I don't know where to start. But different people in both parts of the state have marshaled the same arguments." There were concerns about driving away wildlife, causing cancer, general ugliness, noise pollution from the equipment, and odd research about vibro-acoustic disease—wind turbine sickness. Opponents say there's a constant subtle noise that causes memory loss in little kids and migraines in young mothers.

"And I suppose there's another side?"

"Absolutely. Economics for one thing. Folks who allow companies to use their land for wind turbines get generous payments."

We moved from there to ethanol plants and then to immigration. It was rather pleasant actually, to be discussing something other than killers and intrigues.

But, finally, we came back full circle to the elephant in the living room. Mary Farnsworth's murder.

We traded theories, and shot each one down while we waited for Harold to call back about the witness protection program.

We both jumped like we'd been shot when the phone rang. Josie answered. She listened intently. "When will you know?"

She hung up. "Harold says this will take several days. It's one of those 'why do you want to know' situations."

Keith came home and whistled as he hung his jean jacket on a peg in the mud room. Tosca was ecstatic and nearly wagged herself to death until he reached for her.

"Big discussions going on, I see."

"Not that big. We're just wading through the major issue of the day. The week. Did you have a good day at the office?" I managed to look him squarely in the eye. Keep my voice pleasant.

"Yes, in fact it was rather boring."

"It usually is. But I had an interesting run-in on my way home." I told him about Talesbury. He listened intently.

"There's something terribly wrong with the man," he said. "Or something has gone terribly wrong in his life."

Josie nodded. "Prostration. Deep penance. Unbearable guilt. This disconnect from people. There's something we don't know about."

The next day Keith announced he was willing to be on duty again. "If you don't mind." His glance was cautious.

"Fine. In fact, I'm starting to make a little headway on stories. I have three more tapes to go for Edna before I start on Chip's story. And with any luck at all, Myrna won't phone in any more changes. Thank you for volunteering."

He checked to see if I meant it. Then nodded and headed for the garage. I watched him drive off. He was making the ultimate sacrifice in sitting at a desk with relatively little to do. It showed how worried he was about my safety and how confident he was that no one would ever cross him.

He was wrong. He came roaring back in the drive in about twenty minutes and crashed through the back door. His face was flushed, furious, and he headed to his gun rack.

"What's wrong? Tell me what's wrong?" I pressed my fingers to my throat. Tosca leapt into Josie's arms and we both stood there wide-eyed as he grabbed a rifle.

He started swearing then, and used words he'd never used in front of Josie before. He stood there, shoulders slumped, then put the rifle back in the case.

"Come look," he said finally. "Just come look."

Wordlessly, we followed him out to his Suburban. He drove down the road to his newly planted oats field. He depended on it to start feeding cattle before they switched to corn.

Although Kansas has a moratorium on wells until the state decides what to do about the declining level of the Ogallala aquifer, Keith's family had grandfather irrigation permits. A complicated circle pivot system rotates around the oats field. It's massively expensive and although Keith had once spent an entire evening explaining all the parts and reasons and advantages, most of it was over my head.

But it was clear the circle pivot wouldn't be rotating this year. Someone had plowed swaths diagonally across the field back and forth. A few tracks were circular for good measure. Buying oats on the market would be a major expense. And planting oats was tricky. It was too late to do it over.

Plus, one can't just transfer circle pivot equipment to another field because the set-up depended on a well. We only had one well. And there was no way to harvest any oats that came up now, because the rows were ruined.

Whoever did this, knew what he was doing.

"They used a V-ripper," Keith said. "Can't be too many of those around. I'm going to find the bastard that did this. And it shouldn't take long."

I breathed a little easier. At least he was no longer threatening to blow someone's brains out.

Josie solemnly looked at the ruined field. "It's so mean. So malicious."

"Yes," I said. "Exactly. And this has all the earmarks of a Deal."

"I'm afraid this isn't all that sick son-of-a-bitch has in mind," Keith said. "If this is a sample of what he intends for any of the petition signers, all hell is going to break loose."

Chapter Twenty-Six

I walked into my office at the historical society glad for mundane chores and grateful that Keith had settled down into his thinking mode. Today, he would simply handle calls at the sheriff's office and take notes.

However, it's difficult to deal with crimes committed by someone in another county if the "someone" was a sheriff. There were approximately forty-five Deals, counting little children. The destruction of the oats field would have involved exclusively male adults. Then I amended that to include teenagers. Farm kids started driving at a ridiculously early age.

And realistically, there were more Deals than that. There were married daughters with their husbands' surnames and their teenage sons. Also a lot of women worked in the fields like men.

About nine, a woman arrived carrying a clip board and a back pack purse. She wore skinny jeans with a pressed-in front crease and a snowy white blouse. Her etched leather belt matched the pattern on her silver-tipped western boots. Her shiny black hair was cut in a fashionable wedge. She ushered in an aroma of starch and sunshine.

I rose and introduced myself.

"I'm Zola Hodson," she replied with a soft faintly British accent. "I'm come in response to your advertisement for a housekeeper."

"It's a big place," I stammered. "Two women come once a month to do heavy work."

"That's always appreciated." She checked a square on her clip board.

"I'll need references, and I'm also a law enforcement officer, so there will be a background check because I have to be sure of your immigration status."

"Of course." She smiled.

"We're just starting to screen applicants." A little white one, but surely there someone else would show up. Someone with a little more heft and a strong back. Then I was deeply embarrassed that I had prejudged on the basis of her appearance. "And employment forms. I'll pay social security taxes, of course."

She frowned. "Perhaps you don't understand, Miss Albright. I need to see your place before I decide to accept you as a client. I'm an independent contractor. I will bring all my own cleaning supplies and equipment. After I evaluate your situation and *if* I decide to accept you, we will agree on a rate."

Too dumbfounded to speak, I nodded.

"You also must understand that I take pride in my work, and will insist on implementing a few changes that may involve extra personnel. At my discretion."

"For instance?"

"If I see a wasp nest on your porch, I'll call an exterminator. If a faucet drips, I'll call a plumber."

Heaven. A glimpse of heaven. Uneasily, I eyed her checklist. I gave her directions to Fiene's Folly.

"My sister is there. She can show you around."

She punched my number into her cell phone. "I'll get back to you," she said pleasantly as she breezed out the door.

Frantic, I called Josie. "Make the beds and do something to my bathroom. Now."

"Shall I make tea, too?"

Determined to concentrate on the job at hand, I donned my earphones and inserted one of Edna's tapes in the player. She had been so proud of her son and daughter. I listened to accounts of music lessons and sports events and making costumes for school plays. She skipped around and backtracked through the years and there was no mention whatsoever of her feelings toward her husband. It was as though he didn't exist. She spent her entire marriage working around him. Putting things over on him, for the sake of the children. Actually, she managed to do that very well.

I couldn't shut Talesbury totally out of mind. I got up and located the photo of the nineteenth century Catholic Bishop, Salesburg, whose fearsome name often came up in Kansas priests' memoirs.

His beard was much longer than Talesbury's, and his eyes were deep set, but the resemblance was uncanny. I'd known that from the moment I saw him, and now I knew to trace Talesbury's mother's lineage. Not his father's. Talesbury's great uncle or great-great or some weird kin connection.

Chip Ferguson came through the door at about eleven o'clock, bearing a load of family photos. He had selected the one he wanted in the history books for his own entry and asked if I wanted to copy the others which were behind convex glass.

"Do I ever!" We collected as many photos as we could for our files and a quick glance told me these were a real treasure. There were pictures of Gateway City from the early 1900s, including ones of a rare flood when water had poured into businesses.

I went to our Beseler Digital Photo-Video Copy Stand and attached my Nikon D700. By now, I'd invested a fortune in equipment for my underpaid job.

"Would you mind if I took them out of their frames?" This part was always tricky. Persons imagined that I would somehow trash their precious photos. But it was difficult to do a good job through some types of glass.

"Be careful," he said.

With jewelers' tools, I carefully wobbled the tiny pins from the back of the frame and removed the protecting layer of fiberboard on the back. I centered the photo and took a series of pictures. When I'd finished duplicating everything, I placed the photos back in their frames and gave the collection back to Chip.

Then I uploaded the images to my computer, printed out every one of them on good photo paper. We had a comb binder. I put the pages into an album, printed a cover entitled "My Album," with "Chip Ferguson" in script at the bottom and handed it to him.

"Well, I'll be damned," he said, staring at the book. "God's sake. Thanks. Wasn't expecting this." He fumbled for an old handkerchief and dabbed at his eyes.

"You are very welcome," I said. This was excellent PR and once we had the equipment we could make these books in about fifteen minutes. It had led to some unexpected and generous monetary contributions to the historical society, and through word of mouth, a cascade of fantastic photos came in that ordinarily would never be shared.

"I'll remember this," And I hoped he would. He had no heirs and this stingy, miserly man had to give his money to someone or something. He vigorously shook my hand again and left.

I wanted this man to talk about his parents. How they happened to come to Carlton County, how they made a living. He would soon. I'd learned to take one step at a time.

I listened to Edna's tapes until noon, and then called Keith to see if he could join me for lunch. He agreed and as I hung up, I was struck with a pleasant realization. For a full hour, I had not thought about Mary Farnsworth.

That changed a minute later.

Bishop Rice called my cell phone. "I'm on my way to Western Kansas," he said. "On business related to issues other than St. Helena. But there has been a very strange development. I would like to discuss this with you personally. Will you be home this evening?"

"Yes, of course."

"I understand that your husband is now a deputy?"

"Yes, he is." The news must have traveled with the speed of light.

"Would it be possible to have him there also?"

"Yes. That's not a problem."

"Fine. And your sister? She's still a KBI consultant?"

"Yes." I wondered how he had put all this together and if he knew the dog's name also.

"Fine. I'd like to include her in the conversation. And my wife, Sara, will be with me, helping me drive."

"Please plan on having dinner with us. We would love to have you both."

We agreed on a time. I hung up, and called Josie. I told her the Rices would be there for dinner.

"Is Zola there yet?"

"Yes, she's right here in the kitchen. She says the floorboards on your east porch need replaced. And she says no."

"Put her on the phone."

"I'm so sorry," she said. "So very sorry, but I will not be able to accommodate you."

"If it's a matter of money."

"No, Miss Albright, it's a matter of integrity. The answer is no. I require a certain level of cooperation."

Anything, I thought. *We'll cooperate like crazy.* I could imagine the amused expression on Josie's face. Envision her elaborate smoke rings formed to keep from laughing out loud.

"Frankly, this place requires a great deal of work and I could only give you one day a week. A Tuesday. It's a quite undesirable day. Most persons prefer to prepare for weekends or recover from them."

"Once a week would be wonderful." Tuesday was wonderful. Today was Tuesday.

"One day a week is not enough time to set Fiene's Folly to rights. My great-great grandfather managed an estate in England and my grand-father Tompkins…"

"Tompkins? Tompkins? You're one of the Studley Tompkins?"

"Why yes, I am. Did you know them?"

"I know *about* them. I wrote an article about the English in Kansas." A foot in the door. Finally. I shamelessly exalted her illustrious ancestors, and praised their noble accomplishments. I omitted references to any drunken reprobates. By the end of my self-serving manipulative recitation I had myself a housekeeper. When I mentioned a visiting bishop, she agreed to start at once.

Then I spoke to Josie again and begged her to dig out a recipe book and come up with something elegant and manageable. Especially manageable. No gourmet concoctions because our little grocery store would not have the ingredients.

Their little Honda Prius pulled up our lane early evening. The bishop and Keith hit it off immediately. His wife was a pleasant brown-haired woman with a trace of a New York accent. Sara Rice wore a cream cotton pullover over khaki cropped pants. She was a very gracious lady and I suspected she had a keen intuitive feel for setting people at ease anywhere in the world.

Josie had decided that grilled kabobs and a fruit bowl made more sense than a formal meal on short notice. It was just the right touch. The Rices were skilled conversationalists, and Keith and I enjoy entertaining. The evening should have been absolutely perfect, but curiosity was about to do us all in. There was a lull, then Bishop Rice sighed, stopped smiling, and looked at the three of us.

"It's time to get down to the reason for my visit," he said. "There's been an unexpected complication regarding Bishop Talesbury. And the reason I've asked the three of you to hear this together is because of the time and energy you've all spent trying to make a go of St. Helena."

I didn't groan out load, but inside my stomach little dwarfs started beating kettle drums. How could there possibly be another complication?

"Have any of you ever heard of a glebe?"

Keith knew. I was the historian but I didn't have a clue. Clearly Josie didn't either.

"In England, a Bishop was given a parcel of land for his own purposes," Keith said. "It was called a glebe. It supplemented his living and could be passed down to his heirs. It was his."

"Exactly," said Rice. "And the Episcopal Church in America carried on this custom here for a number of years. There's only one glebe west of the Mississippi and it's in Clay County, Kansas."

I sat bolt upright. I sensed where this was heading. "Please do not tell me that Talesbury is asking for a glebe. Let me guess," I said. "The parcel of land on which we built St. Helena's. The land that had such sloppy documentation."

"Right. That's the land." He looked at us all frankly, like a man used to dealing with strange situations. "It's worse than that, Miss Albright. He claims he already owns it."

"And he claims it's his why?" Josie asked.

"He's the sole heir of his great-great-great uncle, The Right Reverend Josef T. Salesburg, who allegedly owned it to begin with."

"That's why the abstract work was off. Nothing made sense. The land would have been given before Kansas was a state. Territorial times." Alarmed by the excitement in my voice, Tosca ran to Josie. "Paperwork from that era rarely survived. That also explains why an African Bishop showed up in Western Kansas."

"Yes, it certainly does," Rice said. "Forty acres means nothing out here, but they would seem like a patch of heaven on earth to a man who survived the horrible Hutu/Tutsi wars."

I smiled. Land ownership again. It came up over and over in Western Kansas. Forty acres. The number of acres many ex-slaves believed they would own if they could make it to Kansas.

Kansas. The Promised Land. To the formerly enslaved, and now to an African bishop.

Chapter Twenty-Seven

I expected Josie to start packing the next morning. If she couldn't participate in the recall election, there was no reason for her to stay. Instead, I found her at the kitchen table, gazing out the window, drinking coffee and scribbling on a legal pad.

I poured myself a cup and carried it out to the patio. She joined me about fifteen minutes later.

"I'm not going in today," I waved my cup. "Not to either job. Right now I'm worn down by both of them."

"Zola will be great. Sorely needed, I might add."

"Hate to admit it, but I'm exhausted."

"And you're over Keith's stepping in?"

"Mostly. In fact, I'm beginning to see the advantages. I don't have to worry about saying too much or too little. And you? Have you come to love this part of the state?"

"No. And believe me, I want to get out of here, but Harold says we can't back down on the charges we filed against Deal. He's still an arrogant bastard and he still has to go. Spring Break isn't over for another week, and I'll tack on another week if I must. Harold can find substitutes for my classes."

"Maybe so, but you can't hang around here until the next election."

"I know that, but Harold and I have talked. The petitions may be invalid and it was stupid to show our hands before we knew what we were doing, but the sentiments of persons in

Copeland County are genuine. He wants me to talk to each person, explain how we screwed up, and find three voters brave enough to start the process again."

"Deal's sly, Josie. Wicked mean. You'll have a hard time convincing people to speak up after they hear about Keith's oats field. Keith has quite a bit of clout, and if that clan crossed him, they'll target anyone."

"I know that. You think I don't know how to cope with mean people?"

"Maybe, but as a psychologist, you're used to being in charge."

"That's true, but my reputation is at stake. Harold says I've got to see this through."

"We've got a lot on our plates," I said. "Keith is trying to find out who plowed up his oats field, and I'm just sick about the church. All the people who thought they owned these little parcels of land. I still can't believe I was this stupid."

"It wasn't your fault, Lottie."

"In a way it was. I know better than to ignore serious snags in documentation. That land was a nightmare from the very beginning."

"We don't know for sure yet that Talesbury's claim is valid. It sounds fishy to me that this hasn't come up before."

"Me too. I don't buy Bishop Rice's argument that forty acres would seem like a sanctuary to Talesbury after those wars. I can't imagine why he would want them. It's just forty acres in the middle of nowhere. He can't make a living off it. It's not good for anything."

"Are you sure? Is there any oil potential?"

"I didn't think of that. Keith knows some geologists who might be able to make a decent guess."

"Archeology material?"

"Kansas has had great finds all right. The Penokee Man is just a couple of counties away. It's an outline of a human figure about fifty feet long and thirty feet wide. A paleontologist from Harvard thinks it was made by Plains Indians. But archeology is worth checking. I'll call the Kansas Archeology Association and see if they have ideas."

◇◇◇

Harold called mid-morning on the house phone. I was in the laundry room sorting clothes. Enjoying the scent of Febreze, whittling down piles of sheets and towels. Chores that went like they were supposed to. After Josie hung up she hollered from the kitchen. "There's been a new development."

"That figures." I added a capful of Tide to the washer, and walked over to the table. "Do I need something stronger than coffee?"

"No. And I don't know why you insist on calling it coffee. It's a really strange development." She continued after I sat down. "Harold says there is no record of a woman like Mary in the witness protection program. But an American woman resembling her was *supposed* to go in and never did about twenty years ago."

"Folks can't just leave the program, can they?"

"Sure, if you're never in it. Mary might have been this woman, but he says it's doubtful."

"She just disappeared?"

"This woman did. We shouldn't jump to conclusions. He says it's not likely anyone in danger would choose such a conspicuous occupation. He doubts it's the same person."

"Why was the government considering putting her in this program to begin with?"

"Harold is trying to find out. He would especially like to know why everything regarding this woman is such a secret."

"I know where I would start looking first. Bishop Talesbury. I bet he knows plenty."

"I'll call Harold right back."

When Keith got home that evening, he said he'd gotten four calls that day with complaints about Deal. We were helpless, of course, because we were trying to thwart the sheriff of Copeland County. The top law enforcement officer.

"The hell of it is," he said, "a lot of this is propaganda. But when a business is hanging on by a thread, that's all it takes."

He reached for a bottle of home brew and joined Josie and me at the table.

"Mrs. Winthrop called me and said there was a rumor going around that a bunch of people got food poisoning at her café. It was a damn lie, but she couldn't call her own sheriff and we can't do anything about it. She lives in Deal's county and even if I was the sheriff there, there's not a damn thing I can do about a rumor."

"What are you going to do about your oats field?" Josie asked.

"What do you mean do? Not going to do anything." He rose abruptly and walked over to the window and stared outside. He shoved his hands into his jeans pockets. The setting sun accentuated the lines in his face. He looked weary. Older. Beaten down.

"It's too late to replant oats. I'm going to re-till that field and get it ready for corn. It's the only thing I can do. It will be a pain in the ass because a lot of oats will come up volunteer, but I have no choice."

"No, I meant legally. How are you going to find the person?" Josie wouldn't give up.

He turned and looked embarrassed. "I'm discovering that as a law enforcement officer, my hands are tied in a lot of ways."

"Not easy, is it?" I said.

"No. In fact, this whole thing is the pits." He looked at Josie. "Here's the deal. As a deputy sheriff investigating a crime, I need to have probable cause to inspect a man's tractor and equipment and match the tracks in my field. I can't just walk into a man's barn."

"There's got to be some way to do things in counties like this," Josie said, "or police would be victimized all of the time."

"I'm not worried about myself or even you two women right now. I'm worried about all the people who signed that petition. Can't believe I was that dumb. Can't imagine I didn't read all the fine print. Can't believe I've caused that much trouble for people who finally got up their nerve to fight back."

"Don't be so hard on yourself," Josie said. "We were all in on this. And I'm still more upset over the oats field than about the petition signers."

Keith smacked his fist into the palm of his hand. "Before I took this job, I could have just found the bastard and knocked the hell out of him, then dared him to file charges. I can't do that now."

Josie flinched, her eyes widened. "You can't just go around beating people up."

"Keith, that's ridiculous. It's vigilante justice," I said. But he knew that. It wouldn't bring back the oats field.

"No? What else would you suggest? I spent the afternoon reading up on my new occupation. The trouble I could get into as an ordinary citizen, and the trouble I would have doing exactly the same thing as a police officer are different situations altogether."

I pushed back from the table, and walked over to my colorful array of bibbed aprons hanging on pegs. I put one on, picked up a spatula, and waved it at them. "I'm the queen here and this is my kitchen. As my subjects, you are both forbidden to say one more word about crime this whole evening."

Josie rolled her eyes and Keith grinned.

"I've got a roast in the oven. Josie made a pie. Get out of here. Shoo. Go check on the cattle, and by the time you're done we'll have supper on the table. Then let's do something normal. Like play music. For the dog's sake. Tosca needs a soothing evening."

Good food helped. But our conversations faltered.

Later we alternated playing bluegrass, country western, and classical.

I hadn't thought it possible for the three of us to miss so many notes.

Chapter Twenty-Eight

The next day at the historical society I was too edgy to do research. We were all miserable. Keith likes to be in charge and make things happen, but he was trapped by trivia. Spending bored days behind a desk, thinking they couldn't go on forever, but they could. Josie was driving Keith's pickup, backtracking to locate petitioners willing to take charge of the recall election.

On Edna's fourth tape, I finally pulled off my headphones, and stood up in disgust. I rifled through the printouts of her disconnected memoirs, trying to decide if some of the tapes were missing, or she was more addled than I had thought. She had just leap-frogged from her life in Iowa to her life in Kansas.

My cell phone shrilled. I jumped, swore, spilled coffee, and made a mental note to change the ring.

"Sam, here. Dimon called. Some news finally."

"Good? Bad?"

"Neither. Just news. The poison was heavy duty. Totally unexpected. Off the wall. That's what took the toxicologists so long."

My office phone rang. I let it go.

"It's from a poison dart frog. One of the most poisonous varieties known."

After we hung up, I called Josie.

She listened. "I'll call Harold. They are keeping him in the loop since he's still a consultant for Carlton County."

I touched my fingers to the pulse in my throat and waited for her to call back. Bishop Talesbury's face swam before my eyes. I had sworn there was no way there could have been a murder in that little church. No way. But there was and we knew it. The bishop had flown in from Africa. We knew that. And now we knew he'd known Mary Farnsworth.

Ten minutes later, she called with background information. "It's natural habitat is South America," she said. "Not Africa. There has been lots of traffic back and forth between there and Africa since colonial days. Exchanges of products and goods. But even if there wasn't this connection, Harold says there's a thriving pet market for poisonous frogs."

"But how, Josie? How? Let's go for a touch of reality here. Aren't the secretions of these little critters used on the tips of poison darts? We were both there. Talesbury didn't just suddenly whip out a blow dart gun and start firing away."

"No. That's true. But here's what we do know. The KBI says Mary Farnsworth absolutely did die from this poison and no other. She was in full view of over one hundred people. Maybe more. This particular poison is so lethal two grams can stop an elephant in its tracks. She had time to run from the rail to the anteroom. If she had been targeted with this in the sanctuary, she couldn't have taken two steps."

"Is there another way to use this poison other than injection?"

"Actually, there is, but it's not like anyone handed her a cup of poison and told her to drink it five minutes later."

In my heart, I wanted the killer to be Talesbury because I despised the man. But my head took over. "We've got to pull out all the stops and find the man kneeling next to Edna."

"It's a little late for that."

"Yes." I rubbed the bridge of my nose. "I just wish we'd known from the beginning that Mary's death wasn't simple. There were so many steps we could have taken."

"You couldn't have known that, Lottie. You did everything you could."

"Not everything. I'm going to start calling everyone I can think of who was there that day and see how many had cameras. Maybe someone has a picture.

"My money is still on the bishop," Josie said. "But Harold says the KBI is going to send someone out here right away to help with the investigation. Until now, they've just supported us with lab work."

"Our fault on that. One of the agents should have observed the autopsy. But we blew that too."

"Harold told me to warn you not to go off half-cocked. Let the A team take over. We have to do this by the book and not make any accusations before we can back them up with proof."

"I understand." As soon as we hung up, I called Keith.

He listened. "That's incredible. I know a little about toxins from my veterinary training, but an ag vet isn't exactly up to speed on poison dart frogs. I know there's one that secretes the most poisonous substance in the world."

I couldn't remember the Latin name Josie gave me, but I was certain he would call her the moment he hung up.

"It surprised me how long some of these poisons last on the tip of a weapon." I eyed my computer and blessed Google. "I imagine we'll have plenty to talk about at supper."

"Ah hell, there's just no way it could have happened. But you can bet I'll think about it all afternoon."

"Keith, why don't you let Sam take over the next couple of days? I know you're going crazy just sitting there, when you could be tilling the oats field. Or something."

"I don't want to slight my job. Have that old bastard think I'm just dabbling."

I didn't dare laugh. I had used those same words myself, when I was justifying my job to him. I suspected he remembered them. Verbatim.

"Really, honey. Harold says we can't do a thing on our end. The KBI is taking over. There's too many things that don't add up. There's absolutely nothing we can contribute. Nothing." I said again just in case he didn't get it the first time. "Nothing."

"Yes, I can," he said. "I'm going to set fire to that little son-of-a-bitching church. It's been nothing but trouble from the beginning."

I didn't bother to say goodbye.

Myrna Bedsloe came in and asked to exchange her latest story. "I just remembered the great aunt on my Uncle Charlie's side. His third wife? The poor soul doesn't have kith or kin to put in a word about her. Am I limited to one story?"

Her little boy started batting at her eyes and she blinked and tried to grasp his little fists without letting him drop to the floor.

"No, you're not limited," I said. "As long as it's about a different branch of the family, you're free to submit all the stories you like."

I eyed the clock. I wanted to run over to Edna's and grill her. That was the right word, too. So far, I'd been very careful, but with a different kind of questioning she might remember more about the stranger. Besides, by now she trusted me. There was no way a KBI interrogator could do a better job than I. Compiling oral histories was an important part of my training.

"Gotta run," Myrna said cheerfully. "Don't we sweetkums?" The little boy shrieked and giggled and poked her in the cheek. "Mom's in the car. We're on our way to Dunkirk to the podiatrist. She's having a little trouble walking and hollers half the night from the pain in her feet."

The other boy threw a truck across the room and she hurried to pick it up. "At least I think it's her feet. I never know. Last week we went to the stomach doctor, but he said there was nothing wrong."

She grabbed the other kid and left, and I picked up my purse and a stack of files, turned out the light, then whirled around. Chip entered before I could get out the door.

"Miss Lottie, he said. "Am I catching you at a bad time?"

Trapped. I'd been stalking this man for over a year. The little gift photo album had done the trick. Short of spitting chewing tobacco, he could do anything he wanted to right in this office if he cooperated in transmitting his family history. They had even raised sheep.

"Why no, Chip. Come right on in."

Chapter Twenty-Nine

Using the pretext of bringing more tapes, I dashed over to Edna's after Chip left. She took forever to answer the door and for a moment I was ashamed at risking stressing this poor woman even more.

But I had to talk to her before the KBI did.

"Hello Lottie," she said, then invited me inside. "But the house is a mess." It wasn't. Except for the little piles on her dining room table, the place was spotless. Considering the shape her hands were in, I could just imagine how hard she struggled to maintain her standards.

As usual, she wore a bibbed apron over a faded housedress and her feet were shoved into old felted slippers with slits cut to accommodate her bunions.

She seemed even thinner than a week ago. More vulnerable.

"Your stories are wonderful, Edna. There's so much information. It's the kind of details historians love. In fact academics depend on the great journals ordinary persons left behind."

She beamed. "Don't seem like I said anything that would mean much to anyone."

"Oh, but you did." We chatted a bit more. About spring. About flowers. Then I noticed the cloud that came over her face with I mentioned her garden. She shut up. This was clearly the way she handled situations that made her uncomfortable. She avoided them. Changed the subject.

It didn't matter. I pressed. "Edna, I have a few more questions about the stranger in the church." She stiffened. I proceeded. "Sometimes persons remember details after an event when they absolutely have to. I want you to relax while I ask you a few more questions."

"I, I can't," she stammered. "I just can't. I thought you just wanted to bring more tapes. Didn't know you came here to ask questions because you work for Sam."

I felt like a hawk swooping down on a helpless little bird. "The man's skin. Was he dark? Light?"

"He was normal. I don't know." Her eyelids fluttered.

"The color of his tie? The color of his jacket? Do you remember?"

"No." Her skin was so thin that I could see her pulse speed up in her throat. "I can't remember. Please. I can't."

Ashamed, I patted her hands. "That's all right, dear. I just thought there was a chance you might recall more by this time." There was no way I would allow some fierce interrogator to bully this woman. It was out of the question. Her immediate physical reaction scared the hell out of me.

"Have Elmira call me if you think of anything and I'll come right over." I rose and started toward the door.

"I can't sleep at night," she announced. "Can't sleep at all."

I stopped. I couldn't just leave her this way. I turned and went back and kissed the top of her head. "Put this out of your mind Edna. Don't give it another thought. Just work on your tapes." Her chest fluttered with a sharp intake of breath.

"There's so many more things I would like to know about. Did you quilt? I would love to have your memories about quilting groups." She nodded. "And church groups? Did you attend a ladies' aid or missionary society? And by the way, I don't have tapes on how you ended up in Kansas. There's a gap."

She quivered, then trembled and stiffened like she'd been shot. Spittle ran down the corner of her mouth.

I reached for the phone and dialed the hospital. "Send an ambulance to Edna Mavery's house. Immediately. She may have had a stroke."

After they arrived, I called her son.

Later, although her doctor assured me I had done nothing to bring it on and it was a passing transient ischemic attack, I knew better. It was my fault. I shouldn't have gone there in the first place. They would keep her overnight although her symptoms disappeared in a couple of hours and she didn't appear to blame me for ending up in the hospital.

"I'll wait until Stuart gets here," I said.

"No need," she said. "I know you have work to do."

"Edna, I'm so sorry. I didn't mean to upset you."

"Nothing you did, Lottie. Nothing you did."

But again, I simply knew better.

Stuart arrived and rushed to her bedside. When I went back in, I smiled at the change in her appearance. She perked right up.

"I'll go on now," I said.

"I'll be right back." Stuart kissed his mother's withered cheek. "Lottie and I need to talk."

She gazed at him in admiration, then squeezed his hand.

"I ought to be shot," he said immediately. "Not seeing her more often than I do. Leaving her to cope by herself."

"Stuart, you need to know that I was trying to get your mom to remember more details about the episode at St. Helena. I'm so sorry. Despite what the doctor thinks, I'm afraid I helped bring this on. I wish I hadn't upset her."

He gave my shoulder a little squeeze and looked at me sadly with his kind grey-blue eyes. "Life here by herself is simply getting too hard for her. That's what's upsetting. But she won't hear to moving out of her little house whenever I bring it up."

"You've done everything right," I said. "It's best to leave aging parents in their own home as long as they want to stay there. As long as they can. It's the 'can' that's hard to judge. And a lot of them go down swinging before they'll give up their independence."

"My wife and I both work. So it will be assisted living for her, but if she were in Wichita, at least we could visit and have her over to the house. Take her places."

Although I still felt guilty, it was nice to know he understood I hadn't intended to upset his mother.

"Anyway, thanks, Lottie. I'm going over to mom's house and drop off my things. I'll stay there tonight. It will give me a chance to look things over. See how she's been living. I'll check her refrigerator and see what she's been eating."

"OK. Here's my cell phone number." I reached in my purse for my notepad and handed Stuart the piece of paper. "If anything comes up or I can help in any way, please let me know."

"Will do," he said. A nurse went into Edna's room and I stared at her closed door, again struck with remorse.

He followed my gaze. "I would hate to think what might have happened if you hadn't been there. I thought she was getting along great. She was tickled plumb to death when you brought her that tape recorder."

"Don't mention it. I was glad to do it. Her life in Iowa was fascinating. I loved all the details about raising chickens."

His brow furrowed and he looked at me with a strange expression on his face. "Iowa? Mom has never lived in Iowa. She's spent her entire life in Kansas."

By the time I drove home, I had decided what to do. Nothing. Absolutely nothing.

I do not have the right to expose secrets. And I know plenty about people's lives that their children have never heard about. I know about illegitimate children, insanity in families, shameful tales, and about criminals lurking in the family tree. Their secrets are safe with me. It was Edna's place to tell Stuart she'd had another life before she married his father and that he had a half-brother and sister.

The only thing that was my business was learning details about the man kneeling next to her. My distress over upsetting her overwhelmed any desire to push her again. I would simply warn the KBI that she need to be handled with kid gloves and then to leave the questioning to their most skilled interrogator.

Josie had left a note on the table that she was still explaining the muffed petition to signers. I smiled. Her Mercedes was gone and so was Tosca. Apparently she'd decided to quit trying to fit in and had risked going as her natural self.

I headed for my chair, put my feet up on the ottoman, pulled a cotton throw over me, and feeling like a two-year-old seeking the security of a "blankie," I snuggled down with my head resting on a pillow against the broad leather arm.

Keith's movements woke me up. "I wanted to have supper ready," I said. "Make like a decent wife."

"No need. I'm not hungry."

"OK." I smiled and resnuggled. He laughed at my relief and tussled my hair. "I had a terrible day," I said. I told him about Edna.

"I can top that," he said. "I took two calls from businessmen who were madder than hell. An electrician said there's a rumor going around he uses substandard wire in his houses, and the manager of the local grain elevator says the prices he's offering to farmers were screwed with on the local cable channel."

"Rotten tactics, but nothing tangible there that we can charge Deal with. For that matter, we can't even be sure if it's the sheriff or one of his friends."

"Exactly. Even if we were certain of the who, which we're not, we can't charge him with anything but slander. But can you imagine how long that will take? And then we'd have to round up people willing to file charges."

"Not likely to happen, since we blew the petition."

"Shadow boxing. I hate it." With that he left the room and came back with a bottle of brew.

We turned on the TV and watched the evening news. Josie came up the drive and in a few minutes Tosca scampered into the room and headed straight for Keith.

"I'm not cooking," I said.

"I'm not either," Keith echoed. "You're on your own."

Josie laughed. "First break I've had all day. I won't have to go for my run waddling like an overstuffed turkey."

She flopped down into a recliner and kicked off her shoes. "There are some really terrific people out here," she said. "It's surprising how well they handle situations that could fell an ox."

"Going to hang out your shingle here?"

"N-o-o." She drawled out the word. I teased Tosca out of Keith's arms with a single toss of her little ball. She hit the floor running and we all laughed when it bounced against the wall and she tumbled trying to reverse her skid.

Then with a single word on the local news we all stopped horsing around and stood like statues.

Deal.

The anchor on the Wichita television station stuck a microphone in Sheriff Deal's face.

Chapter Thirty

"Copeland County Sheriff Irwin Deal has agreed to this interview regarding the recent mysterious death of Episcopal priest, Mary Farnsworth," the petite anchorwoman said. She looked into the camera and assumed her best relaying-a-tragedy look.

"Sheriff Deal, isn't it true there are unexplained circumstances regarding this woman's death?"

"Just unexplained to some people," he said. His hard black eyes looked directly at the camera. He folded his arms across his chest in a stance he clearly thought conveyed power and authority. "Nothing mysterious about it. It's unfortunate and of course this woman dying right after a church service was very upsetting, but things like this happen."

The anchorwoman looked confused. "So you're saying this was a natural death?"

"Well, no death is natural, I guess." He looked proud, like he'd favored the viewers with a profound insight. "The public can rest assured that my office is in charge of the entire investigation and everything went through the proper channels." He squared his shoulders, then hooked his thumbs in his belt, his fingers dangling like a nineteenth century gunslinger hoping for a chance to draw.

"Sir, it's my understanding that the KBI is now involved."

We have a large high resolution TV with excellent graphics. The three of us exchanged looks, then looked back at the screen as the coloring drained from Deal's face.

"There are some aspects of this I can't discuss," he said sullenly.

I grabbed Keith's hand. "He doesn't know. He doesn't have a clue."

Deal straightened the brim of his hat and started to walk off, but she hurried after him. "Sheriff Deal, we have a few more questions." He waved her away and hustled toward his car.

She turned back to the camera. "In fact, the district coroner, Dr. Joel Comstock, stated to Channel Seven earlier that this has become a homicide investigation. He also appealed to the public to contact his office if they have any knowledge as to the whereabouts of Reverend Mary Farnsworth's family."

The number appeared on the screen. "And now to our weatherman. What's in store for us tomorrow, Paul?" With a cheery change of mood, she waved at a man standing in front of a map. "Well, no good news, I'm afraid, Shelia. In fact, there's a cold front moving in and native Kansans know that can mean anything this time of year."

Keith walked to the TV and turned it off. "So Deal doesn't even know the KBI took over the investigation," he said. "Which makes me wonder exactly what he's been up to on his own."

"I'm on duty today," I announced to my husband two days later. I gave Keith a look, daring him to contradict me, which he didn't. Besides, I out-ranked him. I breezed right out the door, knowing by now he'd come to accept the fact that I didn't have the most dangerous job in the world, and certainly didn't need his twenty-four hour a day protection.

I decided to drive by St. Helena on the way into town. When I topped the hill I recognized Talesbury's Camry. Sheriff Deal's Crown Victoria was parked beside it. The bright yellow crime scene tape left by the KBI was gone. My blood pounded and I tried to steady my breathing. I turned into the lot, then stormed inside. The scent of Clorox wafted over the church.

"What in the hell are you two doing here?" I yelled.

Talesbury came out of the anteroom carrying a bucket and a sponge.

"How did you two get in here? What the hell is going on? And how dare you interfere with a crime scene? Is that bleach?" I whirled around and faced Deal. "Is it? Are you destroying evidence?"

Deal walked toward me, his hands hovering over his pistols.

"I'm cleaning up my property," Talesbury said.

"You are trespassing, lady," Deal took another step toward me. "Get the fuck out of here. Now."

"This is a crime scene. You have no right to be here."

"Wanna bet? It's his property." He waved his thumb toward Talesbury who stood stiff and silent with a miserable expression on his face.

"Are you crazy? We've been down this road before. Are you going to arrest me again?"

"Not this time." His smile was bitter. Creepy. "I'm just going to throw you out of here."

He could easily manage that physically. And I certainly wasn't going to shoot a man over a bucket of bleach. I edged toward the door. I wasn't going to give him a chance to shoot me either.

"Oh, by the way, Agent Dimon gave us the key yesterday after Talesbury showed him the papers proving he owns this land. That put an end to everything."

"You've been to Topeka?" I asked stupidly.

"You betcha, bitch. Do you think I don't know when I've been set up? How much did you pay that reporter?"

His accusation was ludicrous. But Deal waggled the sole key to the anteroom before my eyes. "Dimon says hello and to tell you that this building is no longer a crime scene."

Furious, I eyed the lone key. I should have made copies at the beginning. But there had been no reason to make extra keys because no other woman had shown the slightest bit of interest in maintaining St. Helena.

I walked toward the door, then stopped when he called after me.

"Oh, and Agent Dimon was surprised to know you weren't in charge of the investigation. He had a lot of stuff wrong, but I set him straight."

I walked back up the aisle and faced Talesbury. "Why in the world would this tiny little piece of land matter to you? Why would you want it?"

"Because it's mine. My land. I know of lost children who need a place where they will be safe. A sanctuary. They require isolation and a chance to heal. Child soldiers, damaged souls."

"That war was over twenty years ago. Those children are grown now."

"There is always a war in Africa. With the same patterns. Innocent victims. Children with souls hollowed out. Mine is a sparrow ministry, Miss Albright." His eyes shone. "I save the one, the few."

Here? In Western Kansas? "Who told you about this land?"

Deal stepped in front of him. "I saved it. You're not the only one who can do research. Then I heard about your land grab. Thought you could fire up a bunch of do-gooders to steal it, didn't you? My uncle was plumb grateful when I wrote him."

"You're a priest. You've taken vows." I looked above Deal's eyes at Talesbury. "You presumed to confirm my niece and hold a service in a church that wasn't consecrated."

"I didn't know that at the time." His eyes clouded. "I was misled."

"Get off his property, bitch. Now." Deal drew his gun.

I spun around and headed for my car. Why would Irwin suddenly start doing research on this piece of property? Who told Talesbury the church had been consecrated? Why did Deal care about any of this?

I was beginning to agree with Keith. The place had been nothing but trouble from the very beginning and I wished we had just set fire to it.

◇◇◇

I drove on into town. Emerald rows of winter wheat lined both sides of the road, and clumps of Queen Anne's lace were greening up although it would be summer before the lovely white flower tops dotted the country side.

I walked into the office and called Sam at once and told him about the encounter with Deal.

"They scrubbed down the entire anteroom. With bleach."

"Well, I'll be a son-of-a-bitch."

"Deal claims the KBI released the church as a crime scene."

"Call and double-check. That's probably true. No reason not to if they've checked the place for poison."

The technicians had been at St. Helena last week, but Sam and I had agreed to let the team work without our hanging around. We were rank amateurs and the office in Topeka had all the information we could give them. Which was precious little.

"Sam, I know Deal told the KBI a bunch of lies."

"No doubt in my mind. But Deal was dead right about one thing. This is not our investigation."

"It's not his, either," I snapped. "There's no way he can claim Copeland County has jurisdiction there."

"Now don't get het up. All I meant was that it's in the KBI's hands now. In fact, Dimon called yesterday and apologized after he saw a video of Deal's TV interview. After that, he viewed Deal and Talesbury's jaunt to Topeka in a whole new light. But even so, he said Talesbury had the right papers to claim the key."

"At least I have the satisfaction of knowing after that news interview he's the laughing stock of the entire state of Kansas. I'll bet he's had his ears pinned back."

"Dumb bastard."

"Better him than us making fools of ourselves."

"You mean we're not?"

Brittle from lack of sleep, I assumed he meant me. Sam and Keith were still allies in their shared disgust over the YouTube tape. But I managed to keep my mouth shut.

"How's the new deputy working out?" Sam asked.

So that was how it was going to go. Sam would mask his confusion and frustration by seeing how many of my buttons he could push.

I didn't take the bait. "Best one we've ever had."

I began preparing our report for the *Gateway Gazette*. Sam had issued a couple of speeding tickets. We often omit mention of domestic violence calls. I warned the citizens about burning off fields without notifying the fire department.

About ten o'clock I checked with Margaret and she was surprisingly pleasant. She was busy answering letters to persons who had written requesting information about their ancestors.

"Did any new stories come in?"

"Not a one. Which suits me just fine. Some of the letters are over ten days old."

Stuart Mavery called on my cell an hour later.

"Morning, Lottie, Stuart here."

"Hi, is Edna doing all right?"

"They are sending her home in a couple of hours."

"Great. When I checked her in, the doctor said he thought it was a TIA, a little mini-stroke. Sort of a warning against a future larger one, and with this one all her symptoms would be temporary."

"They were." He paused. Something was off. The silence sounded strained. I wished I could see his eyes.

"Is everything all right, Stuart? Did you sleep OK at your mom's house?" I didn't want to say, "You sound funny," but he did.

"Actually no." He cleared his throat. "Lottie, did you know mom had once been in a mental institution?"

Chapter Thirty-One

"Oh Stuart, no. I'm so terribly sorry. And you didn't know this?"

"No. I didn't. Did she ever mention it to you?"

"No." She hadn't, but guiltily, I thought about Edna's account of her life in Iowa. Obviously she hadn't told her son a thing about that time either. Although I was not under any oath of confidentiality, it was a matter of common sense not to relay secrets that weren't mine to share. She had never told me a thing about mental health problems. Just that her husband was a bastard.

"Stuart, it's not unusual that you didn't know. Years ago, people simply didn't discuss family problems. It wasn't considered in good taste."

"That may be, but you would think a mother would at least tell her only child that there are medical problems in her personal history."

I closed my eyes. He certainly was not an only child either.

"Stuart, now may not be the best time with Edna just getting out of the hospital, but why don't you plan on coming back in a week or so. If she's stronger and getting along OK, you might like to ask her if there are issues that she might want you to know about."

"All right. It's going to take a couple more days for me to iron out some nursing details for home health care. She certainly can't be alone at night."

"No, and I have a feeling she's going to hate that. But there are several ladies who make their living as care-takers for the elderly. Call social services and see if they can give you some names." My suggestion had been automatic before I remembered that the director of our multi-county social services department had been murdered.

"Wait a minute. I'll give you some names." I scanned down the service ads in the *Gateway Gazette* and recognized one that Edna might be comfortable with.

"I don't mind telling you, I don't know anyone less crazy than my mother. I mean no one. She's about as down to earth as they come."

"I agree."

After I hung up the phone, I realized I had meant every word. Edna was evasive and had her petty little subterfuges to conceal expenditures from her first husband, but her life was centered around the farm and every day things. Her tapes might have jumped around, but nearly all oral histories do. They are full of digressions and back-tracking.

She was understandably upset over a murder that had taken place practically right under her nose, but who wouldn't be? And I suspected most younger persons wouldn't be able recall the details of a person kneeling next to them.

I agreed with Stuart. Mental illness just didn't seem to fit.

After he hung up, I walked to the front door and stepped outside for a moment. I needed a jacket. The cold front the weatherman had predicted was on the way. There was a vacant lot between the hardware store and the run-down wreck of what had once been a lumber yard. Weeds grew out of old tires thrown there among the decaying brown stalks of last year's vegetation.

The grass between the sidewalk that fronted the jail and the curb was still brown. The whole main street seemed to be painted in melancholy shades. Deeply unhappy over my encounter with Deal, I knew I had to call Bishop Rice and see if Talesbury's claim was complete. Done Deal? Deal done? I wished.

I was put on hold. When Rice came on his anger was evident in his crisp, sharp voice. He began talking before I could state the purpose of my call.

"I am taking into account, Miss Albright, that no one out there seemed to know a thing about church processes, but this has been unbelievably muddled from the get-go. Just today, I learned I'll need to consult an attorney about this glebe. And this Diocese can barely afford to furnish coffee filters for my office. We cannot afford legal fees."

"I know that, sir."

"Our only hope is that's there's some flaw in passing down this piece of land or that the original Glebe was sold."

I sighed, knowing how tangled things had become when he first checked out the four corner land. "I would like to know if Talesbury has the legal right to claim our church building."

"Oh brother," he said. "I hadn't thought of that."

"I hadn't either, until today." Then I told him about Talesbury and Deal being there.

He said nothing.

"Talesbury told me it was going to be a home for children."

The Bishop made the leap immediately. "Refugee children. Of course. I could not imagine why he would want a piece of property out in the middle of nowhere."

"I couldn't either, but I'm checking out the possibility of oil or archeological finds or some money angle anyway. Just to be sure the refugee angle isn't a front for something else."

"From what you've said, Sheriff Deal doesn't seem like the humanitarian type."

"That's an understatement." I closed my eyes to shut out the quick image of Deal's florid face. "The KBI has taken over the murder investigation, that's no longer the task of either Carlton or Copeland County. Thank heavens the other two counties St. Helena includes have chosen to stay out of this mess."

"All right. Please continue checking out the money angle, I'll call a lawyer and check on the ownership of the building itself if the glebe is valid."

"As you know, sir, I work out of the courthouse. I have easy access to county records. I'll start with mineral rights on surrounding land. It won't take long. But I'm quite sure we won't find anything."

"We need to be sure." He cleared his throat. "Please accept what I'm going to say as speculation. Just first thoughts, OK? Nothing official."

"I understand."

"If Talesbury's claim to the glebe holds, there's not a single thing this Diocese can do about it. Not one thing. Glebes are granted to individuals. They are not owned by the church."

He had already explained that, and if I didn't understand before, I certainly did after extensive research.

"Then as far as the law is concerned, you simply built a structure on land you didn't own. The church is his also."

Luckily no one crossed my path the remainder of the day. I caught up chores, thought, cleaned with a vengeance, thought, typed file labels, thought, and finally settled on sorting thumbtacks.

There was no way in hell that I could explain to a throng of earnest women who had busted their butts raising money that St. Helena had been confiscated by a rank stranger. I didn't care how deep Talesbury's roots were in this county, he was not a native Kansan, and he didn't have a clue about life out here.

Where would he find staff? The church was too tiny to hold many children, and the land around was utterly treeless. The whole venture was ludicrous. African children out here? With no wildlife, no vegetation? The man was out of his mind. Images of the lonely schoolhouses I'd seen in the 1800s crossed my mind. Those kids had survived. But they'd had homes to return to in the evening.

Then against my will, I kept thinking of all the children I'd see on TV lately. Haitian waifs with extended stomachs and flies over their sickly bodies. Other regions where little babies lay listless in their ruined mother's arms.

I tried to put myself in Talesbury's place and think like a man who had been through the horrors of the Tutsi/Hutu wars. Mass slaughter, children raped, animals burned alive. Of course they would be better off here, with good food and decent medical care. I thought about Talesbury's expression this morning.

The burning eyes of a fanatic bent on doing good.

The next morning Keith helped Josie carry her suitcases to the driveway.

"All set. Finally." She'd found three registered voters to carry the recall petition. "I'm outta here. And so's my dog. Aren't you, girl? Ready to go home?"

Tosca leaped into Keith's arms and licked his face. He laughed and handed her to me. "Can't stand loose little dogs," he said. "She'll take up with anyone." Tosca then obligingly licked me from forehead to chin. Social duties completed, she ran back and forth from the house to the passenger side of the car and barked. She knew the drill.

Josie laughed, then gave me a hug. She pushed me to arm's length and looked into my eyes. "Don't be too hard on yourself, hear?"

I nodded. She hugged Keith. "Take good care of her," she said. She strapped in Tosca, then went and around and settled into the driver's seat. She powered down the window for a final farewell. "I'll be back. As soon as Harold schedules the hearing to fry Deal. Shouldn't take too long."

She left. The house seemed empty when we went inside.

I coveted her dog.

Chapter Thirty-Two

I checked development permits the next day. There was no point in going over all the deeds again. I had pored over abstract histories and ownership claims for those forty acres when we began sorting out land issues for St. Helena. I wanted to know if anyone had ever applied for drilling permits for oil wells.

They hadn't. Nor had there ever been nearby archeological discoveries.

While driving home, I swung by St. Helena again, hoping to find Talesbury there alone. I had a faint hope that if I approached him in a nonthreatening way, treated him as I would a person reluctant to give an oral history, he might talk to me.

His car wasn't there. But the KBI was now in charge of the investigation and Talesbury was already undoubtedly a "person of interest." During that trip to Topeka no doubt he had gone through an extensive interrogation.

I had my own set of questions, but after Deal had finished denigrating my abilities, I doubted the agency would be eager to share any of Talesbury's answers with me, despite Dimon's apology to Sam. Nor, apparently, were they interested in contacting me to see if I had discovered new information.

◇◇◇

We ate in silence, missing Josie, missing Tosca. Keith rose and carried his dishes to the sink.

He stood braced against the counter, his brow wrinkled, whistling a tune I didn't recognize. "I have an idea, Lottie. While it's still daylight, let's grab that old metal detector I have in the barn and do some snooping."

"Good idea." I sprang to my feet. "Terrific in fact. I understand why Talesbury wants the land, but not why Deal would go to so much trouble to back him." However, I wasn't so naïve as to assume one could just walk up to some old farmer and try to buy a little piece of land. I'd thought that when I first came out here, but land is treated like family jewels.

Irwin Deal wasn't rich and neither was Talesbury, but they seemed to be ready to pay whatever lawyers' bills came their way to lay claim to a worthless piece of dirt.

Keith's metal detector had excellent depth sensitivity. But it was hand-held and heavy and I wasn't able to manage it well for long periods of time. What's more, I had no interest in treasure hunting. Normally, Keith didn't either, but some of his buddies had managed to lure him into an occasional outing.

Although I'd ignored most of his explanations about his detector I knew it could be set to reject iron objects such as nails and other loose trash, and that his model actually could burrow into the ground.

At the church yard we worked for four hours. He moved the instrument and I dug when the frequency indicated some sort of a find. After the sun set all we had to show for time spent was a handful of very ordinary American coins, a couple of spoons, and sore backs.

"There's better equipment than mine," Keith said on the way home. "Riding ones. Really good. Do you want me to check it out?"

"No. I'll tell the KBI we went over the property in case they're interested, but realistically, Talesbury's claim on the glebe doesn't have that much to do with a murder investigation."

"We've covered all the bases," Keith said firmly. "Just like we should. If I get any more ideas, I'll follow up on them too."

I smiled and looked out the window at the full moon. Keith really was the best deputy we could have hoped for. I was thinking about giving him a raise.

Sam Abbott came to the historical society the next day. I glanced at the clock when he stepped through the door. "Am I supposed to be there? Instead of here?"

He laughed. "Nope. Just wanted to tell you that Agent Dimon called again. Betty's dispatching and all ears, as usual. I was about to leave for lunch so I thought I would just come over and tell you in person."

"Well, what?"

"You already know there wasn't a trace of any poison on any of the ceremonial trappings."

"I knew that. But did they look at the items in the plastic sack that Reverend Mary planned to deliver after the service?"

"They did, but there was nothing there either."

"I didn't think there was. I made a list and replaced all of the things and called every family. All of them were expecting Reverend Mary to bring supplies later that afternoon. I couldn't deliver the items then, but I took care of it the next day."

"Dimon says he can't see how anyone could have done this. He'll be out in person to interview Edna Mavery."

"She's not up to it."

"Has to be, Lottie." He dug the toe of his boot on the floor and seriously studied the stitching. "This is a murder investigation. She has to pull herself together. They'll use a hypnotist if they have to."

He left. I had one more idea. I called the KBI and asked for Agent Dimon.

He seemed pleasant enough, so maybe Deal hadn't done me as much harm as I'd thought.

"Were there injection marks on Mary Farnsworth's body?" I asked.

"No," he said. "There weren't."

"Did you check her fingers?"

"I'm sure we did. Why? What are you thinking?"

"There was a diabetic kit in that plastic sack. It was labeled 'Bertha Summers.' She is a new diabetic and Mary was bringing her a monitor, but I'm wondering if there was something on the retractable pen that pricks for blood samples."

He laughed. "We're way ahead of you, Miss Albright. That was one of the first things we looked at. We also tested her lipstick formula, the antibiotic salve, and even the baby aspirin. Everything. I mean everything."

I called Margaret and asked if she would be free to come in a couple of hours. She said she didn't see why not since she practically lived there anyway and people just naturally expected her to be at their beck and call.

It took several minutes to soothe her, praise her, and pamper her enough to coax her to come in. We don't run the historical society like it's a hobby. It's open during the posted hours. But I needed to call on Edna. Perhaps there was some way to prepare that poor woman for a visit from the KBI. I had to try.

Inez Wilson, our county health nurse met me at the door. "Well look who the cat's drug in. Come in, Lottie." Inez twisted her thin angular body to yell across the room. "Edna, you have a visitor."

Edna sat in her overstuffed chair, with a pile of magazines, a jar of Vicks, and her reading glasses on a TV tray beside her. Her feet rested on a footstool in front of her. Inez frowned. She bent over and grabbed a little fold of Edna's cheek and gave it a little shake.

"And I think I know someone who needs cheering up. Someone who needs a little bit of sunshine. Yes we do!"

I took a deep breath.

"Someone is being a little bit stubborn about rehabilitation. Yes we are." Inez folded her arms across her chest and looked resentfully down at her charge. "Someone doesn't appreciate the lovely thoughtful ladies who come over with food every day. No, we don't."

"Inez. I'll be here for several hours. I know you have other people to see. Why don't you go on?" I'm used to being pleasant to people. Used to resisting the impulse to pound the hell out of them.

She brightened. "If you're sure."

"I am. I don't mind."

She walked over to the table and grabbed her purse. "I have two ladies lined up to stay here." She raised her voice, making sure Edna heard. "Perhaps you can convince someone to make caretakers' jobs a little easier by smiling a little. Being mindful of blessings."

She left. Tears stung my eyes. I could see the red light glowing on a percolator in the kitchen. I walked over and poured a cup of coffee and sat at Edna's dining room table opposite her chair for a couple of minutes before I approached her. She sat staring straight ahead.

"Would you like tea? Can I get you anything?

She slowly moved her head to look at me. Tears streamed down her withered cheeks.

I went to her and knelt beside her. I didn't speak, but simply held her hand. Then I reached for tissues and dabbed at her eyes.

"He was here," she said finally. Her voice was weak, but clear. "He was here."

Chapter Thirty-Three

"Who, Edna? Who?" My throat tightened. The man? The mysterious man?

"My son. Stuart. He was here."

Relieved that a stranger hadn't come into her house, I was nevertheless puzzled by her distress. "Yes, he stayed here overnight when you were in the hospital."

She continued to weep.

I stood and walked back over to the table. There was a sheet of dismissal instructions. I picked them up and waved them at her. "Would you mind if I read these?"

She stared straight ahead and didn't answer.

I skimmed the information. "You need to walk a little. Would you like me to help you over to the table? Can you use your walker as well as you did before?"

She did not reply. I studied her tear-lined face, then pulled a straight backed chair over to her and sat down.

"What's wrong, Edna? Why are you upset that Stuart was here." I knew her son and daughter-in-law visited several times a year and her grandchildren showed up once in a while. Just five years ago, she'd had Christmas at her house.

"He went through my things," she said. "My papers."

"I'm sure he felt he had to, Edna. He wants to give you the very best of care and it's important that he have an accurate picture of your finances."

It wasn't my place and it might not have been the right time to discuss moving on to a different life, but I refused to treat this woman like an child incapable of making intelligent decisions. Her body might have deteriorated, but not her mind. So I slogged on.

"Have you given any thought to where you might like to go if you can't stay here?"

"He went through my papers. He found everything. Everything."

I knew at once she was referring to papers relating to the mental institution.

"He thinks I was crazy now. Crazy."

"He doesn't, Edna." Deciding immediately—now that secrets had been broached—I told her how I knew of Stuart's discovery.

"When your son told me about it, we both scoffed at any such diagnosis. Not that it's a disgrace, but in our present society, you would have been given an antidepressant or some other medication if that was the problem."

"There wasn't a problem," she said fiercely. "There never was. Henry did it to me. He just decided. He got meaner and meaner. It didn't happen all at once."

Shocked. I sat there with my hands pressed between my knees.

"It was my fault to begin with. We didn't have kids and didn't have kids and it like to drove Henry crazy. I didn't bring up adopting. Didn't have to ask how he felt about it. I knew. He put great stock in breeding. Pure lines. He wouldn't have married me if he didn't think I'd make a good breeder."

I quivered in the presence of her torn soul, sensing she had never told all this to another person.

"It was terrible. Terrible times. He kept track. Mounted me like…" She shuddered. "We never had no babies, but I had my little chicks. My flowers. Not saying that was enough. Just saying I had them, that's all."

"Could you have gone back to your folks, Edna?" She managed a weak smile and shook her head.

"Why? What would I say? That Henry was disappointed that I couldn't have kids? That he was mean to me? Lots of men was mean to their wives. He wasn't a drunk. He didn't hit me."

"But," I protested.

"No but. There was no good reason to leave that man."

"Then one day it happened. I was able to tell Henry I was expecting. Things changed. I was an older mother. I was in my late thirties by then. We was both worried that something would be wrong with the baby. When little Oliver was born, a dandy little boy. Well, I can tell you, things changed."

She smiled a little half-smile with the memory, no longer as agitated as she was when she began.

It would be good for her to cling to pleasant memories for a little while. I rose. "Be back in second. I'm going to warm up my coffee."

I sat across from her again, hoping she wouldn't stop before she explained being in an institution.

"When my little Mary Claire came along I had everything and Henry didn't seem so bad. A lot of women had it worse. Much, much worse. Now I had babies and little chicks and flowers, and it was plenty. Plenty good enough. He was a good provider. We was never hungry."

Plenty good enough. A phrase I heard all the time from older persons. Perhaps it was. But women didn't have to settle for "plenty good enough" any more. Our standards had changed.

"Oh we was a caution me and the kids." Her eyes misted. Her mouth quivered. "We had fun. I taught them how to fish, and we hunted for mushrooms, and we chased butterflies and fireflies. There were Monarchs then and…"

Alarmed by the sudden cascade of tears, I rose and went to her and pressed her head against my chest. "Let's quit for today, Edna. I'll be back."

Sobs shook her frail body.

"I noticed on your sheet that Mrs. Hargraves will be here in twenty minutes. Do you know her?"

She nodded. "She lives over in the next block."

"Do you like her?"

She nodded again.

"Fine. She'll be here overnight. And she'll be fixing your supper."

"I'm not hungry," she said.

"Not now, perhaps, but try to eat something later. Let me tidy up a bit and I'm going to get a damp washcloth for your face." Appearances mattered to the frail little woman. She had spent most of her marriage keeping up a front. "Then we'll comb your hair. You'll look just fine by the time she gets here."

I went straight home and called Agent Dimon and didn't mince words.

"I understand it's essential to interview Edna Mavery. But as undersheriff of this county, I insist on being present. So will her son and an attorney."

"We are not your adversary, Miss Albright. After talking with you yesterday, we'd already planned to send a woman trained in elder interrogation techniques."

After we hung up, I called Stuart and explained the situation. "Something goes wrong when I ask about that man. She's frightened. I'm sure I caused her TIA by pressing her too hard."

"Nonsense, you didn't cause anything. But I sure don't want to take any chances, especially after learning she's had mental health issues in the past."

Miserable with the weight of the day, I didn't know how I should respond. I yearned to simply get everything out in the open.

"I need to be there," he said. "I'll leave Wichita early tomorrow morning. And I agree about her needing an attorney. Who do you recommend?"

"Curtis Matthews hasn't been in town long, so he's just now building a practice. I've heard good things about him. Try him first. I'll bet he's looking for business."

◇◇◇

When we all gathered at Edna's the next day, Mrs. Hargraves had her charge looking her best. Her hair was freshly shampooed and coaxed into sweet sausage curls. Her soft pink, bias trimmed, starched housedress was spotless. Her walker and the table beside her chair were the most visible signs of her declining health.

Stuart stood in back of his mother's chair with one hand on her shoulder. Edna reached for it, tilted her head and kissed his palm. Then she released it, squared her little shoulders and tried to rearrange herself in the chair. We all instinctively sprang forward to help, laughed, then stepped back to let Stuart hoist his mother into a more comfortable position.

I winced. A mere two weeks ago this woman had managed to walk down an aisle, kneel—although with excruciating difficulty—then attend a picnic.

The KBI agent, Nancy Brooks, looked at me, attorney Curtis Matthews, Stuart, Mrs. Hargraves, hesitated, then took a deep breath. She was a small blond-headed woman with neat short hair. She wore a navy blue pantsuit and carried a brown leather shoulder bag. Dressed normal. That would set well with Edna.

Brooks located a wall socket and plugged in a cassette recorder. She noticed my surprised look.

"Backup, Miss Albright. We don't take chances." She pulled a tiny digital recorder out of her briefcase and smiled as she waved it at me. "In fact, we're just a couple of months away from adding video capability for situations just like this."

She recorded her own preliminary remarks and identification, then asked Edna her name and address.

Edna spoke clearly, but with hesitation. As though recalling even these details made her uncomfortable.

"Were you present on Sunday, March 14, 2010, at the new church known as St. Helena?"

"Yes," Edna said. "And I kneeled too. I managed to kneel. Like I should. Just want everyone to know I was in better shape back then. A lot better shape."

Agent Brooks smiled. I liked this lady a lot. As Agent Dimon had said, we were all on the same side. I was starting to relax. We all were. Then Brooks asked Edna to describe the man kneeling next to her.

"I can't remember," she said. "I just can't. He was normal. Just normal. Average."

Brooks pressed. "What do you mean by normal, Mrs. Mavery? Explain average? Do you mean he knew what to do during the service."

"I can't remember. He just wasn't special. I didn't pay any attention. If he wasn't normal, I'd of remembered that. But I don't. All I cared about was that we was having communion with a real priest in a real church and I wanted to get down that aisle without falling over. And I wanted to kneel like a proper Episcopalian."

Alarmed by Edna's flushed face, Brooks reached to stop the tape.

"No, leave it on," Curtis Matthews said sharply. Brooks drew back her hand. "Finish this up right now," Matthews continued, "ask those questions you feel you must ask, then please leave Mrs. Mavery alone."

"All right," she said. "Do you think you would recognize this man if you saw him again?"

"No."

"For the record Mrs. Mavery, you've told the Carlton County authorities that the man said something to Reverend Mary Farnsworth. Do you recall those words?"

"Yes," Edna whispered. "Oh yes. They caused a heart attack."

Brooks looked at me. I gave my head a miniscule shake, indicating we had simply decided not to tell Edna Reverend Mary had been murdered.

Brooks drew a pen from her pocket and made a quick note on a legal pad and passed it to me. However, she did not turn off the tape.

"It might not matter," she'd written. I looked up at her and nodded, hoping my eyes reflected my appreciation. Brooks was here to gather Edna's testimony. That was all. What Edna Mavery saw and heard that day would not change one whit by knowing it was murder, not a heart attack. In fact, her knowing that might complicate matters.

"Mrs. Mavery, would you please repeat those words?"

Edna trembled and closed her eyes. Then she opened them and pressed her handkerchief over her mouth. Then she put it on the tray and covered her mouth with the tips of her fingers. "They was 'I know who you are, and I know what you've done.'"

She began sobbing.

"That is all, Mrs. Mavery. Thank you very much. This concludes the interview," Brooks said hastily before she turned off both recorders. Beads of sweat dotted her forehead.

Silently she gathered up the equipment and stuffed it into her briefcase. We went into the kitchen.

"Thank you. You did a good job."

"Some days I hate my work," she said. "I didn't sign up to give little old ladies a hard time." She glanced at her watch. "It's a long drive back. May I beg a cup of coffee before I go?"

"Of course. And really, it went better than I thought it would. Are you making any progress finding this man?"

"No. This is the most screwed up investigation I've ever been involved with." Professional, crisp, she was clearly troubled, the kind who wouldn't tolerate incompetence. "Too many bumbles."

She raised the palm of her hand to cut me off when I started to defend our procedures. "Please," she said, "don't take this personally. We're not saying there's something your people should have done differently. We're just saying everything has been screwed up from the start."

"I know that."

"The team has pored over all the details. If any one of us had been in your shoes, we'd have assumed this was a natural death from the beginning too."

"And the coroner had no basis for thinking otherwise," I added. "Or he would have had a KBI agent there to observe."

"We understand that. We do. Lottie? It's Lottie, isn't it?"

"Yes. And you are Nancy?" She'd given me her card when she walked in the door.

"Yes." She inclined her head toward the living room. "I need to get back in there and say my goodbyes before I head toward Topeka."

"It's that locked anteroom that threw us."

"It's the stranger that's throwing me. I can't believe someone didn't bring a guest book that day."

She smiled. "If someone had murder on his mind, I can't imagine that he would have stopped to sign a guest book."

Chapter Thirty-Four

Stuart called early the next morning. I was still at the house. Sam was on duty. Keith was out checking on cattle and I had arranged for help at the historical society so I could spend the morning at Edna's.

"Hi, Stuart. I hope your mother is still doing all right."

"That's what I'm calling about. Yesterday wasn't a great day for her, but she did all right, everything considered."

"I thought so too. But they couldn't have picked anyone better than Agent Brooks."

He cleared his throat. "What would you think of me leaving Mom right here in Gateway City for a while?" he asked. "If we can keep the right help coming in, I think she'll be better off. She just loves her little house."

"Stuart, I think that's a wonderful idea. Good for you. The longer she can stay in her own place, the better."

"Whew. I was afraid you'd think I was trying to duck my responsibilities."

"Not at all. What made you change your mind?"

"After everyone left last night, I helped her outside to the porch. And I kept looking at her flowers. I've never known anyone who loves flowers more."

"She can't keep them up, you know."

"I know that. But she loves children. And I'm going to find youngsters who don't mind being bossed around. She can tell them what to do. It won't be the same as kneeling in the dirt, but it's the next best thing."

"But it will be plenty good enough," I said softly. "Plenty good enough."

"Lord, Lottie. I've heard my mother say that a million times."

"Did she talk to you any about other things?"

"No. And it wouldn't have been good for her. We kept it simple last night."

"I'll be over there this morning," I said. "Please tell her I'm coming and tell Mrs. Hargraves she needn't come back until after lunch. And Stuart, this won't last forever. There are more changes coming."

"I can't give up my accounting practice," he said wistfully. "You know that. But I can come back here once a month. At least."

"Do not neglect your business. You'll need all the money you can make if she has to go to Assisted Living. And as to moving her, don't give that another thought." I thought of all she had endured. "She'll understand when the time comes. Your mother is a realist. A survivor."

◇◇◇

Edna smiled when I came through the door.

"Well, look at you," I said. "And we were worried that yesterday would be too much for you."

"That was a real nice lady. I kind of felt sorry for her. She was trying to do a job."

"You were just fine." I bustled around and looked for chores I might help with, but the place was spotless. "I've brought a seed catalog."

Her smile faded.

"I know you can't plant," I said immediately. "But Stuart and I are going to round up some youngsters who will be glad to earn extra money and you can tell them what to do."

She looked pleased. Then she trembled. "It will have to be annuals. Not sure I'm going to live long enough for perennials."

I started to protest, then stopped. What had I said to Stuart? A realist. Timid in some ways. Tough in others.

"You can go through the catalogue, pick out what you like, then tell me if it can be grown from seeds or if I should pick plants up from the All-Season Nursery."

We spent an hour doing that. Then she dozed while I browsed through journal articles and marked the must-reads.

She awoke with a start. "Did you bring the tape recorder, Lottie? We didn't finish the other day. Do you remember where we left off?"

I certainly did. "We didn't tape it, Edna," I said. "It wasn't official. Did you want me to?"

She shook her head. "I just wanted someone to know. I want Stuart to know, but I don't want to tell him myself. Maybe you can tell him a lot later."

At least now I had her permission. By "a lot later," I was sure she meant after her death. But, I suspected I wouldn't have to. The day was quickly approaching when she would tell him herself.

"You were telling me about the children," I prompted. "All the fun times with the children."

"That's when it started," she said. "The beginning of it all brought the end. Oliver called his sister 'my own little chickie' because she would follow him around. We laughed too much. Those two and me. We was like a little club." Her voice faltered. "I was just like them. Just as bad. Full of giggles over nothing. Anything could set us off."

Her face stilled. "Henry couldn't stand it. He wasn't a part of it. Not at all. We shut him out. He was jealous. Couldn't stand to hear us. We started play-acting when he was around. Like we did nothing but work. But he sneaked up on us plenty. He heard us."

Hiding laughter. Forced to hide emotions. Patterns set for life.

"Well he found ways to put a stop to it. Mean little ways. And it just took about a half a year. He smothered a quarter of my new shipment of little chicks and claimed it happened because I was careless. But I saw him. He took the food out of the children's lunch buckets and claimed I sent them to school hungry. He tripped over Oliver's project he'd made for a science project and said it was an accident."

Her little body shook and she closed her eyes. "He pulled all my flowers out by the roots and told me it was cut worms. My hollyhocks. My roses. My Sweet Williams."

She reached for a tissue, blew her nose and looked at me. "We stopped laughing."

I didn't bother to hide my own tears.

"I couldn't stand to see Oliver and Mary Claire broken down every day. I decided to leave him. For the children's sake. Go live with my sister awhile. She and her husband couldn't have kids. She loved my two like they was her own. I told him and I guess he showed me. Three days later some men pulled up with papers and they hauled me off."

Speechless with grief for this wronged woman, I couldn't move. America's checkered history toward mental illness changed in the 1960s after Edna's time, but we still had a long ways to go. We swung from one extreme to the other. During the fifties it still wasn't a problem at all to have a wife committed. Or a gay son. Or a promiscuous daughter.

No, Henry wouldn't have met with one iota of resistance. And her parents probably wouldn't have objected either. Since Henry didn't drink. Didn't beat her. Was a splendid provider. Of course she was crazy.

"Only good thing was that Henry hated the kids, too. So he just gave them to my sister and her husband. I could rest easy knowing that. If you can call being locked up in a cell resting easy. I wasn't crazy when I went in. But those was terrible times. Just terrible."

It isn't right for a professional historian who has heard about everything to lose all composure. My job requires a measure of distance. There is a fine balance between empathy and maintaining objectivity, but in a heartbeat, I lost that balance. I felt with Edna, became one with her. Heard rats scratch along pipes, endured the screams of terrified women.

Tears streamed down my face. Alarmed, Edna reached for my hand. "Now no point in carrying on, Lottie. I tried to look on the bright side and every morning when I woke up I reminded myself that things could be worse. I hadn't gotten that terrible operation they were doing to a lot of people."

"Lobotomies," I whispered. "They were doing lobotomies back then."

"Yes, that's the one. No brains left at all. Anyway, most of the guards was women and we didn't have to worry about those perverts I've read about."

She stopped. "Then spring came," she said finally. "That first spring…no baby chicks, no flowers. The walls were gray, you see. And the floors were concrete and there was no green and I…it was when they always sent my chicks. Me and the kids always went plumb crazy. We had races to the pond. We planted marigolds and zinnias."

I swallowed hard and pressed my fingers against my throat.

"You're plumb undone," she said. "You need to get hold of yourself."

The wall clock chimed. She looked up. "Meals on Wheels will soon be here. Those are real nice ladies. Real nice." She patted the seed catalog. "Thank you for this. Just wanted you to know I'm not crazy. I never was crazy. I want Stuart to know that. It was all Henry's doings."

"No, you were definitely not crazy," I said finally.

Chapter Thirty-Five

That afternoon I began organizing the meeting from hell. The one where I would tell the Episcopal women in Western Kansas who had worked diligently to build and furnish St. Helena, that they had labored in vain. There was no way to pretty up this message.

Sick at heart already from my visit to Edna, I gave up trying to find phrases that wouldn't incite a lynch mob against Talesbury. I was resting my face in my hands when Myrna Bedsloe came through the door.

"Headache, Lottie?"

I hadn't expected her and could not stand the thought of even three seconds of her screaming kids. The total chaos. Besides, she had already redone her story five times.

"Just thought of a whole bunch of things I left out of the last one. You might want to look this over." She handed me the pages. I gave a weak smile and started reading. She lifted the boy on her hip into the air, shoved her face under his t-shirt into his tummy and blew against his skin.

He shrieked and the one clinging to her leg yelled, "Me too, me too."

"This is fine. A great improvement," I said abruptly. *Leave*, I thought. *Just please leave*. To my credit, I didn't say the words out loud.

"Great," she stammered. "I thought it was better than the last one." She looked around at office: the computers, the printers, the books, the unprocessed pages. A shadow crossed her face.

"Well. I'll be going then."

Something clicked. I looked at her open freckled face and saw Edna's instead. I kicked myself for being so blind.

Myrna making piddling little changes to a simple story five times. Myrna needing an excuse to seek out the company of grown-ups. Myrna laughing only with her children. Pretending her life was just fine, when anyone could see she was practically an indentured servant.

"Wait," I said. "I have a few questions for you. Have a seat, Myrna."

Confused, she looked at her child. "Here, I'll take him." I reached for the boy before she could protest and then grabbed the hand of the other one. "We keep toys here for good little boys," I said, leading them away from their mother. I opened the cabinet where I kept a huge supply of Lincoln logs. They squealed with delight.

"Myrna, would you like coffee or tea?"

"Tea, I think."

I would bet she didn't know what she liked. Only what her kids liked.

"My questions have to do about your family. Your stories have really concentrated on Ted's people."

"Yes, my husband's is much more important." Clearly uncomfortable, she looked at her watch, then sipped her tea. I sensed she was dreadfully self-conscious. Like a child being judged on manners.

I looked. Looked for bruises, dark circles under her eyes. The day was warm and she wore a T-shirt. No long sleeves to conceal injuries. I would check hospital admissions, but I would bet Myrna was not a victim of physical abuse. Her abuse would take another form.

After hearing Edna's story, I looked for other things. Myrna looked like she was ready to bolt. When was the last time she had just sat and visited with another woman? Did she know how?

Since I was collecting family stories, urging her to tell me about herself and her own family was a perfect opening. "Did you grow up in Kansas?" I asked.

"Yes. Lived here all my life."

"How does Ted's wheat look?"

"Depends on which field."

I looked around, searching for another topic where she might volunteer some information. Finances. Henry had made Edna account for every penny. That was a common form of control.

I gestured toward one of my files. "Tax time coming up," I said, hoping I looked innocent. "Budget time. We have to account for every cent we spend to the commissioners."

"It's not that hard," she said. "Not that hard."

Clearly, I had hit a nerve.

"Ted bitches about it all the time."

She did not have to stand for this. It's the twenty-first century. She was entitled to her own money.

"When I was out there the other day, I noticed you don't have a computer yet. Do you do everything by hand?"

"Absolutely. All those fancy-pantsie machines are going to be the death of us."

"We have to prepare budgets for the commissioners. At first I didn't like budgets, but now I'm all for it." I looked at her expectantly, hoping she indicate the extent of financial control.

She looked at her watch. "Ted doesn't like it either, so I just gave up. Now I just give him a set amount every month and figure it's none of my damn business how he spends it. For all I care, he can tear it up and feed it to the hogs."

She looked at her watch again. "Don't mean to be rude, Lottie. Ted is with Mom this morning and he's as likely to let her holler as not while he watches NASCAR. Lazy bastard," she added, with an indulgent smile. "Place would fall to pieces if I didn't keep after him."

She controlled the finances! Chagrined at how badly I'm misjudged her situation, I watched her gather up her boys who had fallen to quarrelling several minutes ago.

She turned to me and frowned as she swung the smallest back onto one hip. "As to the wheat, I'm trying several different varieties this year. Need something more rust resistant. It's a crap shoot."

I recalled Margaret's assessment of that household. That Myrna called every shot. Stunned that I had projected one person's situation onto another, I rose and saw her to the door.

"Been nice visiting with you," she said. "Gotta run. Baking day today." She pulled the little boy's hands out of her hair. "I make all our own bread," she said, her face bright with pride. "I have our own wheat ground at a little mill in another county, so I can tell exactly what we're offering from our farm." She walked off.

Josie would love this. I couldn't wait to tell her about my bumbling. From time to time, she was amused at my attempts at amateur psychology, instead of leaving it to the experts. Namely her. Perhaps I needed to check out Ted for signs of abuse.

I stood in the doorway and watched her child-burdened progress toward the stair. Humbled, I speculated that this energetic happy woman was a modern day version of an old European painting, *Song of The Lark*. Myrna was born for the land, the day. For planning and plotting and matching her wits against the weather, the wind, the government, the economy.

I recalled one of Willa Cather's novels, *O Pioneers*. Her character Alexandra Bergson could out-think, outsmart any of the men around her. Why had it not occurred to me that there were modern versions of the same kind of women. Myrna was also the living, walking epitome of one of the most puzzling characteristics of Western Kansans. A goodly number of them simply wanted to work all the time.

And Myrna Bedsloe clearly adored her undisciplined brood of children and her no-count husband.

She paused at the rack of literature in front of the extension office. Chip came out the door, stopped, removed his hat and watched her sort through the bulletins.

She turned to him and smiled. Her beaming sons stopped their howling and gazed at the "real cowboy" with adoration.

"If you're looking for a rust-proof strain, ma'am, you might want to consider this one." He pulled a brochure.

"Thank you, Mr. Ferguson." She glanced at the literature. "I don't want you to think I'm forward, but I hear you know more about farming than anyone in the county."

He beamed, stood straighter. "Just been at it a long time, that's all. Can't say as I have any special knowledge."

"You do. I've seen your crops, Mr. Ferguson. Car rides soothe my mother-in-law, so she and the boys and I drive around a lot of evenings. Besides, it gives me some idea how other folks are faring. I'd like to know what variety of seed corn you planted. Your corn crop stood the heat better than any other in Carlton County. I would treasure your advice."

Who would have thought? The old recluse seemed to blossom, right before my eyes.

◇◇◇

My cell phone rang. It was Agent Brooks. First she inquired about Edna, then she asked me to help her.

"Even though there wasn't a register, we're trying to make a list of everyone there that day."

"All right. In fact, I've had to compile the names of persons who helped with fund-raising so I can tell them there's been some complications with possession of the acreage."

"Great. You've already got a start on what we want. After you do that, please note everyone that you can remember attending that day. Do you use Excel?"

"Yes. I'll create a yes/no column for those who helped raise money and also came to the service."

"Then we would like you to add everyone you can remember attending who is not on your fund-raising list. Then call those persons and ask who they can remember. They might be able to come up with names that you aren't familiar with. And additional names. That's what we're really after."

"That's a great idea.

"Obviously, if you can remember names and faces, they weren't strangers. It's the strangers we want to zero in on."

When I hung up, I set to work with renewed purpose. It helped, knowing the KBI was not viewing our law enforcement entity as a poor relation. And Brooks' assignment gave me something to do that actually made sense. It might be possible to zero in on Edna's perfectly normal average man.

Chapter Thirty-Six

Keith waved at me as I turned up the lane. He was near the machine shed.

It was a perfect evening. I walked over as he shut the huge sliding door to one of the buildings that housed our implements. He pulled off his leather gloves, wiped his brow and gave me a hug.

"I've got some great news," he said. "Janet Dickman called and they managed to round up enough signatures for the recall petition. It's not over yet. This will involve a special election and it could get nasty. But we're over the first hurdle."

I whooped and jumped in the air. "We can handle nasty. The recall is for the best, and everyone knows it. There's no doubt in my mind, Deal's toast."

"Well, your lawyer certainly seems to think so. He has everything set up for a judge to hear all the charges you and Josie filed against him. And that's my other good news. Harold and Josie will be here tomorrow evening. And I expect there's a certain little dog coming too." He laughed at my delight.

The sunset was a gauzy red and the clouds moved like belly dancers undulating streamers of varicolored chiffon. I whirled around. We were very, very close to defanging a man who had a ruinous grip on Northwest Kansas. The whole family would have to become law-abiding. And it didn't involve vigilante justice. His own county was going to vote him out, fair and square. I reached up and kissed Keith and ran on into the house.

◇◇◇

By the time Josie's Mercedes rolled up the lane the next evening I was checking the windows every fifteen minutes. Jubilant that she would be back, I felt like a kid waiting for company. There was an array of appetizers and snacks on the counter. Harold would do his part to make me feel like a gracious hostess, even if Josie seemed to have taken vows of abstinence regarding food.

They both groaned when they climbed from the car. "Now don't carry on," I said to Josie, giving her a hug.

"Did you hear the one about the Lone Ranger and Tonto riding across Kansas," she asked.

"Yes. Whichever one it is, I've heard. I've heard every driving across Kansas joke in the world."

She laughed and rolled her eyes and turned to unstrap Tosca. The little Shih-Tzu yelped and leaped from the car. Then the Mistress of the Universe ran half-way to the row of cedars and authoritatively announced her presence to the zillion bunnies in the windbreak.

Keith shook his head in wonder, knelt down and whistled for her. Tosca sped like a bullet into his arms and covered him with little kisses.

"Remember me?" I said. She politely came over, for a ritual petting, but it was clear who owned her heart.

Harold and Keith walked into the house together, the two men carrying luggage, with Tosca trotting happily after them. Once inside, Josie and Harold went upstairs to their bedrooms and after they were settled in, we all gathered in the great room area off my kitchen.

Harold and Keith loaded Fiestaware plates with their choices among stuffed celery, Mexican layered-dip and chips, and crab on crackers. Harold passed over Keith's home brew with a faint smile and asked for bourbon and water.

"Hate to break up this fascinating discussion about the weather," Harold said, "but we need to talk about strategy and what's going to happen in the courtroom."

"Show time," I said. He frowned. "Actually no. Far from it. We charged Irwin Deal with false arrest, malicious prosecution, defamation of character, and obstructing a police officer."

"Yes," Josie and I both said together. "And we're looking forward to it," Josie added.

"Well, don't," Harold said. "Here's how it's going to be. We are going to drop every single charge but false arrest."

"What? Why would we do that?" Josie moved to the edge of her chair.

"Because I kept my eye on the prize," he said. "The goal has been to expose Deal for the stupid bastard he is. He's been thoroughly humiliated in the press and through the media. If that hadn't already been accomplished through a certain YouTube video, the television interview certainly did him in."

"But Harold! We can't just let this go."

"We are going to do just that, Josie. Let me go over these charges one by one. Defamation of character is very hard to prove, and you haven't suffered one bit of monetary damages as a result of your lock-up. The District Attorney didn't follow up on prosecution so the malicious prosecution charge in no longer valid."

"What about obstructing a police officer," I asked, unable to hide my disappointment.

"That was short-sighted and precipitous on my part," he said. "And I apologize. We were all madder than hell. I hadn't thought it through yet. Now I have. If we would go ahead with that, and the court went against him, and he appealed, it would be a nightmare of litigation for god only knows how long."

"And the false arrest?"

"It stands. Absolutely. I hope he has to pay a hefty fine. That charge is valid, and even if it isn't, I wouldn't want the judge to decide we were being frivolous."

Even wearing old jeans and a worn faded shirt, Harold managed to look authoritative.

"We've achieved our ultimate goal. We've gotten maximum publicity to give citizens of Copeland County reasons for supporting the recall petition."

Harold's kind brown eyes belied his keen ability to size people up. He had droopy jowls, and a meaty nose. He was heavy-set without straying over to out-and-out fat. Standing before us, with his fists shoved in his pockets, like everyone's favorite uncle, I could see why most juries simply believed he was the most trustworthy man in the room.

"There were 12,600 hits on your YouTube video," he'd said. "And that's at last count. It's still attracting viewers."

Josie and I leapt to our feet and high-fived each other. Harold and Keith exchanged looks of mock disapproval.

"At least confine yourselves to fist-bumps in public," Harold said. "Do *not* blow this recall election by creating the impression this campaign is the frivolous doings of a couple of teenagers."

We responded by stooping and thumping our chests.

He watched and shook his head. "I have no idea what comes over you two when you get together. You act like neither one of you have a brain in your head."

We looked at one another, giggled, and started line-stepping across the room chanting "I heard it on the grapevine, Sheriff Deal is gonna be mine."

"Well," he said abruptly, "Keith and I have a big day ahead tomorrow. He's going to take me fishing." The two men rose and headed for the stairs. Tosca followed with a haughty glance back at us. "And in the meantime Keith says you have top-notch equipment for viewing my favorite worthless baseball team."

I grabbed Tosca's ball and threw it at his disappearing back. "Quitter! We want you to tell us what to wear and what to say. We're interested. We really are."

"His momma didn't raise no fools," Keith called back and then laughed.

◇◇◇

The courtroom was packed. I didn't recognize a good many persons, which was to be expected since the hearing was in Copeland County before Judge Clawson. Although a number of persons would undoubtedly sign the recall petition, by the looks Josie and I received when we came in, I suspected that Deal's relations had come in full force.

Despite our horsing around, Harold had instructed Josie and me about proper courtroom demeanor and attire. I thought he was been a bit condescending, but he reminded us it was always a serious matter when one messed with another person's reputation.

Even Tosca had obediently entered her little portable kennel without so much as a reproving glance at Josie for taking off without her.

We all knew what was coming. The lawyers had met in advance. Harold would move to dismiss all charges expect for false arrest and Deal had agreed to plead guilty to that one. Judge Clawson's demeanor was subdued. He had to be acutely aware that the many of the observers in the courtroom would decide his fate at the next election.

No dressing Deal down this time, and I suspected the fine would be modest and his statement very, very simple. But it wasn't. Not huge, but three thousand dollars. Deal's face darkened. Clawson was a clever bastard. High enough to hurt, but not so high that Deal would risk appealing and being liable for paying more attorney fees.

Keith and Josie and I sat on the front row in the observers section. We all rose when Clawson left the courtroom. When he was gone, Deal turned and gave us all a look so black that I automatically checked to make sure he wasn't carrying a weapon.

A woman who had been sitting behind me stepped out and blocked our row. Tall, with a thinning grey masculine hair cut that accentuated her small head, I suspected she was Deal's mother. "You're going to be sorry you ever stepped foot in this part of the state," she hissed.

Keith immediately stepped forward to block her access and shoved me behind him. Neither he nor Harold spoke and other persons came forward and immediately grabbed her elbow and pulled her away. Friends? Relation?

Keeping her from getting into trouble. Whispering to her, protecting her just as Keith was doing for Josie and me. I looked around at all the faces.

We were dividing into camps. All of us. Each and every person here.

As we filed out, I saw Bishop Talesbury sitting in the back row. As usual, he wore his formal cassock. For an instant, for the very first time, I thought I saw a faint smile on his face.

◇◇◇

Technically this was a great victory. A fine victory. But not a one of us was in a celebratory mood. Instead all four of us were oddly quiet on the drive back.

We had made an enemy. One who had lots of relations.

Keith's Suburban is heavy enough to withstand buffeting by Western Kansas winds, despite being a high profile vehicle. But the wind had increased and a little flurry of last year's tumble-weeds whacked the car. Dust devils rose, then sank, in a summer fallowed field.

"Goddamn this wind," Josie said quietly. She pulled out her cigarettes.

I didn't say a word. In fact, I was thinking of taking up smoking myself.

Chapter Thirty-Seven

"I'll be in the office," Keith said, "trying to catch up on bookwork."

I nodded. Harold and Josie had left before we got up. Before we could wish them a proper goodbye.

Last night, still edgy from the collective ill-will we had incited during the hearing, it was as though we couldn't bear the sound of our own voices when we got home.

Josie and I had both curled up with books in separate rooms. Keith watched old Westerns on the TV in our bedroom and Harold retreated to the media room upstairs. Josie checked on him once and said he was surfing from one channel to another. Tosca had made a few pleading attempts to interest us in a siege with her little red ball, but finally gave up and sat beside Josie, giving her little reproving looks.

Sam was on duty at the sheriff's office and William at the historical society. I suspected Keith had gone behind my back and arranged with Sam for us both to be home.

Where he could look out for me.

I went to the doorway of the office and peered inside. He looked up. A lock of brown hair dangled across his forehead. He looked young. Earnest. He rolled his chair back and held out his arms.

"Come here," he said. "Baby got the blues?"

"You'd better believe it." I eased onto his lap.

I was better after a long, long kiss.

I lay against his chest, getting strength from his heavy steady heart.

"Want to talk about it?"

"I've been thinking about terrorists."

He laughed suddenly and tilted my chin so he could look in my eyes. "Terrorists? Haven't we got enough problems around here without dragging terrorists into it?"

"No really, Keith. I think we underestimate little terrors. I've been thinking about Edna and all she's had to endure." I had told Keith everything about her tragic life. And how much I admired her courage.

"Think about it, honey. Her husband made her life hell, but there was no chargeable offense. There was nothing that anyone could report to the police. But he was killing her anyway. Just killing her. Even if she hadn't ended up in an institution."

"I get it," he said with a sigh. "You're saying Deal does the same thing?"

"Exactly. Little terrors."

"First things first, Lottie. We've got to get that man out of office. Then we'll just have to take things one step at a time."

"Just so we don't have to wait until he does something huge."

"Ruining my oats field *was* huge. To me, at least. Bad-mouthing people's businesses is huge to them."

"I guess by 'little terrors,' I mean secretive acts. When a person murders, or sets buildings on fire, the whole community knows about it. Deal has spent his whole life doing stuff without getting caught."

"It's a family tradition."

The phone rang. I stood so Keith could reach it.

"It's for you," he said.

"Bishop Rice here, Miss Albright. I'm afraid I have some bad news."

I said nothing.

"Are you there?"

"Sorry. Yes, sir, I am."

"We already have a decision on Bishop Talesbury's claim on the glebe and the judge ruled in his favor. He owns everything."

"And the building? Everything we've done there?"

"Yes, that's about the size of it. I'm terribly, terribly sorry."

I knew he was, but it didn't help. "I've already compiled a list of women who helped with fund-raising. I'll notify them right away."

"Excellent. Sounds like you are right on top of it. I'm quite sure Bishop Talesbury will never consecrate St. Helena. They need to know that. It will always remain a mere building."

"I'm so disappointed."

"He has the authority to consecrate it himself, if he so desires. I'm feeling rather displaced myself at this point."

"Isn't there a process for stripping bishops of their credentials?"

"Yes. It's quite lengthy, formal, and a very solemn process. This man has done nothing that would call for such drastic discipline. In fact, he leads an exemplary life."

"Just thought I'd ask."

I thanked him and hung up, dreading the task ahead. Before Rice called, I'd wondered about contacting house-movers to see if we couldn't just hoist up the church and move it somewhere else.

When Kansas was first settled houses, business, sheds, all manner of buildings had ricocheted around the prairie like pool balls. When it appeared that one town would fail in its bid to become the county seat, structures were hauled to the next most likely place.

Josie answered on the second ring. I told her about Rice's news.

"What I can't figure out is why Talesbury and Deal want that particular piece of land."

"Is there a possibility that Talesbury wants it for the reason he says he does, to build an orphanage for African children?"

"St. Helena isn't big enough," I said.

"I know that. But it's a start. He could add other buildings. In fact, he could keep the church as a place of worship and continue with other structures."

"I suppose he could, if he could get the funding."

"Think about it. I've about decided it's the only thing that actually makes sense."

"There's only one fly in the ointment. Irwin Deal. I just can't see him doing this if there isn't some payoff. Money."

Keith and I got back to work. He was gearing up to till the ruined oats field and replant it with corn.

I put in a totally uneventful day at the sheriff's office, which gave Sam a break. Margaret had caught up on answering requests for information at the historical society but was clearly relieved that I wasn't going to be "gallivanting around sheriffing."

There were pages of typeset back from the printers. I clipped the stories apart and started laying them out on pages with ruled grids, filling in extra spaces from a pile of newspaper quotes.

Elmira Howarter came in about the time I was due for a break.

"How's Edna?" I rose to get her a chair. "Giving her caretakers a hard time?"

"Land no. She's plumb enjoying it. And they like her. I'm keeping a pretty close eye on things. Mrs. Hardesty is her favorite. They chat like they've known each other all their lives."

"Good. What a relief. Her son will be thrilled to know everything is working out."

"Well, her son is what I've come to talk to you about. She got plumb excited about it. She says she wants Stuart to know some stuff and you'd know what she is talking about. Whatever it is, she wants you to call him. Says you have her permission. Said you'd know what it was," she repeated. Her eyes gleamed with curiosity.

I did know what it was, but I didn't think it was my place to tell him. I looked at Elmira.

I certainly wasn't going to tell her either.

Mrs. Hardesty answered when I called. She told me it was really hard for Edna to hold a telephone and could she just relay a message.

"Please tell Edna that Elmira stopped by and said Edna wants me to call Stuart and tell him some personal things about his family history. I'm calling to double-check."

"Just a minute, Lottie."

"She certainly does," says Mrs. Hardesty. "Says she wants him to know some things before it's too late." I heard her holler at Edna. "Now I hope you heard how ridiculous that 'too late' sounds. Like you've got one foot in the grave."

"All right. Tell her I'll call him tonight."

"Hope she isn't getting morbid on me. I'm going to cheer her up again."

We hung up. The visit from Elmira was all it had taken to ruin a fairly good day. No real prize of a day, but plenty good enough, as Edna would say. Plenty good enough.

Nevertheless, remembering how Edna's story had affected me, I felt like a surgeon charged with giving bad news to a waiting family. Stuart was a kind decent man. This would break his heart.

It was my last call of the day, timed for when he would be home from work. I began by making sure Stuart understood it was at his mother's request. It took a long time and I did my best, but I doubted that it was possible to convey the tone, the nuances, the overwhelming tragedy of Edna's story.

Little terrors inflicted by a man who didn't beat her, didn't drink, and was a good provider. No reason to leave him. None at all.

"My God," he said when I finished. "I had no idea. I don't know if I can wrap my head around this."

"Frankly, you're doing better than I did when I first heard it."

He was quiet for a while. I wished I could see his face. Was he thinking? Weeping?

Finally, he said. "There's quite a hole here, Lottie. How did Mom get to Kansas?"

Our own little terrors started right away. When I got home that evening, Keith leaned with one hand braced against the side of the machine shed. He should have been in the field. He looked exhausted and didn't bother to wave.

I didn't swing onto the slab into front of the garage, but drove directly over to him.

"What's wrong?"

For a minute he didn't answer, then, "Fucking Deal poured sugar in my tractor's gas tank."

Modern farm equipment is huge and enormously expensive. Keith keeps his in immaculate shape. He didn't look me in the eye as though he was afraid my sympathy would trigger an explosion.

"How do you know it's sugar?"

"There's some spilled here on the ground." He pointed to white crystals at my feet. "I tasted it. Hell of it is, I'd already started the engine before I noticed it. Let everything warm up." He started cussing in earnest and I had sense enough not to ask questions. There certainly was no point in asking "who?" We both already knew.

"Is it ruined, Keith?"

"Yes and no. If I don't have the right mechanic, it will be. But when the engine started making funny noises, I turned everything off. We can pull the engine and get everything cleaned up. If I can get the right men to help. It's the time of year when everyone is tuning up equipment and all the shops are full. So I'm guessing it will be about a week before it's fixed."

"Oh no!"

"And say I get it fixed," he continued. "Let's just say everything goes right for once. Which isn't likely. The point is that unless I want to sit out here with a shotgun for the rest of my life, this kind of thing can keep happening over and over."

"Little terrors," I whispered. "Little terrors."

"Nothing little about this. I've got to figure out some way to stop the bastard or our life isn't going to be worth a plug nickel."

"I know."

"I'm going to call a machine shop and see what my chances are of getting in. Then I'm going to call Harold and we're going to have a serious chat about security systems. And I don't want the kind that posts labels every three feet so intruders can do a little research and figure out how to sabotage it. We're going to spend whatever it takes to catch this bastard in the act."

My husband is a really smart man. He's a veterinarian, reads journal articles in his field, a shrewd farmer, and had been a captain in the army. But I stared at the ground and gave a feeble wave before I got the hell out of there.

I went to the car and drove back to the garage. It wouldn't take more than a minute or two for it to dawn on him that security systems relayed problems to the local law enforcement.

Us.

Chapter Thirty-Eight

I escaped back to the historical society early the next morning and set to work laying out pages. That done, I pulled out my laptop and clicked on my Excel program, then double-clicked on the spreadsheet containing the names of the women who had helped build St. Helena.

Nothing. Absolutely nothing came up. Incredulous, I stared and tried again. I use an off-site back-up system that starts about ten pm. I accessed it, planning to restore the file. But "Fundraisers" wasn't listed among the saved documents.

I couldn't imagine that I'd used any wrong procedures. Panicked, I went to the main historical society desktop and scrolled through all the information. We keep all the technology simple and easily accessible. Nothing appeared to be missing there.

The list of women wasn't very long. In fact, I realized there might be fragments still on scraps of paper I'd tossed into the trash. There was. It wouldn't take more than a couple of hours to duplicate my work. But two hours was two hours. Worse, after finding the scraps, I was beginning to doubt that I had saved it to the hard drive to begin with.

Little terrors. I began again, mindful of every keystroke. My edginess was caused by more than the sabotage at our farm. After coming dangerously close to making assumptions about Myrna Bedloe's life based on Edna's, I was losing faith in my instincts.

I wanted my moxie back. From time to time, a residual fear wells up in my mind; apprehension that I will slip into the state

I was in last fall. A fear that the stability I had previously always taken for granted was fake. Easily demolished like a house built on sand.

When the phone rang, I jumped out of my skin.

"Lottie, can you come? Hurry." Elmira's voice blurted like she'd run a hundred yard dash.

"It's Edna. She fell."

Damn, damn and double damn. "I'll call the EMTs right away and be there myself in a flash. And Elmira, don't try to move her. OK?"

The ambulance beat me to the house. Elmira and Mrs. Hargraves stood crying on the doorstep. They both talked at once.

"I don't know how it happened," Mrs. Hargraves said. "I don't. We've been so very careful. She was holding onto her walker and shuffling along the floor. She didn't trip or anything. Just kaboom."

"It's not your fault," I said. "There's nothing you could have done. In fact, I've heard doctors say that instead of women falling and breaking a hip, the reverse is often true. They break a hip and then they fall."

They calmed.

"Old bones," I said. "Porous. Just can't support weight anymore."

They looked relieved. I took their phone numbers and told them I would call from the hospital.

She had indeed broken a hip and needed surgery. The last time Stuart was at Edna's, she'd given him power to authorize medical decisions.

When I called him, he said "Just a minute, Lottie." I heard him order his secretary to cancel all appointments for the next three days." Then he came back on the phone. "I'll fax Dr. Martin any forms he needs, then I'm on my way."

"All right. You can reach me on my cell. I'll be here with her."

He made the trip from Wichita in record time. Stuart plopped down beside me in the surgical waiting room and glanced at his watch.

"They took her in about two hours ago," I said.

"I authorized them to go ahead with a joint replacement. Despite her age. Mom and I talked about this kind of stuff when I was here the last time. She doesn't want a bunch of machines hooked up to her, but she's not ready to leave this life either."

We both jumped to our feet when the surgeon came into the room.

"She's fine," Dr. Martin said. "It went well, everything considered. Her kidneys aren't in great shape, but she's in decent health otherwise. Not spectacular, but considering her age, she's reasonably healthy. In fact, she'll see significant pain reduction."

"Terrific," I said. "She just loves her little house here." I looked fondly at Stuart. "Her son here has done everything in his power to make it work."

Dr. Martin gave Stuart a lop-sided smile. More like a sympathetic twitch. "Sorry, Mr. Mavery. Everything considered, you're not going to be able to pull that off anymore."

"I'm not surprised," Stuart said. "We both knew this time was coming, we just didn't think it would get here so fast. I've been checking out assisted living facilities in Wichita."

"Edna is very tough," I said. "She'll find new friends. I know she'll love being closer to you."

"I really am sorry. These transitions are hard for everyone, but it's good to know you're on top of it." Dr. Martin clapped Stuart on the shoulder. "Let me know if you have questions. The clinic can always reach me if something comes up."

We thanked him and he left. Stuart said he was going to stay until Edna was out of recovery, then take his luggage to his mother's house and get a bite to eat before he returned.

"I may sleep in the chair in her room tonight, depending on how she's doing."

◇◇◇

I visited Edna two mornings later. Stuart was holding her hand when I stepped into the room. She beamed when I set a lovely spring bouquet on her bed table. She reached out with her arthritic twisted hand and stroked the petals on a daffodil. It was lovely! Bright red tulips and hyacinths combined with baby's breath filled the room with color.

"You look great," I said. "Stuart tells me you're making a wonderful recovery."

"Well, my boy here doesn't let me want for a thing. Waits on me hand and foot," she said tenderly. "Did he tell you, Lottie? I'm going to be moving to a home close to him and Tina. They'll keep me here for about a month for therapy and rehabilitation, and then we'll put my little house up for sale."

"You'll do just fine," I said. I looked at Stuart and smiled. He rose and reached over and kissed his mother's forehead.

"I'm going back this morning, Lottie. She's in good hands here, and I've got a lot of loose ends to take care of. Not to mention getting the house ready for sale." He glanced at Edna. "Got a minute?"

I followed him out into the hallway. He shoved his hands in his pockets and paced a few steps, then turned to face me. "This beats anything I've ever seen. I love my mother and we've always been close. I've done my best to be a good son to her. You would think she would trust me."

"What brought this on, Stuart? What's changed?"

"Nothing against you, Lottie, but I've been here for three days now and she hasn't brought up her past at all. She's told a rank stranger secrets she's kept all her life."

Tears stung his eyes. He pulled out a handkerchief and blew his nose. "She should have told me. I'm her son. I have a half-brother and sister out there somewhere. Kin. Why won't she talk about it?"

"Stuart, this has nothing to do with you. She adores you. She's ashamed. It's the stranger-on-the-bus syndrome. People will bare their secrets on a long ride to someone they've never seen before and never will again."

He said nothing and stared at the floor.

"She asked me to tell you," I reminded him. "She *did* want you to know, she just couldn't bear to look you in the eye."

Wounded, shoulders slumped, he stared at some spot on the wall. Just like his mother would have done.

"It's her way, Stuart. The way she handles things. She evades. Runs away. Tells outright lies, if she must." *Just little white ones*, I thought.

"Before you move her from Gateway City for good, I want you to listen to some tapes. The part that's hurting you the most right now isn't recorded, but I think there's a story about some wee mice that might give you a peek at how your mother's mind works."

"I don't care about some goddamn mice. I want to know where my brother and sister are. And I want to know how in the hell she got to Kansas."

He suddenly gave me a quick glance, as though worried about having offended me. His freckles were stark against his pasty skin. A man who worked too hard, worried. Needed more sunlight. "Sorry, Lottie. None of this is your fault."

Chapter Thirty-Nine

Agent Brooks called that afternoon and asked if I had time to help contact all the people on my list. I agreed to start the next day.

"I hope we can zero in on persons for further questioning, instead of this guesswork leading to nowhere," she said.

"I've scheduled a meeting for next Saturday to break the news about the glebe to the fund raisers." I had kept Brooks posted about anything involving church business, just in case there was a connection to the murder that wasn't readily apparent to Sam and me. "I can ask questions afterwards on an informal basis. Provided I'm not tarred and feathered and run out of town on a rail."

We met at the high school gym in Bidwell County on a Saturday when no activities were scheduled. I certainly couldn't have risked using some Copeland County facility, and under the circumstances my own Carlton County wasn't a good idea either.

Ingalls was the fourth county involved in the St. Helena fiasco. It did not have a public building or even a school. Ingalls had been involved in a bitter modern day county seat fight. It won, but refused to acknowledge that the county was drawing its last breath.

Gove County, another small county in Northwest Kansas had suffered through similar experiences, but went on to develop a keen sense of community. They all pulled together.

However, when the good citizens of Ingalls won the county seat fight and could no longer wage war on outsiders, confused, they'd looked around and happily turned on each other. Ingalls had a sheriff because it was state law, but rumor had it that it was sort of a sheriff-of-the-month system maintained through drawing names from a hat.

About fifty women filed into the gym and found seats on the bleachers. Most were married and their husbands had contributed labor for the church. They intuitively looked around for women from their own county, and clustered as though they were back in high school. When they went home I knew they would tell their spouses how badly we had screwed up. So I wanted to keep the information clear, simple, and final.

I had requested a podium and a gavel. I wanted to sound authoritative, and help them accept the finality of losing this land, this church. There was no recourse.

Having decided to launch right into my talk with no attempts at lame jokes, I whacked the gavel, then announced that I had bad news regarding St. Helena. Bad news in addition to the untimely death of the Reverend Mary Farnsworth. I traced the general history of glebes, and their rarity west of the Mississippi River. I gazed at the unhappy gathering of women.

"As you know the abstract and deed work for the forty acres on which we built St. Helena was a tangled mess from the beginning. I thought it arose from papers lost in fires and the realignment of county boundaries in the 1880s and incompetent survey work. But that was not the case."

The gym had a faint odor of varnish. Basketball goals were on either side, and a scoreboard gave witness to the home team's last humiliating game. It was just the right height for hanging me.

I soldiered on.

"The long and the short of it is that Bishop Talesbury owns this land." I paused. Now for the zinger. "He also owns the church because we built it on his land without his permission. I'm sure we can remove the furnishings, but as you all know, we were just getting started. There weren't very many."

"That's not fair," a woman called out. "Just not fair. My husband will be fit to be tied." God knew none of this was my fault, but I could have bawled. Her husband had built the pews. Real pews with kneelers.

I recalled Edna's words, her pride, "I wanted to kneel." A few others nodded in sympathy, but most just sat there in silent bewilderment. All they had wanted was to build a church. Have a place of worship. A place of their own denomination.

"The pews aren't permanently attached to the structure," I said. "We can remove them."

"To where?"

I couldn't think fast enough. *Our barn? Some other barn?*

"Why?"

"I beg your pardon," I said.

"Why would he want that particular piece of land? It's not worth the powder it would take to blow it up."

"Because it's his," I said. "I doubt he can afford to buy another parcel of land." I told them about his background and that he had come to the United States after horrendous experiences in Africa. I kept my face and my voice neutral when explaining his Deal lineage and how he happened to inherit the acreage. This was not an appropriate venue for politics. We had to keep the recall election separate.

I did not like the bishop, but I believed his intentions were clear. I was convinced he honestly wanted to provide shelter for children who had been through hell. The ladies brightened when I told them what Talesbury intended to do with the place.

"Again, it's important for all of you to understand our legal situation. There is simply no recourse. We're hosed." I called for questions.

"Why?" asked the same women who had tried to pin me before. "Why is this such a catastrophe?"

Did I have to draw a picture? I groped for words.

"We have a priest," she persisted. "We have a church. And we even have a mission project, right off the bat."

Heads turned toward her. "Why wouldn't this fellow want a nice little congregation? No need to run us off." She turned looked up at the woman behind her. "Mabel, isn't this man some of your kin? On your father's side? Why don't you talk to him? It's not like anyone really owns a church anyway."

A solution! Out of the clear blue sky. Thrilled, I took a deep breath. This could work. Chiding myself for underestimating Western Kansan's resiliency and their ability to survive, I flashed a smile. Foolishly I thought it was that simple. The solution would be that simple. He could keep the damn land. He could keep the damn church. We would simply show up every Sunday.

A woman shot to her feet. "How can any of you even think of having anything to do with that evil man or want to support anything he touches? Have you forgotten his sermon?" Then she glared at Mabel Sidwell. "Don't even think of it. I'm never going to set foot in that church again."

Mabel Sidwell rose to her feet. "Now just a minute here, Lucy." A large woman, she wore a fashionable jade green pant-suit with a peacock brooch. Her voice carried well. Her size, the flash of color, her precise diction added weight to her message. "I think you all know my nephew and a wonderful priest who graciously consented to honor our little congregation have been the victims of a vicious campaign."

"Mabel, let's leave politics out of this. I don't have a dog in this fight, but I say Lucy has a point. Who would want to go to church there?"

Several women spoke out at once. Then everything went South.

I pounded the gavel. "I came here today to give you a message. I have done just that. Here it is again. Bishop Talesbury owns all the land on which we built St. Helena. This was decided by the court. He owns the building. All assets not permanently attached will be returned to the donors."

That said, I left the quarrelling assembly and got the hell out of Dodge.

Chapter Forty

I considered taking time off and visiting Josie in Manhattan. That's always great for my nerves, but it wouldn't be fair to Keith. Having three of us on duty was barely enough.

A nurse called from the hospital and said Edna wanted to see me. When I hung up the phone, I called Margaret and asked her to organize a board meeting. The historical society needed to officially cut down hours or find more volunteers. I could no longer keep asking her and William to "fill in" when the hours spent in law enforcement kept creeping up. Reluctantly, I faced the fact that our society was not always open during all hours posted.

Hopeful that this might be the opportunity to get some answers to Stuart's questions, I simply put a sign on the door saying I would be back in a couple of hours, and closed the office.

If Edna wanted to continue telling me about her past, I didn't want to miss the chance. If the time was right, I would probe for an answer to Stuart's question: how did she get to Kansas?

She was always pale, so that was no surprise, but her face had a faint yellowish tinge and she looked tired. I'd stopped by the greenhouse on the way and picked up a fresh bouquet.

"How are you doing?" She turned to look at the flowers and smiled.

"Fine. Why wouldn't I be? They wait on me hand and foot." She didn't speak again for several minutes but just lay there smiling at the purple lisianthus as though the blossoms would smile back.

"Lottie, Stuart...I. I called because my boy is hurt. I can see it in his eyes."

"Yes, he is. He doesn't understand why you haven't told him about all this before." I didn't add that she wasn't exactly telling him now either. "What happened to you, Edna? What happened to you at that mental institution?"

"My heart got broke. And I couldn't put it back together. My little boy. My little girl. My sister wrote letters. She was doing the best she could. They was all just fine. Gerta said the children cried a lot at first, but they settled down. They was always good kids. Sweet. Minded their manners. Did just fine at school. They tucked in little notes and drawings to send along."

She closed her eyes and I thought she had dozed off. "Water," she said. "I need some water."

I picked up the decanter on her bedside table and maneuvered the flexible straw between her lips, then wiped her mouth.

"I was numb. Just numb most of the time. Then things changed. One day one of the nurses came up to my door and said I was going to get to go home. They had heard from my husband. Just like that. He had decided to put me in and he had decided to get me out. I was thrilled plumb to death. I was going home. I could see my children. Go back to my old life."

Edna's closed her eyes again and gave a little shake of her head. "My old life. Then I started thinking about what that meant for me and the kids."

She stroked a purple petal with her finger and looked at it like she'd never seen a flower before. "I changed while I was inside. Before, I'd had been sure things would work out for the best. Now, I knew that wasn't true. I got to thinking about my old life. Got to worrying."

A nurse came into the room with some pills and stood by Edna's side to make sure she swallowed them. I winced, worrying that Edna would lose her train of thought. But the moment the woman walked out of the room, Edna continued right where she had left off.

"Then I got a letter. From Henry. With twelve dollars. He wanted me to take the bus to Cedarville in two weeks. That was the closest town to Gerta. He said he would meet me there at the bus stop and we would drive to Gerta's house together and pick up the kids and go on home. It would save him fifty miles driving."

Edna wore a soft yellow bed jacket. The satin ties were loose and she groped for the ends with her twisted fingers, then she gave up, sighed and lay back.

"That's when I knew," she said. "Knew he hadn't changed. Knew things wasn't going to be better. He had already ruined me and I knew he was going to ruin the children." She turned her head from me and looked at the wall.

"Because what kind of a man doesn't even come after his own wife after three years? Just sends her bus money? Just to save fifty miles driving? I knew!" Her voice quavered. "A man like Henry. I knew the kind of man I was going back to. He had never once even come to visit."

She appeared to doze off. Overcome with pity, I sat quietly musing on this tragic story of ruined lives. Then she rallied and opened her eyes and began to speak again.

"I thought and thought and hatched a plan. Everyone knew I was getting out, just like most of folks there couldn't understand why I was in. After the first year, I even got to set outside for long stretches of time. The sunshine did me a world of good." She looked down at her wasted body. "I wasn't all skin and bones back then."

"All the papers had been signed. Henry had them mailed back and forth. I didn't need to stay there anymore. The place had a little van that took folks to the bus station. There was people coming and going all the time. I had some money now."

I swallowed and blinked back tears.

"About three days before I was supposed to meet Henry, I left. Just left! I took the van to the bus station and bought a ticket to

Kansas City. In about ten days, I called Gerta to let her know where I was. She said when I didn't show up, Henry drove out to the house and was fit to be tied."

I rose and stroked her hair and dabbed at her tears.

"Gerta said he cursed me and my worthless offspring, like they was none of his doings. He threatened to sue the institution, but the folks there reminded him that he was the one who pushed through all the paperwork, coming and going. He was the one who'd had the bright idea of sending his wife bus money."

She chuckled softly. "I knew he wouldn't pay a lawyer just to get me back." Then her eyes filled with tears. "Just like I knew he wouldn't fight to get the kids back either."

She began to sob then. Alarmed, I watched her blood pressure rise on the monitor. "I gave up my kids," she said. "Gave away my own children. I knew my sister and her husband would love them like they was their own. Knew they would be better off. Told Gerta to tell them I was dead. Tell Henry I died, if he ever asked."

A nurse rushed into the room.

"Stuart wants to know how I came to Kansas? I just did it, that's how." She shook uncontrollably. "I gave up my kids."

Shaken by Edna's story, I fled to the historical society where I hoped to work alone for the rest of the afternoon. Find some modicum of peace in my dusty old books.

Edna had not given up her children, I decided on the drive over. She had chosen to give them life for the second time.

Inside my office, the answering machine blinked and I knew I had made the wrong choice. I would have found more peace at the sheriff's office. I grabbed a note pad, pressed the message button, and began listening. After the first three, I could not bear to hear more and clicked off the tape. Angry, furious women, berating me for tricking them into donating to a doomed cause.

I buried my face in my hands, then rose and walked out into the hall into the restroom and used cold water to wet papers towels and pressed them against my face. In the mirror, I looked gaunt, drawn. My complexion was sallow, like I was the one who had been locked up for three years.

No wonder Edna wanted Stuart to hear all this second hand instead of having to look her son in the eye. I promised the wild-eyed stricken stranger in the mirror, that I would make Stuart understand his mother had been faced with an excruciating choice: give up her children or risk them with a cruel man. She had taken the high road.

Then ashamed of my own petty unwillingness to endure a little discomfort, I went back to the office and turned on the answering machine again, determined to return each and every call.

I scratched a little grid as I listened and labeled categories. The calls fell into a pattern. Some understood my helplessness. Some hoped I would help them skin Deal alive. Some offered bizarre solutions. And some hoped I would go to hell for wreaking havoc on the community.

Toward the end, I was jolted by a man's voice. "Miss Albright. I'm…" Then the voice broke off as though having descended into answering machine hell. I knew the feeling well, of bumbling a message and having no way to call it back. "Never mind."

I knew the voice.

Bishop Talesbury.

Chapter Forty-One

Normally, it's easy for me to concentrate on editorial work. But the next day, I was unhappily conscious of the growing pile of unprocessed stories, tackled them, and knew I had reread one paragraph over and over. Talesbury's face intruded.

Then Agent Brooks called to let me know the team had finished calling every person on my Excel file. Fifteen had come up with additional names. However, it was basically a dead end. I told her that rather than the community meeting giving me a chance to ask questions, it had ended in a royal fiasco.

"We're faced with a real problem here, Lottie. We can only hold a body for so long. If no family or friends come forward to claim the deceased, we're required to notify the University of Kansas Medical School and then the head of the anatomy department can receive the body for medical research."

"Please. Please don't let them do that. We owe her more than that. What if someone comes for her and they've already started dissecting her?"

"By law, a coroner, our office, everyone must make a diligent search for 'family or friends' and we've done that. It's like she came out of nowhere."

"I'm her friend,' I said. "I was this woman's friend. If we can't find her family, I'll claim her."

Brooks cleared her throat. "And what will you do with a dead body?"

"Give her a decent burial. Keith and I will pay for it."

She said nothing.

"She was a wonderful person."

"Yes, I know," she said softly. "So you've told me."

"We'll have the funeral at St. Helena. I'll simply announce it and those who are decent Christians and knew her can just come. Put their savage ways aside for a couple of hours and come to that church."

"Which is owned by a very strange man."

"Yes, but he's a priest. Reverend Mary is entitled to a dignified burial and Talesbury is duty bound to perform certain rituals. I can't believe he would just turn his back on us."

"I can," Brooks said. "Because he doesn't view that building as a church. It's his, Lottie. And I suspect he didn't regard Mary as a legitimate priest because of her gender."

"Bishop Rice would certainly conduct a ceremony at Salina." I twisted the phone cord around my fingers and tried to imagine the consequences of family showing up later. Someone out of the blue. A grieving mother or other relatives, wanting to know why their daughter was six feet under in a strange cemetery.

"OK, Lottie," Brooks said. "There's a way around this. Here's what I think you should do. The medical center has to hold a body for sixty days without dissecting it. Let it go there. They will have facilities for storing it."

Sickened by hearing Mary referred to as "it," by talking as though she were slab of meat, I tried to process her words.

"Then when that period is nearly up, you can step in as her friend, claim the body, and give her a church burial. It will buy us a lot of time."

When I drove up to the house, and parked, I saw Sam's Suburban bouncing across our pasture. Keith was in the passenger's seat. They came through the gate leading to the farmyard. The dead animal disposal truck with a winch and pulley system attached to the truck bed came up the lane. Sam parked, hopped out, opened the gate wide, and beckoned at the driver to follow him.

When both vehicles drove off into the pasture again, I knew one of our prize Herefords had died. I went into the house. I had pulled steaks from the freezer early that morning and placed them in the refrigerator to partially thaw. I began mixing salads and turned on the TV to catch the 5:00pm news. We were under a storm watch, which made it an ordinary day.

Keith came in silent and angry. He gave me an absent kiss, but his mind was somewhere else.

"I saw the truck," I said. "Bad luck?"

"It wasn't luck, Lottie."

He walked out to the mud room and began scrubbing his hands. I watched him from the doorway.

"That cow was cut."

"Cut?"

"I found her over by the fence on the south side. The fence had been cut and there was barbed wire around one leg. She bled out. It was a piss-poor set-up to make it look like an accident, but anyone that knows anything could tell it was deliberate. Whoever did this knew I'd know that at once. It doesn't take a vet to see that gash couldn't have been caused by barbed wire."

And anyone who knew my husband would know that attacking him through animals was a sure fire way to stoke the fire.

"I don't know what to say. It's got to be Deal. It's the kind of thing that family has done for the last hundred years."

"It's going to stop," he said. "Right now. That's why I called Sam and had him come over. We've been going over laws and procedures and it's important that I go through all the steps a man would take if I wasn't a law enforcement officer. I need to file all the paperwork and document everything."

I nodded. "Sam needs to be the one to do the reports and take pictures."

He nodded wearily. "He went back to town to write everything up. Another long day for the poor old son-of-a-bitch." I glanced at him and went to the refrigerator and handed him a bottle of home brew.

"I'm going to call Sam," I said, "and ask him to come right back over here for supper. We have plenty. I'll hold the steaks until you two get your work done." I looked around at my spotless kitchen. Zola was a wonder. She went far beyond weekly upkeep and was already making a dent in deep cleaning and repairs.

I walked outside to fire up the grill. Keith went into the great room and picked up his guitar. Soon the mournful tones of "The L & N Don't Stop Here Any More" drifted out to the patio.

Sam drove up again a half hour later. The two men drove off to the pasture again in Keith's pick-up. Grim-faced, they washed up in the mud room after they came back.

After we'd eaten and carried the dishes inside, Sam reached for his pipe and Keith lit the fire pit.

"We've got to catch the bastard in the act," he said finally. "This can't go on forever and I think it's about to come to an end. A lot of folks have told me that he's madder than hell about this recall election, and that he's going to lose out. Don't know how he'll manage to make an honest living."

"So why would that mean anything is coming to an end?" Keith asked. "He's a sneaky bastard. That won't change."

"Sneaky bastards are planners. I think this is going to set him off. He's going to lose control of himself. It will come to a head."

"Something else is coming to an end," I said. "Up until now, anything he's done has focused on equipment, inanimate objects. He's moving up to animals. That means something. I don't know what, but I'm going to check with Josie."

◇◇◇

Josie came back for the big election event. The evening was hot, disturbing, and we sweltered as we stood in the Copeland Courthouse while the ballots were counted. The room was packed and voters spilled out of the courthouse onto the grass. It was better than a Fourth of July picnic.

There were no stars and inky black clouds blotted out the fading moon. Josie cradled Tosca in her arms. It had been a mistake to bring her and the little Shih-Tzu nervously growled when strangers reached to pet her.

Deal and his relation formed their own little cluster of on-lookers. If looks could kill.

Mabel Sidwell stared at Tosca, then turned to whisper to Deal. He glared at our little dog like she was vermin.

In my purse was my Smith and Wesson .640 Airweight Special.

When the tally was complete, the clerk rose and announced that there were 406 ballots cast in favor of recalling Sheriff Deal and 274 votes against it. Cheers and clapping filled the air.

Deal's face went white. I looked at the stunned faces of his gathered relation. Their dominance was coming to an end.

No longer would this families' crimes be treated differently than other members of the community. Tyranny toppled in a single night.

On the ride back to Carlton County, Keith told Josie about his Hereford.

"He's changing," she said. "Accelerating."

"Well, we're changing too," I said. "And so is Copeland County. I don't know who they are going to elect next, but you can bet it won't be any of his kin. Now, everyone is going to get a chance at due process."

Chapter Forty-Two

Keith was on duty and had left for the office before I got up the next morning. Josie sat on the patio drinking coffee. She smiled when I came outside bearing the pot and refilled her cup.

"Don't tell me this place is growing on you."

"You know, it actually is," she said. "It's the space. The incredible space. I understand more about the connection between landscape and the psyche every time I come here. No wonder people from the plains see endless possibilities. Endless is all they've ever known."

"And the wind? The endless wind?"

"That's another story altogether."

"We're bent, you know, out here." She looked at me and smiled at my words. "No really. Kansas was named for the Kansa Indian, the People of the South Wind. It's always present. Look at our trees. They lean slightly to the Northeast."

"And that has what to do with the people?"

"I don't know. Something, though. I haven't figured out what yet. There was a great book published awhile back, *Leaning into the Wind*. Having to cope with the wind all of the time changes women. Sometimes I think women who come here even now..."

Her face turned toward me. I recognized her bright-eyed psychologist's curiosity. A trace of sadness passed over her face.

"We could team up," I suggested cheerfully, abruptly rising to my feet. "Team up for a knock 'em dead journal article, but for right now, I'd better get a move on. Pages due for the printer and a stack of bills to pay."

She closed her eyes and turned her face up at the sun. Tosca sat alertly at the edge of the flagstones, protecting our property. She suddenly dashed wildly toward some invisible critter and then trotted back, head held high, preening over her success.

On the drive in I thought about Northwest Kansas' wind issues. They were the newest in a string of controversies about energy and resources since the state was first admitted to the Union. The wind was coming up again now, and Josie would soon abandon the patio. Tosca would see to it.

During lunch hour, I swung by the green house to buy a plant, then drove to the hospital to visit Edna.

I laughed when I stepped into the room and saw the volume of plants and flowers. "Whoops! Look's like you don't need any more foliage. It's like stepping into a jungle."

Her color was better. She beamed when I walked over to her table. "Folks is so good to me. Just lovely."

"Any why not? I hear you're a perfect patient. Have you been sleeping well? Getting rest?" Her big move was coming up and I worried about the physical strain.

"Yes." She glanced at me. "I'm just fine. Fine here, and I'll be fine there."

I smiled and nodded. Then I gave her hand a squeeze. "I know that. You would be fine anywhere."

"You know a lot about me. More than anyone else in the world. And I've been thinking about what you said about Stuart being hurt." A spasm of coughing racked her frail body. I reached for some tissues and patted her mouth. "I'm going to talk to him myself next time, Lottie."

"Good," I said. "That's the right thing to do. You know, the part that bothers him the most is having a brother and sister out there. Siblings he's never met."

"They are both dead," she said. "Oliver and Claire both." Tears rimmed her eyes. "But he needs to know. Don't want him to spend the rest of his life hunting for them."

"I'm so sorry," I said. "Did you follow them through the years?"

"Yes. Gerta was real good about writing. When I got to Kansas City, I had just enough money left to get a room in a boarding house. I cleaned rooms but couldn't get ahead much. Then I saw an ad in a newspaper for a housekeeper in Western Kansas. So off I went. I worked for Stuart's father. We fell in love and got married and everything was just wonderful."

She had scooted downward in her bed and I lifted her under the shoulders and pulled her back up.

"Wonderful except that I had given up my own children. As far as they was concerned I was dead. When Gerta told me Henry died, I couldn't just show up. There was some money." Her voice softened. "Money for college and money for decent clothes. Stuart's dad didn't know a thing about them. I didn't want my kids to think I just showed up for the money."

Stunned, I realized this woman was a bigamist. Married to two men at the same time. No, I corrected myself. Had been a bigamist. No longer, because both men were dead.

"Gerta sent me clippings and I kept track of everything. Oliver died in Vietnam. And Claire, she came to a bad end. Took a wrong path. Died way too young. She should have been old like me."

Edna looked up at me. "I'm over Oliver because he died serving his country, but knowing Claire died before her time for no good reason…it's hard."

"Edna," I smoothed her hair and awkwardly reached across the protective rail to hug her. "Stuart will understand all this. You've raised a fine son. He's a wonderful man. He loves you."

She had talked enough and drifted to sleep. I tip-toed out of the room.

A bigamist.

◇◇◇

Agent Brooks called shortly after I got back to the office.

"I'm about an hour away from Carlton County," she said, "on my way to Bidwell County. Would you have time to go with me to Mary Farnsworth's house?"

"Yes, but I thought your team was all through processing the place."

"We are. Even though it's not a crime scene, we inspected everything. But now it's time to box up all her belongings and turn them over to the agency that handles unclaimed property."

"I'll make time."

"Good. We prefer to have someone local there as a witness."

"To keep you from stealing?"

"Something like that."

Margaret was already in the courthouse, but when I called her cell hoping she could fill in, there was no mistaking the tone of stiff reproach. The board had met and voted to cut down our hours. None of them, other than William Webster—who was already a volunteer—offered to help staff the office. Margaret was furious. "I really must get on home, Lottie. Please try William."

I sighed, understanding that she had been burdened by my frequent expectations that she would just drop everything. But prevailing on William was akin to walking over hot coals. An elderly man who counted every penny, William had served on the historical society board ever since I'd moved here. Sometimes he was my champion, sometimes my adversary, but he always played the Grand Lord Inquisitor.

He came promptly, and blessedly, did not ask where I was going and what I was doing, but simply settled into his usual chair and pulled out his ever present whittling knife and a block of wood.

I drove to the sheriff's office to meet Agent Brooks. Sam looked up from the legal pad in front of him. I told him where I would be.

"Ask her if she still wants us to keep Mary's car here. It's OK with me and it's not bothering anyone but I don't think this has come up before."

"She said unclaimed property goes to a particular agency, so I imagine someone will get the details and it will go up for auction like everything else."

"Ok. I'll look all that up while you're gone." He pushed his swivel chair back from the desk. "That's all I get done lately," he said, his voice thick with fatigue. "I look things up." Even his mustache seemed tired. But his shoulders never drooped, and I suspected that was due to pride, not natural perfect posture.

I headed for the door when Nancy arrived and waved goodbye at Sam. "Maybe we'll find something, see something," I called back over my shoulder. "Get this whole miserable case off our consciences."

"Maybe," he said. "But it still won't help me figure out what to do with a mean ex-sheriff that commits little crimes just for the hell of it. An accumulation of misdemeanors."

I turned. "Keith's cow was hardly a little thing."

"Maybe not, but think about it. It's not like Deal shot the critter. It's going to be hard to prove the gash wasn't accidental."

Brooks rolled down her window and hollered to me. "You good to go?"

"Yes." I shut the door to the office and hurried over to the passenger side of her Suburban.

"Is this a step up or what?" I asked, admiring the leather seats.

"Definitely up," she smiled. "We figured this Suburban would hold everything so I got to take it instead of a Crown Vic. From the description I received, it didn't sound like she was big on possessions."

"The only thing I can vouch for is her clothes. When she was in her office at the agency, she wore pant suits that I'll bet came from Wal-Mart. I've seen her about three other times when she obviously had come from some kind of function having to do with the church."

I recalled how surprised I'd been. She had looked almost elegant, born to command. A woman used to being in charge. Her black suit jacket was smartly tailored. Her coordinating knee-length skirt was of the same fine light wool worsted. She wore a black clerical shirt with the obligatory white collar and the usual stylized cross she was never without.

It appeared to be of fine sterling silver and rather than a traditional crucifix, the outstretched Christ was smooth and elongated along the lines of Art Deco. There was a small ruby heart on the chest.

Keith is a devotee of the Sacred Heart of Jesus. When we were first married, I'd suggested replacing the sentimental picture in his office which I disliked with one by the French artist, Odilon Redon. He had given me a withering look. Ashamed, I never mentioned it again, nor did I quiz him when he went off to participate in rituals and feasts from which I was excluded.

Since I refused to join his church.

However, the only time I had seen Mary Farnsworth in full vestments was during the doomed ceremony in St. Helena. Although her snowy alb and chasuble robe were unremarkable, her stole appeared to be woven from coarse threads, and the primary colors, the primitive religious images, suggested a hand loom.

"We've tried every method we can think of to locate this woman's family," Brooks said. "I mean everything. She obviously has no criminal history or her fingerprints would be on file. And the poison frog angle is about to drive the forensic division nuts."

"And they can't find any connection to her and Talesbury?" I had filled her in on every aspect of the Bishop's background and Brooks personally had verified every detail separately that was transmitted through the Diocesan investigation.

"No. Besides, the poison we're talking about comes from South America, not Africa."

"That's what Keith said."

"And of course the forensics people have looked at every possible way someone could have done this. But we're talking about a small windowless room locked from the inside. There's simply no way someone could have gotten to that woman."

"Exactly. That's what I tried to tell everyone from the beginning."

"You were right. So that leaves suicide: she did it to herself. There's no evidence of that either. Our examiners did find a tiny site that they thought was evidence of an injection, but it wasn't. They tested the tip of the blood sampler pen and even the extra lancets."

She steered around a turtle slowly making its way across the highway, then braked and eased over to the shoulder of the road. She got out and picked up the turtle and carried it across, then resumed talking.

I smiled. I liked this woman a lot.

"Anyway, we even took out the needles and pins from her little mending kit, but there wasn't anything on those either."

"It's almost impossible for me to believe that Mary Farnsworth would have committed suicide," I said. "I didn't believe it then, and I don't believe it now. A woman who was going to commit suicide would not have a sack full of medical items waiting to deliver to persons in the community after the service. She just wouldn't."

"And Edna Mavery's theory? That someone gave her a heart attack?"

"That would make as much sense as anything if your people hadn't found poison in her system."

"So see where we come back to? Round and round we go. She could not have been murdered. There's no discernable method by which she could have committed suicide, and even if there was, there was no indication that she intended to. So we're back to harassing a little old lady to remember details she can't recall."

When we arrived at Mary's house Brooks used a key from the collection I'd left with the KBI, and opened the front door. She looked around the sparsely furnished combination living and dining room. The layout was typical of other houses built during that era.

"Naturally we'll keep an eye out for anything the team might have missed," she said. "Some connection to her identity. But the chances of that are slim to none. We've used our very best people on this case from the beginning because, frankly, it's attracted so much interest within the agency."

I said nothing.

She gave me a swift look. "I'm sorry, Lottie. That was tactless of me. I know to you it's hardly an intellectual exercise."

"No offense taken," I said tersely. We sat the foldout packing boxes in the middle of her living room and went from room to room before we began. I stood in the doorway of Mary's bedroom. I would bet every piece of furniture in the house was self-assembly.

On her walls were cheap mass-produced prints that might have come from Wal-Mart. Even her office in Dunkirk had contained more individual touches. I went into her bedroom and my eyes were drawn to a crucifix hanging on the wall across from the foot of her bed that was in the same style as the elongated cross she wore on her person.

"Isn't this sad?" Brooks commented. "It's as though she wasn't a real person." She went to Mary's closet and looked inside. The clothes were cheap, drab, with the exception of a tailored black suit. A black clerical shirt hung next to it. There was a grey coarse-clothed muumuu and a collection of cotton scarves. I examined a black one enclosed in a plastic sack, then placed it with the others in a storage box.

I was struck by the lack of color. The austerity of her surroundings was a strange contrast to the generous attention she showered on children.

"I'll bet everything here falls into the insubstantial property category," Brooks said. "The state is required to store possessions for three years, but if the estimated value isn't worth the expense of selling, it's all destroyed."

"And the furniture?"

"The type she has? They might try for ebay, but I'm not sure. We'd like to just leave it here, of course, or let her landlord buy it, but again, since we haven't located the family we have to keep it. Unfortunately, the landlord wants to rent this place out immediately."

We wasted no time packing up the house. Then we drove to a U-Haul center and rented a trailer. The manager maintained a list of high school boys who welcomed a chance to earn extra money.

Brooks secured the trailer hitch onto the Suburban and drove back to the house. She gave quick directions to the two eager young men, who were clearly happy to lend their muscular assistance to the KBI.

In a very short time, Mary Farnsworth's house was stripped bare.

It was as though she had never existed.

Chapter Forty-Three

I couldn't fall asleep. Keith moved constantly from his front to his back, then each side, and frequently adjusted his pillow. "We're a mess, aren't we?" I whispered softly. The clock hand pointed to 1:30.

He grunted, and sat up and switched on the light on the bed table. "Mind if I read?" He turned and kissed my cheek.

"No. Mind if I do?"

But I couldn't concentrate. I finally put down my book and reached for a notepad. I made a little flow chart of all the people who were involved with this entire fiasco. There were very few logical connections and none at all that led to Mary Farnsworth's death.

The KBI was the A team. As far as I knew, there was nothing I could contribute that they could not do better. But I kept coming back to one name. Or rather a pair of names. Keith put down his book and glanced at my list.

"What?" he asked.

"Nothing."

But there was. In the space of a few seconds, I decided to tackle Bishop Talesbury. That man had called the historical society and wanted to tell me something. What was it? He had chickened out. Changed his mind. Tomorrow I would track the bastard down and wring it out of him, if necessary.

The second person I need to extract information from was Irwin Deal, but I wasn't that gutsy. Thinking about his cold lifeless eyes, I shivered.

I was up before dawn the next morning, and in surprisingly good shape. Deciding on a course of action does wonders. At some point between waking and sleeping, I had decided to confront Talesbury and force him to answer questions.

Sam and I had the right to do that despite the fact the KBI no longer considered Bishop Talesbury a person of interest. And Keith, I reminded myself. And Keith. As an official member of the Carlton County sheriff's department.

We had a copy of Talesbury's and Deal's statements to the KBI taken during their earlier trip to Topeka when Agent Dimon had turned over the keys to the church over to Talesbury. Since the bishop had presented court papers proving the land and the church legally belonged to him and St. Helena was no longer a crime scene, Dimon could not have done anything else. Besides, at that time Deal was still a sheriff and had insisted his county was in charge of the investigation.

All coffeed up and braced for a fight, I drove over to St. Helena, hoping to find Talesbury there. The sky was clear and across our pasture chartreuse yarrow buds sparkled with a touch of dew. It made a deceptively pleasant setting for the bizarre tableau before me when I topped the rise on the road that went past the church.

In the lot in front of the church were four cars and four people! Talesbury, Deal, Myrna Bedsloe, and Chip Ferguson. They were standing outside the church and appeared to be arguing. It was the first time I could recall seeing Myrna without a child on her hip. She shook her finger at Deal who was waving his arms. Chip stood with his fists clenched and his arms pressed against his sides. Talesbury paced, with his hands behind his back.

They all heard my car, of course, and stopped and stared. All thoughts of having a conversation with Talesbury vanished so I simply gave a feeble wave and drove on past the church. Simply Undersheriff Albright doing her duty. Simply making her rounds.

But what the hell?

◇◇◇

I wanted to talk to Margaret Atkinson. Immediately. I called Sam. "I'll be late. Probably won't be there until around ten. I need to swing by the historical society." It was a statement, not a request.

"No problem," he said.

Margaret would be more than willing to answer my questions. No matter what interpretation she made of a person's motives, she was a walking database of seemingly unrelated tidbits.

"I thought you were on duty today," she said, when I walked through the door.

"I am. I have a few questions. Not related to anything that has to do with the sheriff's office." I hastily held up my hand, palm outward, in what I hoped she would take as a gesture of peace. "Something else. Just something I'm curious about."

She relaxed. Whenever she suspected she was being quizzed about anything to do with my "other job" she immediately clammed up. As though it would be held against her in a court of law, whether she had committed a crime or not.

I sat opposite her, chin in hand. "There's something I want to know. Do you know of any connection at all, I mean *anything*, between Chip Ferguson and Myrna Bedsloe? Anything at all those two have in common?"

"Greed," she said immediately. "Naked greed." Her lips thinned with disapproval. "Land hungry. Both of them."

"I'm sure you're right about Chip, Margaret, but Myrna?"

"Absolutely. It's in her blood. Tim may be the front man sneaking around to all these auctions, but you can bet Myrna is the mastermind. Acre by acre. Same as her father before her."

I leaned back and gave it some thought, then wandered over to the coffee carafe. It was full of hot water and I needed more than a cup of timid tea. Margaret's assessment certainly didn't explain what I'd had witnessed this morning.

"Is there something more direct than shared personality traits? A lot of people in Northwest Kansas are land hungry."

She carefully laid down her pencil, then looked up at me with feigned reluctance. "Well, as a matter of fact, according to my husband, there's a rumor going around the boys at the coffee shop that those two have become thicker than thieves."

"My god."

"Not that way. Chip is old enough to be her grandfather. It's not that. But they say folks have seen them together at seed stores and equipment dealers, and a couple of folks have driven by the Bedsloes and seen them together walking around in fields."

"Why?" I sat back. "What on earth is going on?"

"You asked if there was a connection," Margaret said primly. "There is something. Something there, but I don't know what. Why? Is it important?"

"No, I was just curious," I said honestly. "I saw them together this morning and I thought it was peculiar. More than peculiar."

I suspected their friendship began the day Chip handed Myrna the brochure on rust-resistant wheat. She'd seemed genuinely eager to hear his advice. He had been all too happy to give it. And those adoring red-headed boys!

He'd been adopted.

"Going fishing," Sam rose when I walked through the door. "I'll be at Lake Pleasant. For the whole rest of the day. With any luck at all."

"Well if anyone deserves a little time off…"

He gave me a sour smile and slapped his Stetson on his head. "I'll be out of range."

"Cool. Besides, I think I know an overanxious husband who will be here in a flash if anything comes up."

Josie called mid-afternoon. "I don't suppose there's been some miraculous break in the case in my absence?"

"None." I told her about Brooks' trip back to pack up Reverend Mary's house. "She said the agency has to move on to other cases. They are at an impasse."

"Are you?"

"No, I'm not. In fact, there's a number of things I want to check out." I told her about Talesbury's incomplete message on my answering machine. "I'm positive he intended to tell me something and then changed his mind."

"Would he, could he, if he wasn't staying with Irwin Deal? Is it a matter of not wanting to bite the hand that feeds you?"

"I don't know."

"Lottie, I been thinking and reading about Irwin Deal. I doubt if he was the kind of sadistic child who tortures animals, then progressed to more violent crimes. I think he's the kind of man who gains control over others through threats against their pets."

"There's a difference?"

"Yes. Sadly enough, we see it all too often in children who are in foster care. Their own parents, or the substitute parents they are placed with, threaten to do terrible things to their dogs and cats. It works like a charm. Produces practically perfect children."

I shuddered and closed my eyes to shut out the image of cruelty. Utter helplessness. Desperate children willing to do anything to protect their pets. "Monsters."

"Exactly. But the persons capable of such actions aren't attracted to this behavior if there's no pay-off other than witnessing torture."

"That's comforting."

"Just wanted to give you my latest thinking on this whole mess. I'll see you this weekend."

"You're coming out here again this weekend?"

"Yes, didn't Keith tell you? He asked me to be his partner in the Homestead Fiddlers competition this weekend."

We hung up and my head reeled. Keith had asked Josie to be his partner? Without even telling me?

I felt left out. Although I was aware that he and my sister had moved from a frankly antagonistic relationship when we were first married to one of mutual respect, my response was pure envy. Childish, unnerving.

Already unsettled by Josie's carefully parsed description of people who tortured animals for fun, and those who did it to gain control over others, I spent the next couple of hours compulsively typing labels for files. Irwin Deal's face kept coming to mind. His cold black eyes. His spiteful relations. But there had been only one murdering ancestor that I knew of, and that had been within the family.

Then I brooded over sibling relationships. Historical ones and my own. As twins, Josie and I had been constantly scrutinized and compared when we were children. Identical in appearance, we had always known we shared the same heart. Came from the same egg. Yet, as we aged, differences emerged. At first they were subtle, then they became more obvious, and by the time we were shipped off to finishing school, we flaunted our individuality.

We even chose different sports and, to our hovering parents' dismay, we refused team involvement. Neither one of us wanted to kick a soccer ball or join a rowing crew. To spite our father, Josie took up fencing and I became a crack shot. Both were utterly useless activities and we were quite pleased with ourselves.

Then against our will, the split went deeper. Although we both soared academically, Josie's affinity for music surprised everyone except me. I had always known this about her, even before our parents were aware that this one daughter deserved the finest instruction. She might have been a concert pianist. Would have been, if she had chosen that route. She progressed to a certain point, then stopped short of a life on the stage.

It was complicated and we had never discussed it. But I've always known she would only go so far along a path that would leave me behind. And beyond that, she was too private and self-protective. She would never be able to bear the emotional exposure required of professional musicians.

Josie had to contend with my easy ability with words, my ability to make connections, my easy recall of information that teachers had praised since I was in grade school. By five o'clock, I had settled down.

We all have our crosses to bear. She and Keith had dueled to a musical stand-off last fall. And if I didn't like feeling like a little waif peeping through a window, I would have to get over it.

They were both simply superior musicians.

Chapter Forty-Four

All duded up for the contest, Josie wore a sparkly turquoise shirt sprinkled with rhinestones. Her slim jeans were tucked into embroidered boots. Keith had found a coordinating plaid western snap-button shirt that accentuated his shoulders and complemented her star-spangled attire.

Vendors had set up booths at the west side of the park and offered an abundant supply of junk food: hot dogs, popcorn, cotton candy, snow cones, funnel cakes, nachos with cheese, and giant pretzels.

The violin or fiddle is Keith's best instrument. However, he's an excellent guitarist. Although Josie was a concert- level pianist, she was also an exceptional violinist and a recent convert to bluegrass fiddling. She had assumed that bluegrass and country/western were one and the same before Keith set her straight and bested her in their classical music showdown.

Sam and I were in full uniform, which meant jeans, medium blue shirts, badges displayed prominently, and guns anchored on our belts.

This contest was sparsely attended but would generate money to purchase equipment for our county-owned theatre. Today's event was minor compared to our county fair which took place the last weekend in July. There were no rides or carnival attractions at the Homestead Fiddlers contest. Most of the organizations did not bother to put up booths as the event attracted mostly amateur musicians and bluegrass fans who were notoriously cheap.

Josie had brought Tosca. I would take care of her while she and Keith played. Until then, she trotted at Josie's side until another larger dog showed interest in her perfumed, beribboned presence.

Amused, I watched my sister evaluate the persons she would contend against. The Anthony sisters, lively brunettes, wearing red-tiered skirts with white peasant blouses, played very well, but usually chose safe, crowd-pleasing tunes. There were three men who played in separate bands, but were very good friends and called on one another to cover in emergencies. There was the usual assortment of beginners and youngsters and older men who sawed away at old time dance tunes. None were professional musicians.

Keith and Josie walked up to the platform and found their way down the line of chairs. Next to them, at the very end, sat Old Man Synder, toothless, ageless, dressed in old blue chinos with a yellowed white shirt and a shiny green tie of indeterminate age. "How do," he said to Josie as she sat next to him. His tipped-back stained old fedora seemed glued to his head.

Keith had coached Josie on the finer points of the contest and talked hard to wean her away from complex arrangements that he didn't feel she could master in a short time. She'd scorned "Orange Blossom Special" when he insisted they play it.

"Look, this is your debut. Do you want to learn to play bluegrass or not? This song establishes your credentials with the crowd," he'd argued. "At some point, some time, somewhere, someone is going to request 'Orange Blossom Special.' That and 'Fire on the Mountain.' You can count on it."

She'd made a show of tilting back her head and raising her bow upright to the tip of her nose like she was a seal balancing a ball. "And I mus' go 'tru zis humiliating ritual, why?" She lowered her bow and dramatically lifted her elbow to her brow. "Why 'mus I sacrifice my art to ze masses? Why?"

I'd coughed and spurted scotch and Keith looked at each of us in turn and shook his head. I could count on one hand the number of people who had ever seen this side of my sister.

But she had tackled the complexity of double shuffles and double stops and he had coached her until she understood how simultaneously to captivate the crowd and overwhelm the judges.

Now the audience politely applauded "Twinkle, Twinkle, Little Star," and other squeaky juvenile classics and nodded in the direction of the contestants' beaming parents. The adult section began an hour later with the Anthony sisters and other players who were generally considered to be of medium ability.

All had some sort of rhythmic accompaniment such as a guitar or upright bass. A few brought boom boxes that served the same purpose. This was not a major contest, so anything was allowed.

Josie and Old Man Snyder were the only ones left.

"No, you're not seeing double here folks. Here from the grand city of Manhattan, Kansas is Miss Josie Albright, sister of very own undersheriff, Lottie Albright. And I see the one little lady is armed? See that, judges? Now, I'm not telling you what to do, but a word to the wise if you know what I mean."

"Oh, brother," I whispered to Tosca before I gave the crowd a feeble wave.

Keith counted, then began the heavy undulating base roll of chords that emulated a railroad engine. Josie hung her head then picked up the bow and executed the multi-stringed stroke that signaled the beginning of "Orange Blossom Special." She casually lowered the bow to her side, fingers extended, counting measures before she lifted it again and added more swipes to Keith's relentlessly accelerating rhythm.

"She's a ham. Don't look," I whispered to Tosca. But I was thrilled with the audience's sudden intake of breath as my sister finally began the melody. Her fingers flew up and down the neck of the fiddle and the bow was soon gyrating and vibrating at an incredible speed.

When she finished, the crowd went wild. Triumphant, her eyes shone and she bowed her head and she and Keith walked back to their chairs.

Old Man Snyder had remained expressionless throughout, but he turned and gave Josie a pleased nod of acknowledgement before he rose. He walked over to a cheap boom box with a cassette deck, adjusted a few knobs and walked up to the microphone with his scarred old fiddle.

He gently tapped his foot. The crowd hushed with anticipation. I closed my eyes. I had heard him before and had imagined Old Man Snyder was the reason God created music. When the worlds were formed and the Creator realized human beings needed something more, this old man had stepped forward.

With the first note he launched into an incredibly complex arrangement of the ultimate fiddle challenge, "Limerock." His bow floated over the strings and his fingers traveled so rapidly across the frets that it did not seem possible that he could produce such a clear melody and still stay true to the subtle rhythm.

When he finished, a chill ran down my spine. Stunned, like the rest of the audience, it was several seconds before I rose to award him a standing ovation. Awestruck, Josie gaped, then leapt to her feet and joined the clapping and chorus of bravos.

Snyder won.

He had never lost a contest.

Keith and Josie climbed down from the platform, then walked over to where I stood with a goofy smile on my face.

"You were set up," I said to Josie.

"You told me the selection had to be bluegrass, not classical," Josie said to Keith.

"'Limerock' is a bluegrass tune. It's traditional."

"That was the most astonishing performance I've ever heard," Josie said.

"Didn't Keith mention this old man when you were settling on your number?"

"Ladies! No, honest-to-god, I swear I didn't know that old man would be here today." He started backing away with a laugh and aped covering his head as though he was in mortal danger.

"Do you think I care about losing this contest? I want to know how more about that man. That was amazing. Beyond amazing. And you're fired, my friend. I want to know if that old man gives lessons."

"He just shows up," Keith said. "He's from Bidwell County and he's a farmer. We can't tell which contests he will enter."

My cell phone rang.

"He's dead." For a moment I was disoriented, unable to make the transition from hearing mesmerizing otherworldly music to dealing with the reality of harsh sobbed words.

"Who is this? And who is dead?"

"Myrna. Myrna Bedsloe. Chip. Chip is dead."

"Where are you?"

"I'm on the county road leading up to Chip's place. He's in his pickup. And he's dead. I don't know what Jimmy is going to do. What any of us are going to do."

"Myrna, I'll be right there. Are the boys with you?"

"Yes. They are."

"OK. Take them on home. Right now. I'll be there in a flash and take care of everything."

I hung up and told Keith, then ran over to tell Sam who was directing the orderly departure of vehicles from the park.

"Keith and I can go," I said, "unless you want to. I can take over here."

"The poor bastard. No, it's not my favorite job."

Chapter Forty-Five

Slumped in his pickup on the shoulder of the road, his arms circling the steering wheel, Chip appeared to have simply pulled over to take a nap. I walked over and looked at his clenched jaw and pressed my fingers on the side of his neck and glanced at my watch and called the EMTs.

Another unattended death. Another job for the district coroner. Another trip to Hays. In fact, another death of a person with no family.

But this time, I had a full record of his life story. I knew exactly who his people were. While we waited, I told Keith about Myrna's and Chip's unlikely affiliation. "Her kids were just crazy about him."

When the ambulance sped toward us, I waved, directing the driver to park directly behind Chip's pickup. They unloaded the stretcher and pulled out a body bag.

"Wait, Lottie," Keith hollered suddenly. "Tell them to wait a minute. Don't anyone touch one single thing."

"What are you talking about?"

"That," he said. "That. On his neck. There's a little gouge mark there. On the back of his neck."

I whirled around and went to Keith's Suburban and used OnStar to call Sam.

"I'll call the KBI immediately," he said. "We're going to do it right this time." He called back. "Stay there. Everyone is in high gear. They'll have someone there as soon as possible. Do not touch anything."

I went over and stood by my husband a short distance from Chip's pickup. We did not want to muddle the crime scene with our footprints.

Keith looked at the road. "There are no skid marks, Lottie. Chip simply pulled over. He knew the person that did this."

Keith stayed there and I went on over to Myrna's.

"I'm so terribly sorry for your loss," I murmured, wishing I knew a more effective, more comforting canned phrase. "I need to ask you some questions."

Tim Bedsloe stood in the doorway, looking like a needy child. The children began quarrelling fiercely over a yellow dump truck and Myrna started to rise and tend to them.

"Wait. Sit back down. Tim, were you with her when she found Chip?"

He shook his head.

"Then please take the boys to another room. I need to ask your wife some questions."

Startled, the boys looked up and then took off after their father.

I pulled out a notebook. Myrna wept uncontrollably. "I just loved Chip. He was like a father. Or a grandfather. He took me under his wing. He told me what to plant and when, and my little boys, they just lit up when that old man came around."

I let her talk.

"He was lonely, Lottie. He didn't have a family. Not another soul in the world. Just worked all his life."

"So tell me what happened, Myrna."

"Chip called and asked me to meet him at the church. He said there were some things he wanted me to know. Some things he wanted to show me. Said it was time."

St. Helena again. All roads led back to St. Helena.

"I started over there, and saw him parked. I supposed he'd seen me coming and had pulled over to talk to me. I drove up behind him and parked and got out and went up to talk to him. He was dead! Then I went back to my car and called you."

"You did everything right."

She shuddered and her aching sobs subsided into hiccups. "Was it a heart attack?"

"This was an unattended death," I said carefully. "So I can't speculate, but we'll know soon enough. Sam called in the KBI."

She nodded.

"I have other questions, Myrna. First of all, do you have any idea at all, any indication whatsoever why he would want you to come over to the church? He wasn't a donor to the project. Wasn't an Episcopalian. I know that because I just finished compiling a list."

"He wasn't religious. I know that because we talked about everything. He came over here to the house a lot after we got acquainted. He played with the boys, ate supper with us."

"And Tim?" I asked carefully. "Did he get along with Tim?"

"That's another thing I loved about Chip. He was nice to Tim. Real polite. Not everyone is." She stopped and blew her nose. "Oh, I know what people say behind my back. That I wear the pants and my man is hen-pecked."

Yes! But I suspected Chip was a shrewd judge of character and struck just the right chord. One doesn't amass a fortune without being able to read people.

"Sometimes Chip asked me to meet him at implement dealers, and he pointed out different features of the latest tractors and drills and combines." She began to sob again. "He's the only one I've ever met that loved the land as much as I do."

"And Tim?"

"He doesn't care as much. When we were first married, I was disappointed. Then I looked on the bright side. I'm a better farmer than Tim. He talks a good game, but if he was in charge, we'd be ready for the poor farm." Her eyes misted again. "We were meant for each other. Most husbands wouldn't let a wife just plumb take over."

Most wives wouldn't want to, I thought. "Back to the church," I prodded.

"This was the second time Chip had asked me to meet him there."

I pressed. "I assume the first time was the other day when I drove past St. Helena and you were there with him and Irwin Deal and Bishop Talesbury. You all seemed to be quarrelling. What was that all about?"

"That all broke up right after you drove past us. We all saw you and just left. Have you ever felt like things are going on you don't understand? It was weird. I got there late because Mom had a problem."

"But you were right in the thick of things, Myrna, shaking your finger at Deal. I saw you."

"Damn right, I was. I walked up just as Deal started calling Chip names. Terrible names." She looked away. "No need to mention them all here. I lit right into Irwin and told him what I thought of his whole inbred family. That bastard isn't worthy of breathing the same air as Chip Ferguson."

I rose and grabbed a fresh batch of tissues and handed them to her.

"Anyway, it turned out Chip wanted to buy the church land and Deal just blew up. Just freaked out. Then Talesbury said it was his land. His and his alone. Then he and Deal got into it. Deal said he was imagining things."

"Myrna do you have any idea why someone like Chip would want those worthless acres?"

She lifted her tear-stained face and looked at me with her red-rimmed hazel eyes and shook her head. "No. Not a clue. But I'm sure of this. If he'd lived long enough today to make it to the church, I would now know. That's what he wanted to tell me."

After the KBI processed the scene, they transferred Chip's body to Hays. Both Brooks and Dimon were present to witness the autopsy. The Forensic Department at Topeka had anticipated certain complications.

Brooks called as soon as the lab was completed. "Chip Ferguson was murdered, Lottie. The gouge mark was from a very thin instrument."

I took a deep breath. "Like a stiletto?" I asked.

"Yes, but that's not what killed him. It was tipped with poison from a poison dart frog."

"Like Mary Farnsworth? Just like Reverend Mary?"

"Actually, no. This poison came from the *Dendrobates azureus*. A bright blue frog. The poison that killed Mary was from the *Phyllobates terribilis*. A bright yellow frog. One came from Africa, the other from South America."

I couldn't speak.

"Drag Talesbury in for questioning. Right now. He's much more than a mere person of interest. We'll help. But especially in light of what Myrna told you, we want him off the street."

"I agree, Nancy," I said unhappily, "but he still couldn't have killed Mary. There was simply no way."

◇◇◇

Sam and I went to Irwin Deal's together. I watched Talesbury's face when we told him he was wanted for questioning in connection with the murder of Chip Ferguson. Stunned, he took a faltering step forward and braced himself on the door jam. When Sam launched into "you have a right to remain silent," he stiffened, his face no longer a self-protective mask, but distorted with grief.

"I want a lawyer," Talesbury said immediately. Deal stood to one side, his arms across his chest and watched as we arrested his uncle.

"I'll get you a lawyer. Right away," Deal said at once.

Talesbury shook his head. He whirled around and gave Deal an angry look.

"No. A lawyer of my choosing, not yours." He turned back to me. "I am not a killer." His eyes begged me to believe him. "I do not kill people. I save them. In the name of Jesus Christ."

It was I who remained silent, feeling that any words I uttered would somehow be used against me.

"Please contact the Diocese," he said. "I want a lawyer furnished by the church."

When we arrived at the jail, he sat at the little table in the room where we now questioned persons. His elbows were braced on the table and his fingers laced through his long hair as though his head would topple if he removed their support. The county commissioners had upgraded our facilities. We now had the kind of mirror the men had so admired on various TV shows. This was the first time it had come in handy.

I called Bishop Rice and told him Talesbury had asked for a lawyer from the Diocese. Rice's first stunned response was carefully worded as he sorted through the ramifications of a second death that might be tied to the Diocese of Western Kansas. "Miss Albright, Ignatius Talesbury is simply not attached to this Diocese and we have no responsibility to protect him."

"I understand that, sir. But apparently he does not."

"And furthermore," he said thoughtfully, "despite what this man seems to think, this is not the Diocese of New York and we do not have attorneys on staff. Apparently he has no concept of how little money is available."

"He's out of touch, sir. It's as though he doesn't understand how anything works."

"Nevertheless, he needs a lawyer." His voice softened. "He's a brother in Christ. He needs our help. Whom would you suggest? There has to be a lawyer in your area."

I thought of Curtis Matthews who had been present during Edna's questioning, and said I would call him.

"Let me know how it goes," Bishop Rice said. "How is he doing?"

I gazed through the mirror. "He's terrified, sir. Absolutely terrified."

Curtis Matthews arrived and spent fifteen minutes conferring with Talesbury, then Sam and I joined them. We slogged through a fruitless monosyllabic interview. Yes, he knew Chip

Ferguson. Yes, he was familiar with lethal poisons obtained from frogs. Yes he owned a stiletto. No, he had not killed the man. We questioned him for about three hours without extracting any confession or pertinent information. Matthews intervened frequently.

Sam glanced at me and jerked his head toward the door. I followed him outside.

"We're getting nowhere."

"I agree." There was no point in holding this man until we obtained a warrant and searched his car and Deal's house.

We went back into the room. "You are free to go," Sam said.

Talesbury stiffened and sat motionless, his eyes trained on a spot on the far wall. Then he broke his trance and beckoned to Matthews to bend down. He spoke to him in a low voice. Startled, the lawyer shook his head then bent and whispered in Talesbury's ear. The bishop did not reply, but simply resumed staring at the wall.

Matthews looked at him, shrugged, picked up his briefcase and the three of us left the room.

"Bishop Talesbury requests protective custody," Matthews said after we closed the door. "He would like to remain here."

"I know your communication is privileged," Sam said, "but do you have any idea what in the hell is going on? I would like to remind you this man is not under arrest. Yet. So far we have no reason to charge him with a thing."

"I know that and he knows that. But he still wants to stay here."

"Lottie? Have you noticed anything I didn't?"

"Only that Talesbury was petrified when we picked him up and told him there had been another murder. Scared to death. But I'm sure you saw that too."

Sam glanced through the glass at Talesbury. Then he went over to the ashtray on his desk and tapped old ashes out of his pipe. "Well, Curtis, you're the lawyer. You tell me. Can we do this? This hasn't exactly come up before."

"They didn't cover this in law school."

All three of us trooped over to the window and studied the man. He hadn't moved since we left the room.

"We've had homeless people work for us for a place to stay overnight, but I believe this is the first time I've had someone want to stay here that had another choice," Sam said. "But after the KBI does a search, if they don't find anything, he has to leave. I'm not running a hotel."

"He's scared."

"Doesn't matter. We can't do this."

"I would be terrified if I had to stay with Irwin Deal."

"No," Sam said. "It's not Deal. Talesbury wasn't frightened when we first went to the door."

Chapter Forty-Six

When I got home, I found Keith listening intently to a recording of "Limerock," Old Man Snyder's winning song. He held the remote in one hand and his fiddle in the other.

"Going to try it?"

He paused the recording.

"I shouldn't. But then plenty of other folks do who shouldn't."

I walked over to the crock pot and lifted the lid on the beef vegetable mixture I'd set simmering early morning.

"Josie called," Keith said. "You're to call her back."

After adding more seasoning to the stew I dialed my sister.

"We were wondering."

"And 'we' is?"

"Tosca and I, of course. We were wondering if we've worn out our welcome. We have a three-day weekend coming up."

"Are you kidding? I'd love it." Thanks to Zola, she would have fresh sheets and would not have to suffer through my usual mumbled explanation that I planned to have the cord repaired on her favorite reading light as soon as I had time.

"Good. Keith and I have talked and I've decided to take on Old Man Snyder."

"You'll lose."

"Maybe."

I laughed. It was a toss-up as to who was the more competitive, Keith or my sister. But beyond that, I knew neither one of them could resist mastering this piece. "I'll love it for whatever reason you're coming. Besides I want to pick your brains." I told her about bringing in Talesbury for questioning.

"You can't keep him," she said. "There's no probable cause for arresting him. You've risked making a first class mess out of any conviction."

"You're right, but he's not under arrest. We've just agreed to sort of keep him for a while."

"God, Lottie. This sounds loony."

"Don't I know. Sam's relieved that we're not in charge of this investigation. Since Ferguson's death occurred in our county, we had full authority to request the KBI's help from the very beginning. So they are the ones who will snoop around Deal's house."

"Ah yes, Deal. What has he been up to without his badge?"

"We may have dealt him a death blow. When we picked up his uncle, he just stood there and didn't put up a bit of resistance. He didn't even threaten us. It was like confronting a high school bully."

"He was used to hiding behind his badge," Josie said. "He probably feels powerless without it. Harold believes once that man reorganizes his thinking, he's going to be dangerous. He's worried that Deal will explode if the right trigger occurs."

"And do you agree?"

"I don't. I think he's a different kind of crazy. A planner, not an exploder. Since he relishes getting to people through animals, he's into a sly kind of torment. Psychological torture. That's a lot different than someone who blows up."

"But he's so damn stupid, Josie. This is the great mastermind who ended up a laughing stock by throwing us in jail. He can't think his way out of a paper bag."

"Evil stupid people do as much damage as evil smart people. The only difference is, the former often self-destruct in the process, and the latter get away with it. But the damage to innocent people is the same, either way."

"If I had to vote, it would be for planner, not exploder."

"Exactly. He got to Keith's oats field, his equipment, and one of his cows. Deal knew right where to stick the knife."

"We got him in the end. Nothing could have hurt him more than losing that badge."

"We've got him if he stops. Nevertheless, I'm sticking to my perception that Deal is remarkably talented at figuring out what will cause his enemies the most pain."

◇◇◇

Margaret's eyes brightened when I walked through the door the next morning.

"You have something to tell me," I observed. "What? God's truth according to the coffee shop boys?"

"Yes. But it really is this time."

I poured the dregs of yesterday's coffee into my cup and heated it in the microwave. Then I took it to the chair opposite Margaret's desk.

"Chip had a will. Quite recent. And you'll never guess who he left his money to?"

"The historical society? I can always hope."

"No. Myrna Bedsloe and her kids. Specifically to Myrna. Left her husband plumb out of it."

"She's worth millions now!" I tried to imagine the impact this would have on her life. Would she put Tim's mother in an Alzheimer's unit? Travel? None of the above, I decided. Myrna would buy more land. "Wow," was all I could manage.

"That's not the big news," Margaret said. "I mean it is big news, but that's not what everyone is talking about. It's Irwin Deal's reaction when he heard about it. He's at loose ends since he got booted out of office, and madder than hell at anyone in Copeland County who voted against him. So he comes over here to Carlton County to buy gas."

She eyed my coffee cup. "You know, I really don't know how you drink that stuff."

I wrinkled my face. "Never mind. And then what?"

"So the other day, after he filled up, he just strolled over to the booth where my husband and his buddies were sitting, and asked 'what's up?' like he was the most popular man in Carlton

County and they should all just scoot over so he could sit in their booth."

I laughed. "I'll bet no one moved an inch."

"They told him they were just talking about Chip leaving all his money and land to Myrna and then according to Leroy, Deal just blew up."

"Blew up?"

"Looked like he was going to pass out. Then he started cussing and left. Leroy said a lot of the men were shocked anyway that Chip was worth so much."

"Margaret, you usually know as much as anyone what's going on in the county, do you have any idea why Irwin would be so upset?"

She leaned toward me. "Irwin has been sidling up to Tim Bedsloe. This came straight from the horse's mouth, Lottie. Tim himself. He told the coffee shop boys that Irwin had heard that Chip hung around their house all the time. Then he asked Tim to talk Chip out of donating building materials to that bishop."

"Chip was going to help out Talesbury?" It made no sense.

"Yes, at first Chip wanted to buy those forty acres. Then when the bishop wouldn't sell to him, Chip asked him not to sell out to anyone else."

"So where does Irwin fit in to all this?"

"I don't know. According to Tim, Irwin was fit to be tied when Chip volunteered that building material. As you can imagine, the boys had a big laugh over Irwin assuming that Tim made the decisions in that household."

"That's Irwin," I said. "He never gets anything right."

Land again. It always comes up out here. A perennial question: who owns the land?

Brooks stopped by the sheriff's office the next morning. She waved a search warrant at Sam.

"That fast? What? You have some judge in your pocket?"

"As good as. Magistrate Judge Willard Clawson didn't bat an eye when we told him why we wanted to search Deal's house. He simply reached for his pen and wished us luck."

"I'll bet he did. It took all the self-restraint he could muster to stay out of the recall election."

"We want you to come too, Lottie. Everything is set. In fact, it was the information you gave us about Talesbury using the stiletto at the church that gave us the specifics for the warrant. The tip of the weapon used in the murder was unusual. A triangular shape."

"Sure you don't want in on this?" I asked Sam.

"No." Then he raised his eyebrows and tapped his lips with his finger, and jerked his head indicating he wanted us to follow him. We stepped outside. "I want to stay here with Talesbury."

"You know you can't keep him here," Brooks said. "If we don't find anything, you'll have to let him go."

"Not let him go, make him go," I said. "He's not under arrest. We got around a few little minor considerations such as state law by charging him with vagrancy. But what's changed, Sam? A couple of days ago, you complained that Talesbury seemed to think we were running a motel."

Sam stared at the sidewalk and thrust his thumbs in his jeans pockets. "That was before I saw his back. And other body parts too. I let him use the shower this morning and brought him a different shirt. Something bad happened to that man. Maybe he's not so crazy wanting to be locked up."

"Nevertheless," Brooks said, "if we don't find anything that might be the basis for filing charges, he has to leave."

"I know that," Sam muttered.

"But in the meantime, having him here for a couple of nights was a lucky break. He didn't have a chance to dispose of anything, because Lottie said Talesbury seemed stunned when you picked him up. Apparently he wasn't expecting that at all."

◇◇◇

"We have two men waiting at the rest stop," Nancy said as she drove toward Copeland County. "The warrant is limited to Deal's house and Talesbury's car."

Caught off guard, when Deal came to the door he glared at me like I had engineered the search instead of the KBI. He stomped off to his pickup.

We searched the entire day without finding the weapon. By evening we were exhausted, and after looking through Talebury's car, Brooks clearly felt like a fool. I did too. No doubt, she had trusted my information about Talesbury's owning a stiletto. She dropped me off at the office and headed for the motel.

"You know what you have to do," she said. "Tell Sam to get that man out of there before we all get sued for something."

I went inside and told Sam we didn't find the stiletto. His guest had to leave. Then I went back to Talesbury's cell, but of course he was already on his feet, having heard everything that said in the dispatch office including my comments about the botched search.

"You are free to leave. But I suggest you don't take leaving too seriously. It's best if you stay around here."

A strange look came over came over his face. "You didn't find what you were looking for?"

"No. Go. We can't keep you here."

"Were you careful with my things?"

"Yes. Despite what you've seen on TV, the police don't delight in destroying property when they do a search." *What things?* I thought. I'd never seen a man with so few things.

"My sacred items. My vestments, my cross. The items in my satchel. They were all in the car. You've touched them."

I froze. Was he implying that his so-called sacred items had somehow been soiled by contact with mere mortals? A man had been murdered, and he hadn't volunteered one whit of information and all he cared about was our having touched his precious things?

I spun around. "We left everything in perfect shape." I wished we hadn't. Then I looked at him hard.

He was no longer afraid.

Chapter Forty-Seven

"Don't worry, I'm not going to tell you about my day," I said when Josie pulled in the next evening.

"Does that mean you're not going to let me tell you about my drive across Kansas?"

"Better not." We laughed and Tosca yelped and threw herself into Keith's arms.

"I told Sam I would make the rounds this evening," Keith said. "I think our fiddling session can wait."

I looked at him gratefully. "And take the mutt with you."

He laughed and rubbed behind Tosca's ears. "How about it, pooch? You want to be a police dog tonight?"

They left. I fed Josie leftover stew and told her about my perfectly horrible, very bad day. When we were kids, we used to compete with each other to see whose was worse.

After she settled in, I read and she took her fiddle out and looked at the sheet music Keith had left on the stand.

"So. 'Limerock,' huh? Looks like he's trying to get a head start here."

"You'd be better off listening to the CD he bought," I said. "It's very well done."

She listened and hummed and concentrated. "I'm still not following something right here. I'm going to give him a ring. Let him know he can't get the jump on me."

She went out to the kitchen and used the landline and came back in a few minutes.

"Bastard," she said cheerfully, "he's going to keep everything to himself. Didn't help me a bit. Just said he would be a while and to start *Tosca* without him."

"*Tosca?*" We weren't planning to watch *Tosca*. He was making rounds so we could go to bed early. And he didn't like that opera.

The hair rose on the back of my neck. "He said *Tosca*, Josie?"

"Yes. He'll be back in time for his favorite part, the last scene."

"He hates that scene," I said slowly. "Betrayal. It's all about betrayal." My skin prickled. "What number did you call?"

"Oh damn. I forgot and called his cell phone. That's funny, it worked."

"You didn't use his OnStar number? "

"No, I don't even have his OnStar number."

"Did you hear your dog?"

"No."

I went to the kitchen. Josie followed. I looked at the call list and hit "redial." The number that came up was Keith's cell phone. If she'd have called OnStar, the call would have gone through the speakers and Tosca would have started barking like crazy.

"Something is wrong," I said. "His cell phone shouldn't have worked out in the country."

"But it did."

"The only place with good reception right now is along the county line. By St. Helena."

We looked at each other. I called Sam and screamed out four words when he answered, not waiting for his reply. "Keith, trouble, St. Helena." We ran for the car.

I couldn't talk, could barely think. I concentrated on keeping the Tahoe in the middle of the road. The radio crackled. "Pick up the mike, Josie, tell Sam we're almost there."

"I'm on my way," he said. "Don't take any chances."

I kept my eyes focused on the road. "Tell him to call Brooks, too. She's staying at the motel. EMTs. Everyone." I choked back a sob. Brooks' men might still be there too. We would have all kinds of manpower if we weren't too late.

I topped the final rise and saw St. Helena in the distance. The moon reflected the sheen from the white car parked at the far edge of the lot in front of the church.

Talesbury's Camry.

Keith's Suburban was beside it.

I pulled over onto the shoulder about two hundred yards away from the church. I was not in uniform, but I had my Smith and Wesson Airweight in my purse. I would have liked a more powerful weapon, but the little 642 would do.

"We can't take a chance on Talesbury hearing us. Let Sam know what we're doing. Tell him to hurry."

I opened the car door and let it close soundlessly then ran toward the church in a crouch knowing Josie would follow.

None of the main lights were on. There was a faint glow coming from the windows at the back of the church.

There was no foyer. The front door simply opened into the main room. Shielding my eyes, I peered through the arched window to the left of the entrance, thankful that we had not been able to afford stained glass yet.

Jolted by the sudden rush of blood to my head, I reached to steady myself. Not Talesbury. Deal.

He was waving Talesbury's stiletto back and forth like a drum major's baton.

Josie came up beside me. I could not swallow. My tongue stuck to the roof of my mouth. Keith was at the very front of the church, directly in front of the communion railing. Deal had spread his arms and bound his hands to the rungs.

Keith was bent at the waist into a semi-sitting position with his cord-tied feet jutting down the center aisle. Christlike, his head sagged forward and blood streamed down his face. Barking continuously, Tosca circled him, trying to get him to stand.

She made little pounces toward Deal with low growls.

"Goddamn dog," he said. "You're next." He turned and scooped up Tosca and grabbed the rope and started wrapping it around her neck. Tosca twisted and bit Deal's hand and immediately leaped to the floor when he lessened his grip.

She ran down one of the exterior aisles. Deal plunged after her. He dropped the stiletto beside Keith and pulled his revolver from his holster and took aim.

The little Shih-Tzu was an impossible target. She dashed in and out under the pews. Furious, Deal stared at the last place he had seen her, then suddenly gave up his prey, and turned back to Keith.

He picked up the stiletto. Terrified that it had been tipped with the same poison, used to kill Chip Ferguson we watched Deal move toward Keith.

Keith stirred and raised his head.

Tosca came out from hiding and began a whimpering crawl down the aisle on her stomach as though she were offering herself as a little doggy sacrifice. Deal snorted and watched her edge toward him.

"Come here, you worthless piece of shit."

I couldn't think. Could barely breathe.

Tosca would run to us if we stepped inside. The distance from the door to where my husband lay prevented me from entering and running down the aisle, because Deal would kill Keith. Or me.

The glass would deflect my bullet if I fired through it with my Airweight and Deal would hear the glass if I tried to break it.

I had to burst through the door and shoot Deal in seconds before he could react and prick Keith with the stiletto. Kill him in cold blood.

"Take your time, Tosca, baby." I whispered. "He loves little animals. Keep him distracted."

I closed my eyes for a second and calculated the moves. Fixed the sequence in my mind.

Run, door, aim, fire.

Run, door, aim, fire.

No warning, my entry had to be lightning fast. No wild shots, I had to aim well.

I turned toward Josie and tears stung my eyes. My little Smith and Wesson Airweight was no match for Deal's .375 Magnum if I was too slow. She knew that.

Someone would die. I or Keith or Deal.

I stooped into a runner's stance then raced from the window to the steps, slammed through the door, crouched, and took aim.

Tosca was faster. Josie was one step behind me and the little Shih-Tzu leapt ecstatically, sailing toward my sister. She jarred my arm as I fired.

Deal recovered immediately and called on training as sheriff of Copeland County. He whipped out his .357 and trained it on us instantly.

"Drop it, bitch."

I did.

"Kick it down here."

I did that, too.

Tosca whimpered in Josie's arms. "There's nothing in this for you, Deal," Keith said. "Nothing to gain. Let us go before you're in any more trouble."

"Shut up, Fiene. Do you think I'm stupid?" His round face, drenched with sweat, quivered with self-pity. "There's nothing I can do anymore that will help. Do you think I'll get a break if I let you go?"

He was right. There is absolutely no one more dangerous than a person at wit's end. He had nothing to lose. I thought he had nothing to gain either. Then I realized he did.

He would have the ultimate satisfaction.

Sam was on the way, but it didn't make any difference. Like other cornered killers, this evil man was going to take as many of us with him as possible. He planned to kill us all.

Deal had to know we'd called up the cavalry before we came and that somehow Keith had alerted us when Josie phoned.

Then Tosca rallied. Gathering courage from the sanctuary of Josie's arms, she lifted her head and yelped at Deal like he was an errant rabbit she'd decided to vanquish. Deal bounded down the aisle and ripped Tosca from Josie's arms. Dangling her by the hind legs, he went back up to where Keith lay.

I knew then that he planned to drag this out until the very moment he heard Sam approach. Then we would die. Josie was right. He was into psychological torture.

I started talking although Josie caught my eye signaling that buying time wouldn't do us a bit of good. We all knew when we heard the sirens we were doomed.

I eyed the gleaming stiletto. "You killed Chip, didn't you? Not Talesbury."

"Goddamn right. He was going to give money for buildings. A whole goddamn school. He was trying to talk my uncle into putting that land into a trust for a worthless foundation just to help a ragged little bunch of foreigners. Just so I couldn't have it. My uncle was crazy. I was willing to pay him good money for that land. Before Chip started messing things up, I was going to inherit."

Keith took over. "You came here to plant that stiletto, didn't you Deal? Hoping to frame your uncle. Still old Dumb Deal. Still a little short of brain power, aren't you? Penis short too?"

Irwin's face flushed. Horrified I stared at Keith, then realized he was trying to taunt Deal into lunging at him. Giving me a chance to go for my gun. "No," I mouthed. "Please, no." Just a touch of the stiletto meant instant death. I couldn't let Keith do it.

Deal didn't take the bait. "I didn't have time to hide it at the house," he volunteered sullenly, as though it made him sound smarter. Our fault that he was forced into this situation. He glared at me. "Your goddamn whore of a wife is screwing Judge Clawson. That's why she got the warrant so fast."

"Boo, hoo," Keith jeered.

I stared at the black sky visible through the still open door. There were no stars. A sudden breeze scattered some papers on a table in back of the room. Moths clicked against the light fixture. My throat dried, shrank. I couldn't even swallow when I heard the sirens.

Still holding Tosca's back legs, Deal raised her in front of him, stretched out like a pullet hanging from a hook. He turned her stomach toward him and held out the stiletto, and looked at Josie, then me.

A totally worthless little dog. Good for nothing. Her pink ribbons hanging down from her fine silky ears.

Our hearts broke as one.

"You goddamn evil son-a-bitch," Keith said. "I hope you rot in hell."

Josie reached for my hand.

Then Deal looked past Josie and gave a strangled cry.

"You," he gasped. He clutched his throat.

He pitched forward.

Tosca landed on top of him. We turned toward the back of the church and looked into the cold eyes of Bishop Talesbury.

Chapter Forty-Eight

He stood in the open doorway with his arms folded and his hands tucked into the sleeves of his cassock.

"Do you have your phone with you, Miss Albright?"

Stunned, I could only nod.

"Call the EMTs. Tell them to get here immediately."

I stared at Deal's body lying at Keith's feet with the tiny arrow extending from his chest.

"Now," he repeated.

I doubted there was any need for speed. "They are already on the way." My voice shook.

Relief swept across his face. "This was curare, Miss Albright. A paralyzing mixture and not lethal. I save people. I do not kill them. But they need to hurry."

I ran to Keith, knelt, and my hands shook as I clumsily fumbled with the knots.

Josie went to the door. "Sam's here," she yelled. She waved at Sam and Brooks. Talesbury stood in the doorway, waiting for the EMT's.

Sam took one look at Keith, and ran down the aisle toward him, his Swiss Army knife out before he even crouched down next to him.

The last cord cut, Keith rose to his feet. We hugged, clung to each other. "Son-of-a-bitch was behind the door," he said with disgust. "I walked into it like I was a seven year old playing cops and robbers and let Tosca out of the car. I didn't know what hit me. When I came to, I was trussed up like a turkey."

"Josie must have called right after that."

"He held my cell phone to my mouth when Josie called. I told him you'd know something was wrong if it didn't go to voice mail after the first ring or if he let it ring and I didn't answer at all."

His heart raced. I couldn't bear to turn him loose. "All it would have taken was a touch of that damn stiletto. Deal kept waving it at my neck. I counted on you knowing something was wrong. Then I worried I was leading you and Josie into a trap. Which I did. I'll never forgive myself."

"Don't think that way," I whispered. "Put it out of your mind."

He pushed away and walked over to Sam. "Did Deal park around back?" Sam nodded. "I didn't see his car when I drove up. I just noticed a light in the church."

"Josie and I saw only your Suburban and Talesbury's Camry."

"Talesbury wasn't here when I drove up. He must have gotten here after Deal and me, and before you two came."

"I'm going to find out the answer to a lot of things," Sam said.

The three of us went to the front of the church where Talesbury anxiously waited for the EMTs.

"Where were you?" I asked.

"I was still in my car when I saw you approach. Then when you immediately started sneaking up to the church and looked through the windows, I knew all my suspicions about my nephew were well founded."

"I mean when we were fighting for our lives. Where the hell were you?"

He whirled around. "I would like to remind you that I saved you, Miss Albright. All of you." He glanced at his watch. "I looked through the window, as you did. I saw what was going on. The door was still open after your explosive…arrival. I stood right outside it and listened. Your entry was perfect." He gave a weak smile. "I tried to duplicate it."

"Why did you come here in the first place?" Brooks edged in front of him, so she could face him squarely.

"When you released me from jail I stayed the night in a motel and figured it all out. When the KBI couldn't find the stiletto, I knew Irwin had killed Mr. Ferguson. It was not hidden. My nephew was the only one who could have taken it out of my satchel."

"We jumped the gun on the warrant," Brooks said. "We should have included this church in our search."

"Of course Irwin thought I was still in voluntary confinement and he would have a chance to hide it here to frame me. He wanted it to be found. The KBI would think I had done it. I drove to Irwin's house this evening to beg him to ask God's mercy and turn himself in."

"Fat chance of that," I said.

Talesbury glanced at Deal lying on the floor and checked his watch again. "Irwin wasn't at the house. I retrieved my satchel, and indeed, the stiletto was missing. I knew the logical place for him to hide an object that would implicate me would be at St. Helena."

Sam stepped forward. "What did you use on Irwin Deal and where is it? I need to take your weapon."

Talesbury pulled a short slender hollow tube from the left sleeve of his cassock. "A blow dart gun. I'm never without it. Where I come from, there are always children's lives at stake." He flipped a cap secured with jeweler's hinges back over the top of the tube. He reached into his pocket and took out a pointed tip that screwed in the other end. It looked like a pen.

"You carry that with you here? In Western Kansas?" Sam rubbed the bridge of his nose, like he was trying to make sense of it all. "We're not in the middle of an African tribal war. Why?" Then his face flushed. His words broke off and I knew he was remembering the man's terror, the scars all over his body.

"Always. I am never without it." His voice was flat.

"Is that how you killed Mary Farnsworth?" I blurted the words.

Talesbury spun around and skewered me with his cold eyes. "Madame, I've told you. I did not. I am not a killer."

"Are you denying that there was poison on the tip of the stiletto that killed Chip. From a poison dart frog?"

"I do not carry lethal poison. I didn't put it there. My nephew acquired it from the internet. I knew he had been visiting websites and he asked me a lot of questions, but I thought he was investigating Mary Farnsworth's murder. When I picked up my satchel, the credit card receipt for the purchase of the poison that killed Chip was laying by his computer."

I recalled Brooks telling me that someone had their frogs mixed up. No doubt Deal had screwed that up too.

An ambulance pulled into the yard.

"Thank God," he said. He stepped back as they rushed inside and knelt beside Irwin Deal. Talesbury shoved us out of the way and hurried over to the men. "You must act quickly. I used curare. He needs physostigmine immediately."

The men froze. "Never heard of it," one of them said, slowly rising to his feet. "Never heard of it."

"My God," Josie whispered. "Oh my God." She reached for my hand. Western Kansas ambulances carry supplies for situations likely to be encountered, not an array of exotic antidotes.

Talesbury lurched toward his nephew and started to do CPR. The EMTs looked at one another. One of them stepped forward. "Sir, it won't help. He's already gone into paralysis. Defibrillators won't help in this kind of situation either."

Talesbury rose and took a few faltering steps toward the cross in front of the church. He steadied himself on the railing. "I'm not a killer," he whispered. "Not a killer."

We watched the EMTs load the body. Then, Brooks beckoned to Sam and me. "Arrest him. Let him call his lawyer. Matthews?"

I nodded.

"He and the county attorney can slug it out over the charges. And Lottie, there was no little arrow sticking out of Mary Farnsworth's body."

Curtis Matthews made short work getting the bishop released. It was clearly a justifiable homicide, and there were ample witnesses to the fact that the man did not intend to kill Deal.

"Where will you go?" I asked as Talesbury gathered up his belongings and prepared to leave the jail. "Back to Irwin's house?"

"No, Miss Albright, my lawyer has found me a house to rent right here in Gateway City." He looked at me hard. "I'm not leaving, if that's what you are hoping. I own land here, and I plan to create a place where children can be safe."

"I wish you luck, sir." That was almost the truth. I couldn't tell if he was more stricken by his nephew's death, or the fact he had lost his moral purity.

"There's something else I would like to know. You called the historical society and started to leave a message and then changed your mind. What did you want to say?"

He stared at the calendar on the wall, his face sallow with grief. He did not reply.

Chapter Forty-Nine

We live with a number of failures. Just suck it up. Get over it. Go on. It's an American mantra. But I didn't believe I would ever get over our inability to bring Mary Farnsworth's killer to justice.

I tried. Josie went back to Manhattan, Keith continued to serve as a deputy, and the KBI slunk back to Topeka as frustrated as I.

Keith had urged me to go on my favorite outing—the Kansas State Historical Society. After I prowled through the archives, I planned to spend a weekend at Josie's town house.

I had barely gotten started on my research when an attendant passed me a pink slip stating that I'd gotten a call from Nancy Brooks. Our cell phones aren't allowed inside the room, so I stacked my material, left, and walked outside.

"Good morning," she said. "I'm so glad you're here. I want you to drive to KU Medical Center with me." There was no mistaking the excitement in her voice. "They called an hour ago. Mary Farnsworth's family has come to claim her body."

Stunned, I went inside the research center, gave materials I'd checked out back to the archivists, retrieved my purse and cell phone from the locker and drove to the KBI headquarters.

"Did they give you any more information?" I asked Brooks on the drive to Lawrence. "I'm floored."

"None, whatsoever. There's paperwork, and of course the State Coroner called the KBI immediately."

We went to the medical examiner's office and he led us to a small private room. "They are waiting for you," he said. "I told them there would be questions."

Brooks was the first through the door. She stopped abruptly. Inside were two women. One, carrying a briefcase, was petite with silver blond hair. The room was warm. She had removed her suit jacket and carried it over her arm revealing a gorgeous gray silk charmeuse blouse. Her pearls appeared to be real.

Next to her was a tall black woman in a dark mustard-colored pantsuit. Her black hair was close-cropped in a natural Afro. Her queenly bearing enabled her to wear a large amount of gold jewelry that would be ostentatious on a less confident woman.

Neither one seemed likely to be a member of Mary's Farnsworth's family. Brooks and I exchanged looks: *I don't* think *so.*

Then I saw their identical stylized silver crosses with a ruby off-center heart.

The blond gazed at Brooks' badge, smiled, and extended her hand. "I'm Annette Brown and this is Claudette Rodon." We introduced ourselves.

"Well ladies, as you might imagine we have some questions," Brooks said.

"We've anticipated that. So let's begin by proving our connection to Mary." The black woman smiled broadly and nodded her head at the woman holding the briefcase. She opened it and took out two grey gowns and unfolded black headscarves. The gown was identical to the garment hanging in Mary's closet I had mistaken for a muumuu.

Then she reached for a group picture. There were five women in grey habits with black headscarves edged with a white band. I glanced up and studied the two of them. "You're both in it, and this is Mary?" I pointed to the woman on the end.

"Yes," said Annette "That was Mary."

"And the other two?"

"Dead. There are three now."

Three again. Talesbury had said "three" when I first told him about Mary.

"We suspected you would require proof," Claudette said. "Although we never wear these garments now."

"You are Catholic nuns?" Brooks looked skeptically at their expensive clothes before she examined the picture again.

"No, Episcopal sisters. If we were Catholic, Mary could not have become a priest."

"I assume Mary was a member of your order?"

"Yes. She was Sister Maria. I was Sister Claudine. Annette was Sister Anne."

"You're using past tense," I said. "Don't you take vows for life?"

"No, not all of us. Mary did, and so did Sister Theresa. There are many religious orders in the Anglican Communion. Ours was not a contemplative one. We were out in the world. We have two year renewable vows. Annette and I both renewed ours three times." The black woman's voice was musical with a trace of an accent I couldn't place. She smiled at the blond woman. "Annette became a medical doctor, as is her husband."

"And you?"

She shrugged. "An artist. Or so they tell me."

"I know who you are!" The name suddenly clicked. "Claudette Rodon! I should have recognized it." I turned to Brooks. "Miss Rodon is gaining quite a following for her paintings of African village life."

"I'm surprised you would be aware of my work."

"My specialty is African American history."

"I'm an American citizen now, but I was born in Morocco."

"You also have a reputation for humanitarian work."

She shrugged again.

"Where are you taking Mary's remains? You said you are taking her home."

"To Africa. Burundi. To the place where our mother house once stood. This was her request. Most of our sisters are buried there. We also want her vestments for a proper ceremony."

"Once stood? Where your mother house once stood?"

They stiffened and exchanged looks.

"It was destroyed during the Hutu-Tutsi Wars," Dr. Brown said. "Everyone was massacred except us five. Many of our sisters were subjected to rape and terrible torture. Frankly, we would rather not discuss this."

"There's no need to do so," I said. "The garments, the picture is proof enough that you have a claim to Mary's body."

"We've been years trying to put it behind us. In fact, as you might imagine, we are quite reluctant to make the journey back there. But it's a sacred trust. Mary had no living family. Just us. She clung to the memory of happier times when we lived in community. We're bound to make this trip."

"I'm so very sorry." Brooks bowed her head for a second and raised her hand to her forehead as though screening her eyes. "You have my deepest sympathy," she said. Then she recovered and drew a deep breath. "We have a number of questions about Mary Farnsworth." she said crisply.

They froze. Deadened their eyes, as though braced for an ordeal. I was reminded of Bishop Talesbury's inscrutability when he was questioned.

Brooks opened her briefcase. "Would you mind if I recorded this?"

A shadow crossed over both their faces. "We would prefer not to."

Brooks decided instantly. I knew the last thing she wanted was for these two women to consult a high-dollar attorney, and by the looks of them they could easily afford it.

"All right," she said. "No tapes. Provided you answer all my questions fully and do not withhold any information."

They exchanged looks again. Then Claudette nodded reluctantly. "We no longer have any reason for secrecy. The war is over, but habits remain. It's difficult to retrain our thinking."

"Ask away," said Dr. Brown. "Let's get this over with so we can do what needs to be done. We are busy women with a long trip ahead of us."

"There's a table in the next room where I can take notes." Brooks rose and held the door open and we filed out. She placed her pad in front of her, pen ready. "You are not under oath, but of course we expect you both to answer our questions fully and honestly."

They nodded.

"I'm giving you fair warning, however, Mary Farnsworth's death has attracted a great deal of attention within the bureau. Do not risk being held over for any reason. If you refuse, I can hold you over for obstructing an investigation. A session with Agent Dimon will be very unpleasant."

"We're accustomed to unpleasant interrogations," Claudette said. Her eyes sparked with contempt.

Brooks softened. "That was thoughtless of me. I apologize." Embarrassed, she lowered her eyes and stared at the table. "Let's get down to business."

"Please start with some basic information," I said, hoping they would relax. "Tell us about your life now."

Both were married, although only Dr. Brown had children.

"Please tell us how you both learned about Mary's death."

"After we fled from Africa we located in a South American region, Suriname, for a very short time. There's a priest, Fr. Reilly, who's been there for years. It's generally known he's the one who passes along information." Claudette's voice was flat, her eyes expressionless.

Dr. Brown glanced at her and took over. "This is the first time we've heard from him since we've made new lives in America. He told us about Mary."

"Suriname is a rather odd place to go," Brooks said. "Why would you have felt the need for…"

"Such cloak and danger stuff?" There was no mistaking the bitterness in Dr. Brown's voice. "Because we were being pursued by a vicious consortium of men. Our order rescued children. You've heard of the legions of child soldiers recruited by both sides?"

Brooks nodded.

"We helped them escape this terrible entrapment. Tried to put their souls back in their bodies. We kept lists of these children to help their parents find them. But when the Hutu army was defeated, the leaders panicked and worried they would give testimony. They wanted our lists. Two of us were..." Then Dr. Brown stared straight ahead.

"I doubt these details are relevant to this investigation." Claudette trembled. She glared at Brooks. "You want me to tell you what all these savages did to those two sisters? You enjoy hearing about gang rape? Torture? Mutilation? Or perhaps you would prefer that I catalogue what's possible to do to little boys? Do you enjoy that more?"

"I..." Brooks stammered. "No...please, you're right. Let's move on to how you got to Suriname."

"A bishop placed us there. We did not work with him, but word reached him that the five of us had survived. A Tutsi man hid us, then helped us escape. Bishop Talesbury made all the arrangements. We were in Suriname for a very short time before we all moved to America and went our separate ways."

Brooks and I exchanged looks. "Tell us more about this Talesbury."

"We only saw him once and that was when we left Africa." Claudette wiped a stray tear from her cheek. "We would have known him anywhere if we had ever seen him again. But we didn't." She reached for a tissue. "His eyes. That beard. A haunted man."

I recalled my first impression when he walked down the aisle at St. Helena. Like he had stepped out of an El Greco painting.

"He would have recognized us too, I think. If not our faces, our terror. He stood on the dock and watched us sail away. He risked his life for us. No one could ever know he was the one who arranged for us to be relocated. Theoretically, he was on a different side in that insane war. We were in a Tutsi region and he a Hutu area. We both did the same kind of work, but there were no sides really. Both tribes were bent on destroying the other."

Dr. Brown chimed in. "But we were pursued. Even in Suriname. That's where they got Sister Theresa."

"They are all gone now," Claudette said, her voice thick with tears. "We thank God. The war has flared up over and over, but every single one of the persons pursuing us has been captured.

We bless the freedom of this country. Our lives. Even Mary found peace."

Brooks lifted her head from her notebook. "Who helped you relocate?"

"Fr. Reilly helped all three of us. After Teresa's death, we knew we could no longer stay together in Suriname. We didn't need any fake ID's or such, because in Africa we were only known by the names we assumed in the mother house. Besides, all records of our previous lives had been burned. And obviously, we look different without our habits."

Claudette rose and walked over to a pitcher of water on the stand in back of the room. She filled a glass and went back to the table.

"Fr. Reilly told Mary that Bishop Talesbury kept in touch with an aunt in Western Kansas and that she knew of an opening for a social worker. Mary had been ordained a priest in Burundi. It was a perfect fit. She adored children. All children." She shuddered. "So many dead now."

Dr. Brown reached for the group photo and put it back in her briefcase. "Of course the Bishop Talesbury never knew where any of us ended up. Nor did he know about any of our backgrounds or abilities. We were among many who fled. Fr. Reilly must have helped a thousand refugees relocate."

Brooks glanced at the clock. "You've already identified the body?"

They nodded.

"OK. Let's move on to the most crucial questions. We're hoping you can shed some light on the circumstances surrounding Mary's death."

They looked at her with puzzled expressions.

"You do know, don't you, that Mary was murdered?"

Dr. Brown gasped and reached for Claudette's hand. "No, no, no. That war is over. We're safe now. We're safe. All those evil men were killed. All of them. God in Heaven. I have children. I have children."

"God in Heaven," Claudette whispered. "They found her."

Stricken, Brooks stood and turned away. I leaned against my elbows and held my head. I could not look them in the eye.

God help us all. No one had told them.

Chapter Fifty

"How did she die?" Claudette asked. "How was she murdered?"

I was afraid she would fly into pieces if I gave the wrong answer. "She was poisoned. Killed somehow with…"

"With the poison of the golden dart frog," Dr. Brown said before I could get out the words. "There. In Western Kansas after all this time."

Claudette sobbed. Terrified, they both rose and tried to comfort the other.

"We are desperate to find the person who did this," Brooks said. Her face had become a death mask as she struggled to keep her emotions at bay long enough to do her job. "What can you tell us? I hate having to question you, but we are so very grieved over this death. Clearly you both know details we don't. Do you know who killed Mary Farnsworth? Can you give us a name? A motive? A method? Anything at all?"

They said nothing.

I tried asking a less threatening question. "Was Mary ever in the witness protection program?"

"No. She considered it but after Sister Teresa was killed she worried that about the reliability of people in the FBI." Annette gave a weak smile. "But there are other groups who can help one disappear. Where better than Kansas?"

"You must understand," said Claudette. "There was no one we could trust. They used everyone. Old women. Children. Persons you would least expect."

"Old women were the worst," said Annette. "They had no strength, no ability, but they were the spies, the messengers."

Claudette agreed. "The very worst of all, and they did it to protect their children and grandchildren and great-grandchildren. Who could blame them?"

"Someone had to have been there in that church that day," said Annette. "Someone."

"Talesbury was," I said.

"Bishop Talesbury? Back in America?" It was as though I had announced the presence of a ghost.

"How could he be alive?" Claudette stammered. "After we left Suriname, we heard he was captured and tortured. No one ever survived their torture. The soldiers heard about our rescue, and his role. They tracked him down."

Brooks' lips trembled. She took a quick note.

"How did he escape?" Claudette raised her tear-stained eyes. "It must have been a miracle." She turned to Annette. "Mary must have been terrified when she saw him there."

"But you've just said that Talesbury helped you," Brooks said.

"Then. But now we can't be certain what he told those men." Dr. Brown stood unmoving, tears streaming down her cheeks. "If they let him live, it's hard telling what compromises he made. Mary couldn't have known where he stood."

"Someone else was there," Brooks glanced at me, knowing I would understand how much she detested pressing these women. "A man. We haven't found him. The old woman who saw him is in poor health. She doesn't remember much. He didn't stand out."

"Not all Africans are black," said Claudette. "Americans tend to forget that. There were wealthy white men backing up some of this search."

"He spoke to Mary," Brooks said. "He said, 'I know who you are, and I know what you've done.'"

"My God, my God. After all this time." Claudette bowed her head in sorrow, then clenched her fists. "Fr. Reilly swore to us every one of those men had been captured. Brought to justice. All of them."

"Ladies, I can't tell you anything about that man, but can assure you, Talesbury had nothing to do with Mary Farnsworth's murder."

"Oh we know how she died," said Dr. Brown. "She was our Prioress. The big fish. She was never truly out of danger."

Brooks pressed. "Whatever you tell me is safe with the KBI."

"We're sworn to silence."

Brooks simply stared at them. "You must," she said.

Claudette toyed with her cross. Suddenly, I knew. "Your crosses. Mary's cross. She killed herself. But how?"

Annette blanched, then reached down and held up the crucifix. "The heart," she said. "The Sacred Heart of Jesus. It opens. We had them specially fitted when we reached Suriname. To protect the children. There's just time enough. Just time before the poison takes effect to close the lid. We practiced. We all practiced. Opening the compartment, licking the poison, closing it again."

"Oh yes," said Claudette with bitter smile. "Even now, we are never without our crosses."

I recalled Talesbury saying he was never without his blow dart pen.

"Mary was spared," Annette's face shone. Tears welled up. "It worked. Whatever danger that man presented, she was spared."

"There was a full congregation there. She could have cried out for help." I could not take this in.

"And be believed?" Annette's voice rose. "And say what? That an unarmed man kneeling in a church was really a vicious thug? That she needed protection in a church in broad daylight? And the bishop also might be part of a conspiracy?"

"We have to keep her cross," Brooks said, when she could finally speak. "For evidence. But I'm sure it will be ruled a suicide."

She cleared her throat. "I have a few phone calls to make, but I believe you will be able to leave tomorrow."

Chapter Fifty-One

Sam and Keith and I threw a victory party for three. Deal was dead and his whole family would have to follow this country's laws, just like everyone else. In fact, according to the boys at the coffee shop, Deal's family now claimed he had been an aberration. A lone twisted twig on their magnificent family tree.

KBI had verified the presence of poison from the golden poison dart frog in Mary's cross. Although the wind was picking up, the evening was pleasant, and there was a possibility of our resuming what passed for normal lives.

"It's still not really over though," I said. "Mary may have killed herself to escape torture, but we still haven't found the man who triggered it." Sam scowled, annoyed that I couldn't leave it alone.

The kitchen phone rang.

"We're not here," the two men chorused together.

It was the hospital. "Lottie, Edna has taken a turn for the worse. We don't know how much longer she has. We've called her son and he left Wichita immediately, but she wants you to come right now."

"I'm on my way."

◇◇◇

The head of Edna's bed was elevated and she lay in a quilted pink bed jacket, too large for her frail body. She stirred when I came in.

"I knew you would come," she said. "My blessed Lottie. If Stuart doesn't come in time, please tell him."

She closed her eyes and I thought she had dozed off. Then, "I killed her," Edna whispered. "I killed Mary Farnsworth." I reached for her hand. She was delusional. Rambling. Old. Frail. She had been so crippled with arthritis she could scarcely move that day.

"I gave my own little girl a heart attack."

My blood froze and all the saliva drained from my mouth.

"I'm the one who said those words. 'I know who you are, and I know what you've done'."

"Edna. I don't understand. Mary Farnsworth was your daughter?"

She nodded. "My own little Mary Claire. My little girl." She began to sob. "I didn't mean to do it Lottie. Didn't know she had a weak heart."

"My God, Edna, why would you have said anything at all?"

"I wanted her to know how proud I was. Gerta wrote me. Through the years. Told me what a fine daughter I had."

"Edna, how did you know who she was?"

"When Gerta's husband died Mary came back to Iowa for the funeral. I saw a picture of her in the paper. So I knew what she looked like all grown up. She was such a loving child. I was so proud of her. What she had done. She saved children, you see. Over in Africa."

"But why didn't you get in touch with her earlier? She's been in Northwest Kansas for nineteen years."

"I didn't know she was here. Why would I know that? I didn't need no social services. Wasn't no reason for us to bump into each other. Last I knew, she was in Africa. She came to a bad end dying of a heart attack in a church instead of marrying and settling down. She should have had her own children. Like I had with my husband here in Kansas. A son like Stuart."

I squeezed her hand, knowing she had never heard of the wars ripping Africa apart.

Tears streamed down Edna's face. "But when I saw her coming down the aisle I knew who she was. I thought my heart would burst I was so proud."

Her breath was faint and I bent to hear her soft speech.

"I wanted her to see me kneel," she said. "I was going to tell her who I was after the service. And I did it. I managed to kneel."

"Yes, you did," I whispered. "Yes, you did."

"There wasn't no stranger," she said softly. "I said those words. Me. And I gave her a heart attack. I just wanted her to know how proud I was."

I know who you are, and I know what you've done.

The words of Annette and Claudette's testimony about using old women seared my mind. "They used old women. They used old women. As messengers. As spies."

And more words. Mary Farnsworth already shocked by the presence of Bishop Talesbury. "She couldn't have known what compromises he had to make," Dr. Brown had said. *Couldn't have known. Couldn't have known.*

Then the next horror.

I know who you are, and I know what you've done.

The fatal words that sent Reverend Mary running into the anteroom.

"Oh Edna, why did you even tell me there was a man? Why would you do that?"

"I didn't want you to think poorly of me. I thought if you knowed it was a heart attack, you wouldn't go poking around looking for some other reason. Wouldn't cut up her insides. It's not decent. My little girl didn't need to be cut up."

She sniffed again. "Course she thought I was dead. I was going to break it to her real gentle after the service."

"Edna," I asked, not wanting to make her close up, "did you say something else? What else did you say?"

"It was nothing. I didn't have time to say much more before she dropped the chalice."

"What else, Edna?"

"Just, 'You'll tell. You're going to tell.'"

My lips began to tremble. "Tell what Edna?"

"Just that she would tell Stuart about how our life was…we had baby chicks…and raised flowers."

There was no man.

My gentle, lying little mouse murderer, who simply could not bear for people to think poorly of her, had made up the mysterious stranger. Sent us on a wild goose chase because she couldn't bear for us to know she'd given her daughter a heart attack.

Old woman, old woman.

There was more. Much, much more to it than that. She'd spoken words that trigged her daughter's suicide. A daughter who understood torture.

Old woman, old woman.

Webbing through life like a spider heedless of tangles and tendrils.

Seen through my tears, her face was hazy, unfocused. The door opened. "Mom," Stuart called softly. "I'm here."

I left.

◇◇◇

She was buried here in Gateway City. An overworked priest from a community ninety miles south conducted the service in our local funeral home.

I had called Agent Brooks three days earlier and gave her "the rest of the story."

"Will this never end?" She gasped, incredulous. "I'll call Annette Brown and Claudette Rodin immediately and let them know they are not in danger."

"I think this just about does it. For you, at least, but not for me."

There was a son. And a mother who had trusted me to pass on information. And I wasn't sure it was the right thing to do.

Nancy Brooks' search ended with our conversation. The KBI would no longer expend energy chasing after a man who didn't exist. But it hadn't ended for me.

◇◇◇

Two days later, I drove over to St. Helena hoping to find Bishop Talesbury. According to Margaret, the boys at the coffee shop said he practically lived there.

He was working outside cutting boards with an old fashioned hand saw. He looked Amish in his full beard and suspendered pants. I stood apart until he stopped, straightened, and waited for me to approach.

"Sir, I have questions. But they have nothing to do with my duties as a police officer."

"Then there's no need for me to answer them."

"Yes, there is. The people of this community built this church. It's yours now. I understand that. But I believe I'm owed a little consideration."

He hesitated, then nodded.

"Why did Irwin Deal want this land? What was it about these god-forsaken forty acres that was so valuable?"

For the first time ever, I saw a spark of humor in his eyes.

"What do you have more of than anything else out here, Miss Albright?"

Exasperated by his riddles, I felt like I was burdened with a trig problem.

Then he bent and plucked a dandelion stem and gently blew the seeds into the air.

"Wind," I said. "Our wind."

"Exactly. My glebe stands directly in the path of a proposed wind farm. Irwin would have made a decent living for the rest of his life if he could wrest the glebe away from me. Not a killing, but a living."

"And there's no way you would have done that."

Talesbury nodded. "He thought I would sell it to him without giving the matter a second thought. He contacted me and informed me of my inheritance, assuming I would prefer the money to the forty acres. He had already signed a contract to lease a strip of family land for the route if the company decided to locate their wind farm out here. He thought my glebe was the only impediment to closing the deal. But it wasn't."

"Chip and Myrna," I said. "They would never, never give up their land."

"Exactly. He was livid when Chip offered to donate material. He knew it would make me even more determined to stay. Irwin kept whittling at me, telling me there was no way I could support the children I planned to bring here. Chip was going to change all that. In addition to building materials, he offered to fund me."

I remembered Chip's miserly handwriting, the money-centered narrative. "A major change of heart."

"I've known many men like Chip." Talesbury studied a distant patch of grass undulating in gusts of wind. "Greedy. Calculating. All their lives. Then when they see the end coming they want to be remembered for something. Or think they do." His lips lifted in a slight smile. "At heart, I suspect he was more interested in protecting his own land, than benefitting my children. But Myrna's family certainly brought out the best in him."

"That's true," I said.

"When he killed Chip, he had no idea that Chip would leave his land to Myrna."

"Irwin bumbled everything he did," I said. "Everything. But then what *did* he think would happen to Chip's land. It would have been tied up in court for years since he had no direct heirs."

"Not years. Not out here. And you can bet any heirs would sell out in a heartbeat."

Talesbury pulled out a handkerchief and wiped the blade of his hand saw. The wind ruffled his beard. He closed his eyes and could not disguise a shudder. He bowed his head. The saw dangled at his side. "So many deaths. And now I've killed too."

"There's a difference in wanton murder and what you did."

His head snapped up, his haunted eyes condemned me for my attempt to rationalize what he had done. "I killed, Miss Albright."

I swallowed and could not speak.

"Is there anything else?" His tone was formal, polite. As though dismissing a child or a fool.

Now. Now when he was wallowing in guilt would be the ideal time to ask if he would consider holding services in St. Helena. Ashamed at the impulse to take advantage, I decided to call Bishop Rice instead. Talesbury needed confession and absolution. My compassion did not stop me from pressing forward with one more question.

"Yes. You were frightened at the jail. Scared to death. Why?"

"When Chip was killed, I thought the man everyone was looking for had returned. I believed he was the one who had killed Mary Farnsworth, then Chip, and I was next. To be killed or worse. I could not go through that again."

"What made you change? You weren't frightened when we released you."

"I heard Miss Brooks say two separate poisons were used to kill Chip and Mary. When she didn't find the stiletto, I immediately suspected Irwin had murdered Chip. I figured Mary was the hit man's only target and that he had fled after she beat him to the punch."

"You know the truth now?"

His eyes fluttered, warning me not to press him too much.

"I heard." He did not mention the sisters.

"One last question. The time you called at the historical society. What did you want to tell me?"

"That I had notified Sister Mary's family. Through a Fr. Reilly in Suriname." There was a tell-tale bob of his Adam's apple. "They would take her home." He picked up his saw.

A week later, back at the historical society, I finally decided. Burdened by my promise to Edna, I reached for the phone. There would be no more secrets in the Mavery family.

Stuart was still at his mother's house, preparing for the sale. He answered on the first ring.

"Would you mind coming by? I have something to tell you."

Acknowledgments

Lethal Lineage required synthesizing a peculiar blend of research. Kansas has a number of communities that sociologists and historians refer to as hamlets. Hamlets have a population of 250 and under. Police techniques and procedures used in these tiny settlements are quite different from those followed in cities and larger counties. A number persons involved in law enforcement in various sizes of communities have shared their expertise for this book.

I would like to thank Ellen Hansen, Chief of Police, Lenexa, Kansas, and Ron Greninger, former Field Sergeant with the Lenexa Police Department, for helping me work my way out of a swamp of often conflicting information. Mark Bouton, a career FBI agent with a law degree, helped resolve jurisdictional issues between the FBI and KBI. Bouton worked criminal and terrorism cases, helping to identify the Oklahoma City bombers.

The following priests answered questions about frontier and contemporary Catholic and Episcopal churches: Fr. Ben Helmer, Fr. Frederick Sathi Bunyan, Fr. Don Martin, and Fr. Jean-Jacques D'Aoust. Kansas was a particularly difficult assignment for pioneer priests sent across the prairie to locate scattered communicants.

Mortician David Leopold provided information about Kansas County and District Coroner systems and the decisions involved with "unattended deaths." Luci Zahray, the well-known "Poison

Lady" advised me on the poison issues. Jimmy Stewart coached on farming and planting techniques.

I owe a special debt to fellow knitter and good friend, Judy Cunningham, and her mother Nola Hall, for passing down one of the most peculiar family incidents I've ever heard. I met Barbara Booth at the state Kansas Authors Club Convention and she told me about the only glebe in Kansas. It's located at Clay Center.

The Kansas State Historical Society is outstanding. I plug this amazing organization in every book. It was founded in 1875 and has one of the largest newspaper collections in the world. As a Kansas historian, I could not ask for a more valuable resource. The Lottie Albright series has been greatly enriched from help given on the state level, and through the hours spent by dedicated workers in small county historical societies scattered across Western Kansas.

A special group of Episcopal women have made my transition from Kansas to Colorado much, much easier. I'm grateful to the Hood: Janis Davis-Lopez, Nancy Riddell, Sharon Robertson, and Maureen Ford.

My editor, Barbara Peters, and her husband, Robert Rosenwald, publisher, richly deserve the cascade of honors showered on them by the literary community. I owe Barbara special thanks for her keen editorial eye, and Robert for his superb support in all the stages of publication. This manuscript was greatly improved by suggestions from Editor Annette Rogers. Associate Publisher Jessica Tribble has an amazing ability to coordinate all the complex stages of getting a book to market.

As always, I cannot express enough appreciation for my steadfast and savvy agent, Phyllis Westberg, of Harold Ober Associates. She has unlimited patience with my extraordinary curiosity that requires her to coordinate a variety of projects.

Hugs and kisses to my wonderful daughters who were raised assimilating the twists and turns of my peculiar writing career.

God bless them, they thought our household was normal.

To receive a free catalog of Poisoned Pen Press titles, please contact us in one of the following ways:

Phone: 1-800-421-3976
Facsimile: 1-480-949-1707
Email: info@poisonedpenpress.com
Website: www.poisonedpenpress.com

Poisoned Pen Press
6962 E. First Ave. Ste. 103
Scottsdale, AZ 85251